RUIN'S DAWN

Book 3 of the Resonance Tetralogy

Hugo Jackson

Published by Inspired Quill: April 2020

First Edition

This is a work of fiction. Names, characters and incidents are the product of the author's imagination. Any resemblance to actual events or persons, living or dead, is entirely coincidental. The publisher has no control over, and is not responsible for, any third-party websites or their contents.

Ruin's Dawn © 2020 by Hugo Jackson
Contact the author through their website: hugorjackson.com

Chief Editor: Sara-Jayne Slack
Cover Design: Katie Hofgard (patreon.com/Eskiworks)
Typeset in Garamond

All Rights Reserved.
No part of this publication may be reproduced or transmitted in any form by any means electronic, mechanical, photocopying, recording or otherwise, without the prior permission of the copyright owner.

Paperback ISBN: 978-1-913117-98-6
eBook ISBN: 978-1-913117-99-3
Print Edition

Printed in the United Kingdom
1 2 3 4 5 6 7 8 9 10

Inspired Quill Publishing, UK
Business Reg. No. 7592847
www.inspired-quill.com

Praise for Hugo Jackson

"[Legacy] is very satisfying. Jackson brings a complex and colorful anthro world to life. His descriptions are full of lush detail."
— Fred Patten, *Dogpatch Press*

"I can't say enough good things about this book. The writing is great. The world is fascinating. The heroes are intriguing and lovable. The villains are terrifying, and the fight scenes are written as if by a fight choreographer. I loved it. A perfect book for adults, teens, and children alike."
— M. Shaw, *Amazon Reviewer*

"I loved it! This book honestly gave me a huge nostalgia rush – a lot happens once things start rolling. […] A fun fantasy romp with a great cast of heroes."
— David Popovich, *Bookworm Reviews (Youtube)*

"Overall, a very well written story that kept me entertained from start to finish. Every once in a while, you stumble across an amazing gem, and this is one of those."
— J. Poole, *Bestselling Author of* The Bakkian Chronicles

"[Fracture is] An epic anthro-fantasy […where] Jackson tenders relatable albeit convoluted motivations, heart-rending tragedy and an all-too-familiar feeling of unease in this dismal chapter of our heroes' history, closing as friends old and new commit themselves to a brighter future for all Eeres. Eagerly anticipating RUIN'S DAWN!"
— Mark J. Engels, *Author of* Always Gray in Winter

To those who are gone,
who brought us light,
may we create a future
built with the strength of your love

Prologue

"How much did your father tell you about Nazreal, Faria?"

"Only what you heard before he died. The rest... I still don't know. There was nothing left for me to read from, no time to learn before the Dhrakan siege, and I remember very little of my mother. You're all I have, all anyone has, of the history."

"I see. Do you feel ready?"

"I have to be. I've been healing enough. I want to hear everything, Osiris. All that you can tell me."

"All right. Please, sit. We will be here a while."

"I have time."

"For now, at least."

Chapter One

A ball, small and wooden, rolled clumsily down a sloping sand bank in the desert of burnt red. It hissed and bobbed quietly across the shifting surface, leaving a light, broken trail in its wake. The young fox at the top of the dune smiled playfully as it gained speed, then slid to a halt a few feet from his home. Not much older than two, his bright blue eyes were alight with glee.

He sprinted down the bank as fast as his stubby, uncoordinated legs would carry him. Misjudging his own momentum, however, he tripped at the base of the dune, rolling twice head-over-heels to land neatly on his back, staring into the brilliant clear sky. Stunned for a moment, he wriggled around to sit facing his house, a modest, squat building of red sandstone with semi-circular windows and a lush, billowing tree breaking through its roof. He brushed the sand from his ears with a tiny huff of frustration. Thankfully his mother and father, although talking by the window, had not seen him fall, or they would cordon him inside again.

A bright glint in his mother's hand caught his eye, a shimmering blue shard of rock.

The magic crystals!

He had seen her make brown plants green with it, and she was the one who had grown the massive tree that stood in the centre of their house. His father was just as skilled, having made small shelves come out of the wall, and made a chair appear from a pile of sand, which he compacted and hardened with little more than a flick of his wrist.

The young fox rocked onto his hind paws and picked up his ball again. Shielding his eyes from the sun, he assessed the dune he wished to conquer.

He had an idea.

While his parents talked, he trotted boldly and unnoticed into their small kitchen, his eyes on the chunk of crystal he'd found last week while digging. It had a smooth, pointy section poking out of a rocky hemisphere, glistening with blue iridescence. It was his favourite discovery, and he'd screamed excessively (although still not enough to convince them otherwise) when his parents said he couldn't play with it, and placed it on a high shelf. They would probably say no to his current plan as well, but they were conveniently inside, rapt in each other's conversation, so for now he would just play, and surprise them later.

The shelf loomed over him, austere and forbidding, shielding his prize.

His mouth lolled open in concentration as he reeled his arm back, then tossed the ball up as high as he could. It bounced lightly off the wall at just the right angle, toppling the rock from its hemisphere and sending it tumbling down.

Aidan caught it, barely, and the ball bounced off his head with a hollow *thunk*. He withstood the urge to cry out, because his plan was worth more than to be discovered.

Collecting his mildly traitorous ball, and with tail flicking confidently, he marched back outside. He was almost giddy, his breath pushing from him in hurried, whispered laughter. This was going to be the best thing they'd ever seen; he knew it!

After clambering to the dune's summit (planting his face in the sand three times on the way and treading on his tail once), he twisted the ball down, so it made a little nest-like indentation and stayed put. This was his fifth or sixth ball, as he had a habit of losing them between boulders, or sometimes the desert lizards would mistake them for eggs and carry them off, leading to a wild chase that his parents often got involved in and didn't find very amusing, (although neither did Aidan after the second theft).

He'd seen his mother use the crystal before; she held it to the leaves and ran her paw over it in a certain way. Within moments the plant had turned green and crisp. His father had done the same with the shelves and chair, but all he'd done was hold it to the wall and push.

The kit turned the sparkling lump of crystal over in his hand and pouted. It wasn't as smooth and shiny as his parents' rock. He ran a digit along the planed surface, then tried to dig his claw between it and the bulbous rocky protrusion it was stuck within. The stone tickled his finger, and although he couldn't see it move, he could almost *feel* it about to come free at any moment. He pushed harder, pressing his pads to the blue, willing the mineral deposit to fly off the end.

What occurred was slightly different. It happened so fast he barely knew what he did. Within a second, a spark fizzed at his finger and the rocky half twisted and elongated to a perfect hexagonal prism, with pointed ends. He blinked at it for a moment and turned it over, examining every surface.

Now it looked like his parents' crystal: exactly what he wanted. He shook his paws excitedly, keeping a firm grip on his prize.

He knew from experience that sandcastles couldn't be made from dry sand because it all slid into a pile, but he didn't have any water. If the sand was hard, like rock, then he could shape it like his father had when making the chair. Standing atop the dune and thinking about his father's actions, he stuck one end of the crystal into the sand and pressed down hard.

He lifted his paws away for a second to view his progress. Nothing but a barely visible blue glint, embedded in the sand. He gave a frustrated huff, then dug it free and pressed down again, focusing on the dune below, and how he could make his ball run more exciting. He remembered running his finger along the pretty wave carvings by the elders' hut, thinking how fun it would be to slide all over them if they were huge and climbable. Large, undulating waves and curves, slopes of all sizes, spread before him in his mind's eye.

BOOM.

His parents sprinted outside, fur on end.

Towering before them in newly-hardened sandstone was an enormous, uneven ball run, and standing atop it was their son. The force of the transformation had left him a little shell-shocked, but he picked himself up and shook his head free of the ringing in his ears. He waved to his parents, who could only blink in reply. A triumphant giggle rippled down to them as Aidan reached for his ball.

If his mother's eyes had been any wider, they would have dropped into the sand. His father kept looking the structure up and down, examining the surface with disbelief. Neighbours from nearby homesteads peered around corners at the rumble, and were equally shocked.

"Aidan..." his mother called. "Did... did you do this?"

He nodded proudly. "Look!" he beamed, before dropping his tiny wooden sphere into the top of the run.

As his parents watched the ball sweep, twist, and slide jovially towards them, the young fox put his paws on his hips and admired his work with an enormous, satisfied grin.

Chapter Two

"Even that young? He was... incredible."
"He was certainly talented, but in his youth it was not always best applied."

The red desert had an unforgiving sun. Even though Mahrae was on the sand's edge, carved out of the winding crimson rock faces that led to a life-giving river, the heat was punishing, and when the wind blew, it was relentless. Many of the first homes were hewn into the cliffs themselves, on the sides the wind bettered less often. As the township grew, homes were built further out, moving or growing as the sand dunes shifted in the punishing gusts. During bad storms, some houses would be completely buried; this was where Aidan would see his parents, Freya and Llufrio, work most diligently, using the fantastic blue crystals. He hadn't yet been allowed to help, but he experimented with them at every opportunity he could. His family's abilities weren't unique, but Aidan's parents were two of the most adept, and worked together to keep their village safe, fed, and sheltered. They did their best to credit others' natural craftsmanship, though, and made sure their powers were always used in service. Together, they pulled rocks out of the sand, created narrow windstorms to uncover buried pathways and structures, and were currently constructing rocky baffles that would help protect the outlying houses from sand exposure.

It had been seven years since Aidan had discovered his own affinity for the shining gems while playing in the sand dunes, and his adventures had grown in scope from that day.

An unruly proportion of his grand quests came from his parents' attempts to store the crystals away until they could supervise his training, and hence spawned from new schemes to retrieve them from various hiding places. This set him in trouble in a myriad of ways. From breaking ornaments and furniture, stealing tools, stacking books to reach forbiddingly-high shelves and forming stairs out of the wall with the retrieved crystal to get back down again; or attempting to unearth them from deep within wooden chests, getting stuck inside, and exploding his way out in a panic, he had undertaken numerous dangers that threatened to turn his parents' fur grey. Usually he just wanted to play, and when they supervised him his freedom was only curtailed when they sensed something dangerous about to happen, and could counteract his powers with their own. He was not strong enough to undo their work or overpower their energy, but he'd had some dangerous tantrums when he was younger that came close.

His favourite trick, upon hitting that volcano of frustration, was to form a stone cage around himself and scoot around the house while inside it, like a skeletal turtle.

That backfired swiftly once his father managed to disarm Aidan of the crystal he'd been experimenting with and forced him to negotiate calmness through his accidental prison in the middle of the hallway.

He'd been better since then, mostly. He could tell his parents were eager to see him learn, but at a pace much slower than he wanted, and the frustration built as he longed to help around the house and village. He'd constructed basic chairs and furniture, and made intricate patterns on the floor, but their usefulness was superficial; thus far he was limited to stone and sand sculptures, and if he was tired or unfocused their structure would collapse after a time. Water was too taxing because it wouldn't stick together outside of a container. He had dismembered multiple plants in anticipation of being able to create a forest in his bedroom, but once had success with creating a leaf big enough to fall asleep underneath.

The worst setback came when he happened across a small desert woodrat that had wandered into their house, and decided he would transform it into something large enough that he could ride around the village.

He trapped it in a small basket pilfered from the larder (leaving a trail of dried fruit that needed ejecting in favour of his captive), and rushed to find a hidden crystal. He'd deliberately left some hiding places untouched to use for later, and hoped his ingenuity would pay off.

His father had a leather work apron, which normally had tools and materials stuffed in its many pockets, adorning a hook in the hallway by the front entrance. After shaking the apron free, Aidan rummaged through the deep chambers, ejecting scraps of metal and rock, and a rolled bundle of fine detailing tools. As he laid the pouch aside it flopped open; inside he saw the familiar blue glint, glowing timidly in the shallow leather pouch.

He glanced over his shoulder. Clear so far. Stuffing the crystal into his waistcoat pocket, he scurried back to the basket, then whipped a claw inside to clutch his experiment.

"It's okay," he said in soothing tones. "You can stay, you'll be safe. I'm going to make you bigger. You'll be my pet and I'll ride you." His paw wrapped around the small shard, the tip poised above the rat's back. He wiped his moistening nose on his arm, as his tail flicked excitedly.

The rat's beady eyes widened as Aidan lowered the crystal. It quivered, its tiny ribcage pulsing with fearful breaths.

Flash.

His parents had been outside talking with neighbours. When they heard their son's chilling cries they sprinted into the room to find him screaming, wide-eyed, with the crystal and a bubbling, fleshy mass dropped at his feet. His paws and face were splattered with the blood of the rat, which was now unrecognisable, and unmistakably dead.

Freya picked up her son immediately and ran him to the water pump to clean him off. His screams echoed through the house as his father slid the animal's remains into the bloodied basket, and buried it in the sand behind the house.

Aidan hadn't talked until the evening, when the three of them were nestled amongst the roots of their big house tree for the night. The cub stared solemnly at where the rat had been.

"I'm sorry," he whimpered.

His mother's arm was already around him. "I know you

are."

"It won't... it won't come back, will it?"

"No, it was buried," Llufrio said quietly. "What were you trying to do?"

Tears welled up in Aidan's eyes. He sniffled. "I just wanted to make him bigger, so I could ride him."

Llufrio took his son's hand. "Growth is more than size, especially for animals. It takes time, patience, and a lot of energy. Some things aren't made to be big like we are."

Aidan wiped his eyes. "But you did it with the plants. I thought the rat would work too..."

Freya gently stroked her thumb across his shoulder. "Plants are different. They take energy from water, light, and the ground, so if you're very careful and can feel the way they change as you pull them up, you can help them change quickly. But that energy still comes at a cost. Do you remember that big leaf you made?"

Aidan nodded.

"What happened to it?"

"It was all broken when I woke up."

"And the plant was all grey, too," she continued. "When we change energy in a living thing, we can destroy it if we're not careful. These crystals are very powerful, and animals, plants, us, we aren't connected to the ground like stone is." She leant her head back. "We made this tree grow very quickly, but for a long time after that, it needed even more care to keep it alive. Trying to grow it too fast almost killed it. It's strong now, but it took a long time to heal properly."

Aidan sniffed, his nose at his chest. "I don't... I don't think I want to use the crystals. I want to grow up properly."

His father sat up. "You can still use them if you want

to," he replied softly. "If you use them well, and keep a kind heart, I'm sure you can do amazing things. That's how your mother and I try to live. But if you want to leave it for a while, we understand, and that's okay too."

Aidan nodded, and flopped over to bury his head in his father's side. "I'm still sorry for the rat. Do you think it had a family?"

"I don't know, love," Llufrio replied. "But if we see some, how about we leave out some rice or seeds for them?"

Aidan nodded. "Lots of seeds."

That night was not kind to Aidan, nor were many others. Nightmares and flashes of memory crashed into his mind as he tried to sleep, and he awoke crying.

"Don't use them any more Mum, Dad, please!" he bawled. No amount of placation would settle him. He eventually slept again, out of exhaustion, gripping his father tightly.

Several months passed, the first of which Aidan spent diligently following his parents around to make sure they weren't using any crystals, and trying to hide them if he thought they were going to. Freya and Llufrio had taken to distracting him in turns to conduct repair work around the village, or when they wanted to peacefully practice honing their own resonance, or meditate near the river.

One day in autumn Freya was reading Aidan a story, while Llufrio gathered supplies to create an orchard nearby, so the village could cultivate the land into something more than desert and carefully-tapped cactus. It was getting towards evening, and the sky's deep, rich blue grew darker.

Almost at the end of the book, the door to their home swung open, and Llufrio lumbered inside, cradling his right paw. His bag slipped from his left shoulder, hitting the floor with a heavy thud. Immediately, Freya cast the book aside, startling Aidan as she leapt to her feet to attend her husband. Aidan strained to see, but his mother kept an arm out to bar him from closing in.

"Found some nice flint by the river, but it didn't want to be taken without a fight," Llufrio winced, nodding to the gash on his paw. "I already cleaned the grit out, but I thought this might help Aidan if he saw what *else* the crystals can do."

Freya frowned. "I don't know, he's been calm all day, maybe you should just go to the healers."

Llufrio rubbed his muzzle. "Whatever you do will be fine. I want to show him. With luck, none of us will ever *need* to know how to do this well, but I would rather be prepared than lucky, and it may help him unlearn his nightmares a little."

She considered this for a moment, then escorted her mate to the roots of the tree, where he sat as she knelt in front of him. Aidan, still holding the book, peered over her shoulder.

"Dad, are you okay?"

Llufrio nodded. "In a moment, I will be. Come here, sit by me. Don't be scared, I just hurt myself a little."

Aidan obliged, worry wracking his face at his father's injured paw as he opened it up. Carefully, his mother slipped a crystal from her waistband. Aidan whimpered.

"No no *no*, Dad, don't let her do that!"

Llufrio gently wrested his arm from his son's terrified grip. "It's fine, love. Look."

While he pinched the edges of the laceration together, Freya touched the tip of the crystal shard to the injury. It pulsed in a soft glow, like a heartbeat, and gently, slowly, she moved it along the cut. Aidan's eyes were wide, his fists balled so tightly under his muzzle that they were shaking. His tail curled and quivered. But, as he saw where the cut had been, his terror turned to astonishment. Blood had stopped ebbing from the line of red, and gently Llufrio squeezed his paw to test it. He held his hand closer to his son, who leant in and gently stroked his finger along the almost-healed cut.

"These aren't evil," Llufrio said softly, holding the crystal to Aidan. "In the right paws they aren't even dangerous. You can learn to do this too. For anyone, and anything you need."

Aidan nodded, and threw his arms around his father.

Several months later, the village was preparing for some 'special guests'. Aidan wasn't sure where they were from, but they sounded incredibly important, and he'd overheard whispers of their fearful nature. Uneasiness hung in the air like a fog, but his parents wouldn't discuss it. They were 'just busy' or 'just tired', whenever he mentioned that they looked serious. The village had rationed food for several weeks, stockpiling the rest as though for a famine or party. But nobody was excited enough for it to be a party, and it wasn't the right time of year for any kind of solstice. Aidan had seen gatherers bringing more wood from the far forests than usual. The trips were so long that they normally only left once a month, but now groups were travelling every week. The biggest trunks were being smoothed into huge poles, while smaller pieces were cut into thinner rods, like the shafts of weapons.

Since seeing his father healed, Aidan's desire to learn had returned; with trepidation at first, then incredible fervour, once again outpacing his parents' time or patience, and sometimes their ability. They put it down to his creativity and energy, and promised more time with him, but in the days preceding the guests' arrival they'd been returning home later and later after their respective tasks, sometimes when he was asleep.

Aidan insisted he could help if they let him, but he was denied until the frustratingly vacuous time of 'after they'd gone'. As such, he was left almost daily in the care of an elderly fennec who didn't so much walk as slither upright, and whose selective deafness pertained only to conversations you had with her directly – she could still hear the slightest delinquent movement from the next room over, and could recall every detail of the salacious conversations across the street even though you could tell her three times to her nose where the blankets were kept. Her name was Hapi, and she was anything but, unless she was exposing some kind of gossip. To that end, there was no use bargaining with her for leniency, and letting your guard down meant she'd recant the entire hushed conversation with your friends to the returning parents to guarantee scorn and admonishment after her departure. Getting around her attention required intense planning and perfect execution, or she'd dash into the room as a viper would and sink her piercing voice into your ears like razor-pointed teeth through a young calf's hide.

Such was Aidan's current position, on a day that had been a 'particularly bad day to ask to help on', sitting with a pile of books and a chalkboard, to study from or create art with, whichever he felt most inclined to do.

They were equally bothersome. He couldn't concentrate when the promise of bigger things lay just outside the walls of his house. If these guests were important, he wanted to help the village. He wanted to do something amazing and show them that *his* village was the best there ever was or could be. He wanted to create the same sense of marvel that had exploded with his sandstone ball run.

He glanced up from his book, checking his surroundings to secure a plan. Hapi was tablet weaving on the old, cushioned bench, the long tufts of fur on her cheeks moving softly with the soft breeze from the window. He rubbed the current page between his pawpads in thought, then looked back to the short bookshelf in the opposite corner. He had stashed a small crystal back there a few days ago in case of emergency, and right now boredom and his missed potential was the combined crisis.

He slapped the book shut and made a hearty tutting sound, then marched over to the shelf.

"I just need more ideas," he said deliberately, as he caught sight of Hapi's raised eyebrow and swivelling, discerning ears. He stroked a young claw over the spines of the roughly-bound books, while his other hand slid into the gap to retrieve his illicit catalyst. Feeling the shard between his claws, he shuffled it into his palm and knelt on the floor to 'inspect' the lowest shelf, placing the crystal against the ground and covering it with his hand.

While he kept his gaze on the books before him, his focus was elsewhere.

On the back of the wall behind him, in the opposite room, a wooden shelf kept some small cultivated plants and a basket of tools. Aidan visualised the tool basket, and laid out a path in his mind for the energy in the crystal to follow to get there. The crystal thrummed beneath his hand; he began to feel the room, its space, and the borders beyond it. He could see the shelf, sense the thickness of the wall, and how much it would take to push a section of stone out to send the basket and its contents all over the floor.

Taking a deep breath, he gripped the crystal tightly. A ripple of energy burrowed under the floor and up the wall to an adult's head height, and from the other room came an enormous clattering. Hapi bolted up; even Aidan jumped, giving her a fearful look. Thankfully her attention was on the noise and not him. The moment she turned her back and strode across the threshold, Aidan pressed the crystal to the wall beside him.

"Goodness me," he heard Hapi groan, and there began a scraping of tools, the sound of collection.

With another burst of energy, the wall opened; Aidan rolled through, and immediately sealed it behind him as he entered freedom in the warm desert air. He shook the sand from his fur and placed his clenched paws on his hips in triumph.

Time to help!

He danced around the back of his house and began searching for work to be done, eager to leave before his absence was discovered.

Baskets of fruit glinted under a big awning in the village centre, adjoining the tall, wooden-roofed stage that acted as the community gathering place; used for services, announcements, dances, and various other things Aidan fell asleep through. The smell of fish and other meats in the smoker filled the air with a tasty, earthy smell. His face lit up for a moment upon catching scent of it, but he quickly darted back behind the building next to him. He was bound to be seen if he crossed the circle, so he dashed between buildings, skirting the periphery while scanning the stockpiles to find opportunities to help.

Everything seemed to be assigned for preparation, and he couldn't cook anyway. He could start a fire, but even he knew that wasn't what people wanted right now. He tapped the crystal idly against his leg. There had to be *something* to improve.

He leant against a house, whose blank walls were crumbling slightly. Dusty residue slid down his shoulders. Barely even thinking, he swiped the crystal across the marred surface and the crack disappeared.

His eyes gleamed.

He leapt across to another crack and smoothed it over. The next, a bigger one, he pulled together like stitches. He flattened rough, uneven sides and softened sharp edges.

He patched up everything he could find and stood back to admire his work. Neat as it now was, it was still a simple, boring house.

It didn't even have any window ledges.

Yet.

He extruded the stone underneath the first window, forming smart little shelves. On the other he scooped the wall out into a sort of well, for planting flowers. It was a little uneven because his paws were tingling, but it still looked better than a plain box. He turned in anticipation of his next task, then instantly whirled back round to face the house again.

It needed more.

He formed little scallop-shaped reliefs along the ground, and pulled the corners of the roof out to make neat ornate points. Then he pulled at the edges of the roof, to make a shelter over the door. Then he made a row of decorative finials along the arch of the door. Then he made a big flower shape on the wall under the window. Then another flower on the other side. And drew some grass, in stone. Then he cast a big sun relief over the door and added clouds over the windows.

Perfect.

He turned to the next house, and, knowing now what it should look like, his work was a lot faster. By the time he'd got to his fourth house, he was doing several things at once. He sprinted up the street to each dwelling, his additions becoming more elaborate and outlandish each time, making one door look like a scary monster, and another as if it was covered in leaves and flowers, another like an ocean in relief. He managed to modify the sides of some of the houses overlooking the centre, but not the fronts, for fear of being noticed.

He stood back and admired his handiwork, flexing his fingers and shaking his paws to try and make the itchy, tingling sensation leave them.

It seemed odd to him that so few adults were at home. Were they really all at the village centre?

He shrugged, and looked to his biggest task, the houses carved into the cliffside. He had always wondered why the rock was so rough and layered. He was sure he could make it all change at once if he concentrated hard enough, despite its vast surface.

He turned the crystal over in his paw. It felt lighter, in a strange way. It didn't *look* any smaller, but something in it felt… emptier, almost. But maybe that was the sensation in his paws, which had spread into a numb stiffness in his elbows now.

He pressed the crystal to the cliff.

"Aidan!" came a shrill voice. Hapi was on the warpath, shuffling towards him as fast as she could.

He grimaced and zipped around a corner, then slammed his paws onto the wall in front of him to conjure a set of stairs on the edge of the house. He sprinted up, and slid to the floor to push the stairs back in. He started from the bottom, so Hapi couldn't clamber after. She suddenly veered into the pathway and he jumped, such that the stairs he was moving jolted upwards and into him, knocking the crystal from his hand.

Hapi glanced about, grumbled something mercifully inaudible, then continued on.

Aidan took a few deep breaths and shuffled his paws about him for the blue shard.

It wasn't there.

Breath caught in his throat, he peered over the edge. The key to his escape lay about twelve feet below him, glimmering in the sand. Too high to jump, and thanks to his 'repairs', the walls were too smooth to climb down now.

As he rolled onto his haunches to form a plan, he saw

an assembly of creatures entering the circle around the awning. His unintended sentry position was only one house behind the buildings that encircled the gathering space, and with a little shielding from the sun, he could see fairly clearly. Five towering creatures with gold and white plumage and enormous wings were accompanying a big group of adult villagers. The new creatures wore shimmering robes adorned in gleaming metals, and their eyes were unfathomably vivid and sharp.

"Gryphons!" he gasped.

The magnificent creatures were the tallest things he'd ever seen, standing higher than the accompanying villagers by at least a head each. Gryphons, although revered as a magnificent sight, were generally forbidden to approach, considered fickle, aloof, and not particularly friendly. Some warned they would play cards to decide whether to coat you in liquid gold, eat you, or help you. Aidan had always been instructed, if he ever saw one, to leave immediately for home and call for help. The gryphons lived in gigantic towers on the sea, and were incredibly powerful and secretive. But here they were, plumage dazzling in the sun, wings bristling brilliantly.

Walking right next to them were his parents. His mother was holding a short metal spear of some kind; he recognised the tip of it immediately, a shining blue crystal.

He dug his claws into the stone in excitement as the villagers began to gather around the hall, standing to greet the gryphons with gestures of equal reverence and nervous anticipation. He scrabbled around for a place to jump down, and as he returned to where he'd dropped the crystal, he saw Hapi inspecting the gem. He shrank back from the edge and turned to the gathering at the centre.

A tall gryphon with red streaks of plumage on their crest, was looking at him. They leant their head to the fox next to them, Aidan's mother, and pointed.

Aidan could see her shoulders drop from here, and in seconds she and Llufrio were marching his way. He shifted to the middle of the roof and hugged his knees, trying to become as small as possible.

A few seconds later, his mother's familiar voice called to him.

"Aidan?"

He remained silent.

"Aidan, why are you on the roof?"

"I knew he'd hidden himself, little mischief," Hapi rasped from somewhere nearby.

His father was the next voice. "Aidan, we know you're there. Are you stuck?"

The young fox crawled to the edge and poked his head over, just so his nose and ears were visible. "Yes."

His mother held the crystal in her paw. "You shouldn't have this," she scolded, pointing it towards him accusingly. "We specifically told you not today, and you ran Hapi around in a chase."

Aidan scooted forwards and folded his arms, dangling his legs from the roof. "I just wanted to help," he grumbled. "You said today was important, and I was bored. I wanted to make things look nice."

Freya looked around. "What things? Oh…"

Llufrio was already inspecting the reliefs Aidan had adorned every nearby wall with. "He signed his name and everything."

Freya tapped her spear-like tool against the house and a stone platform slid underneath her, then rose to bring her to the roof, where her son curled even further into a ball.

"You can't just put drawings all over someone else's house."

"But they're not inside!" he protested.

"People own the outside of their houses too, Aidan. You'll need to clear it up and apologise to everyone, all right?"

Freya sighed. "I'm sorry we didn't include you, but we just… needed to focus. The gryphons are showing us how to improve what we do with the crystals. They want to help us grow, and have offered us protection if we work together. Eventually, this will involve you too, I promise. Will you come down?"

Aidan sat for a few seconds, staring at his knees, then stood up and took his mother's paw, not raising his head even as they descended to the ground via the stone elevator. Further down the street, Llufrio was freeing some inhabitants whose door had been obstructed by Aidan's spiked decorations in the archway. The young fox squeezed his mother's paw.

"I'm sorry."

"Just stay with me for now, all right?"

As they traipsed back to the gathering place, Aidan felt a light tap on his shoulder. He looked round to see Hapi wearing a kindly, warm expression.

"You can leave the flowers on my house," she whispered. "I think they're very pretty."

Aidan nodded and gave her a shy smile in return.

Chapter Three

"I, er... *very nearly ran around the Tor doing that myself when I was three.*"

"*It is your building to do with as you wish.*"

"*Well, at the time I was very into clouds and sea monsters; I don't think the Representatives would have been happy.*"

"*It is not their job to be happy; their job is to govern so that you, and others, can enjoy such freedoms.*"

"*Don't give me ideas, Osiris.*"

A path cleared for them as they returned to the gathering place and took their place at the end of the table just below the stage. Above them stood the gryphons, in their resplendent attire. Aidan thought they looked angry, but to him most birds did; the larger they got, the angrier they looked, so he hoped it was just their normal face. The red-crested leader cast her gaze to the young fox.

"I see you rescued your little one," she said, her gentle voice still booming with authority.

Llufrio bowed his head. "We did, yes. Apologies for interrupting."

"Quite all right," the avian continued, keeping her eyes on Aidan. "Very resourceful to have climbed so far by yourself. A higher view begets a bigger world."

Aidan didn't understand the last bit, but he nodded politely. The other gryphons stood stoically facing the rest of the village, while she opened her arms to the crowd before her.

"Denizens of Mahrae," she bellowed. "I am Venedreus, Archon of the nation of Arete. It is with great esteem that we present ourselves before you today, as messengers of a great partnership. We hold in enormous pride our quest to see the world grow and flourish. We seek out the most noble of knowledge-seekers and kindest of spirits. Among you will be brilliant voices and honourable warriors, willing to not only find a place of belonging, but to encourage others to belong with us.

"We seek an alliance with you for many reasons, but there are three of the utmost importance."

She raised a claw adorned with simple, but brilliantly shining bracelets. "Firstly, the resources for which a number of you have a natural affinity are incredibly special. These crystals, of which there are a dozen or so types, are immensely beneficial. We wish to guarantee your ability to improve yourselves, and we can, together, discover their full, or indeed infinite, potential."

"Secondly, perhaps the most immediate concern: we, and you, are in the midst of a dangerous struggle for these resources. The struggle has spread wide, and is both unseemly and potentially catastrophic. I am told you have been aware of something stirring beyond your reach, and may have witnessed it among your closer neighbours. We extend our bonds of friendship to you, because your safety above all else is paramount. To many others, it will not be. We wish to pre-empt those who will seek false alliances only to drain you for their own machinations of greed and supremacy, and leave you in desolation."

Murmurs rippled through the swathe of villagers.

"I understand this is an indecent way to address such serious news to you, especially where it may be seen that we are arbiters of our own agenda. That is why we have consulted your elders over the last few months, and slowly introduced ourselves and our motives to you. You do, collectively and individually, have every right to refuse our concordance. To that end I will make our final circumstance absolutely transparent."

She held her golden-scaled claws against her stomach and drew in a deep breath.

"We are dying."

The crowd murmured again, and some shifted uncomfortably.

"The specifics are… complicated," Venedreus continued, "but I promise it is the truth. Despite our best efforts, and exhaustive research from our many scholars and physicians, we have had little reprieve from our gradual decline. Henceforth, we are reliant on new lives, young minds, skilled and able bodies, to help us preserve our past and future, so that we in turn can continue our work and help secure the prosperity of the entire world. This I declare to you with the utmost sincerity."

She gave a great bow, and the gryphons either side of

her followed suit by taking a knee and bowing their heads in solemnity.

"It is long past time Arete opened our borders, and our minds, to you. We humbly offer ourselves to your service."

The village council, led by an older male coyote named Tennax, stepped onto the stage and offered the gryphons a formal bow in return. Tennax turned to his villagers. "We have discussed at length over the last season what Arete can bring to Mahrae and how best to protect ourselves from the ravages of weather, and resist the dangers of nomads and warring tribes. While we have no guarantee of how things may escalate, we believe this will benefit us in untold ways, and I, along with the remaining Elders, have suggested we graciously accept the company and cooperation with Arete."

Tennax reached out a paw to Venedreus, who took it heartily in a bold shake.

Polite, if somewhat trepidatious, applause rang out in the circle as the gryphons rose to a stand once more. Tennax gestured for them to sit at the table prepared for them at the edge of the stage, while he and the other elders sat either side of the delegation. Food was brought to the tables with the exact timing and choreography as a dance; within seconds huge numbers of fish, fruits, baked things, and vegetables had been presented to them all.

Llufrio and Freya were immediately next to the stage, sitting opposite each other. Aidan sat next to his father and kept watching the huge gryphons as they talked and ate, their claws big enough that they could crush his head like a mouldy pumpkin. The younger gryphon with crimson eyes, diagonally across from where Aidan sat, eyed him curiously.

"Have you seen us before?" he asked, with a kind but

deep voice.

Aidan jumped a little, and shook his head. "No, sir."

"You were on the roof, were you not?"

Aidan nodded. "Y… yes. I wasn't supposed to be, though."

The gryphon gave a wry smile. "I leave the judgement to your elders," he said, peeling away a section of fish with a single claw. "For my part, I admire the adventurous. Part of the reason that we came here is because we became mired in obsequious isolationism and stagnant tradition."

Aidan nodded blankly.

"How did you get up there, if I may ask?" he continued.

His voice was deep, but calm, like distant thunder. Despite his imposing size, their guest was a reassuring presence and did not loom as officiously as Venedreus. The cub looked to his parents. Llufrio politely gestured for Aidan to explain.

"I don't actually know how you got there, Aidan, so the story's yours. You're not in trouble for saying anything."

Aidan gave a short sigh and pushed a squash around the table in front of him. "Well, Mum and Dad have these crystals, and I can use them too. So while they were out, I got bored and tried to make things look nice. Then I ran away and made some stairs in the wall to climb up. But I dropped my crystal, and got stuck."

The gryphon raised his crested eyebrows. "You are an adept, even so young?"

Aidan glanced around for help, his head still slightly bowed in deference.

Freya gave a nervous laugh. "He experiments a lot. Between the three of us he has the most natural affinity. I

daresay he may have the most raw power in Mahrae, but…"
She and Llufrio exchanged quick, wary expressions.

"We don't know if he's ready for intense training yet," Aidan's father said hurriedly. "We haven't had the time to–"

The gryphon raised his talon. "I would not dream of taking one so young before they were ready. I value your unity and peace of mind, as without that, we have little else." He twirled a fishbone between his claws and shot an optimistic glance to Aidan. "However, I hope we shall see a demonstration of your prowess at some point."

Aidan bowed his head again; his tail flicked as excitement ebbed back into his demeanour.

"There's plenty of examples of his handiwork still on the walls," Freya said, pointedly, but not admonishing. "I'm sure you can watch him turn things back to normal with us."

The gryphon seemed satisfied, and looked once more to Aidan. "What is your name?"

"Aidan Arc'hantael, sir."

Their avian guest smiled. "It is a pleasure, Aidan. My name is Osiris Tallon. I am a Captain of Arete."

Curiosity lit Aidan's face, but it instantly withdrew when the stern Venedreus leant forwards to join the conversation.

"Tallon is one of our youngest captains. Impetuous, but part of the driving force to changing our methods." She turned her head to her subordinate. "Somewhat of a radical."

Osiris steepled his claws together. "You cannot be of the world and consider yourselves above it," he replied. "Philosophy, if never acted on, is good only for self-congratulation. We are in a position to give, and we have to. It is a far better alternative than the Dhraka."

"What's the Dhraka?" Aidan asked quickly. Venedreus shifted a little.

"They are... difficult. Dragons. An... opposition, of sorts; at least certain factions of them are. Much of our time in isolation has been spent protecting the wider world from their influence, but they have expanded beyond a point we can contain them, and in a much less beneficial way for anyone."

Aidan tilted his head. "So you want to stop them? Is it a war?"

Venedreus paused, the edges of her mouth behind her beak curling down slightly. "We are not venturing into this with predetermined aggression. We have had conflicts in the past, and there is mounting tension, but our intent is to shield you, encourage others into an alliance, and hope we find an end to future... contentions."

Llufrio and Freya assessed each other's concern, but thankfully it didn't appear that Aidan fully understood the envoy's inference, as he went back to his food. The discussion turned to lighter topics, including the promise of forthcoming cultivation projects for the village. Aidan kept looking at the silver staff next to his mother. The sharpened prism glinted proudly, one of the clearest and most precise gems he'd ever seen. But more fascinating than that, down the metal shaft were blue spirals of the same lustre. He couldn't take his eyes from its shimmer, the intricacy of its craftsmanship.

"What's that?" he said eventually, interjecting through another conversation.

Freya gestured to it, without touching it. "This is a tool that makes the crystals easier to work with, and enhances their power," she said carefully. "The gryphons have shown us how others used them."

"Is it yours?" Aidan asked to Osiris, who was sat nearest it.

He shook his head. "I cannot use it. Many in our species are too old, and haven't grown up with the powers like you have. Where the towers of Arete were built, there are very few crystals. It is predominantly those on the land who have access to their power, and the gryphons who wielded resonance before were not as gifted. Our size tends to make it less viable."

Aidan glanced up from the fish he was about to sink his teeth into. "Resonance?"

"Our term for the power in the crystals. You are very much a conjurer of this power." He looked to Freya and Llufrio. "You have quite a legacy here."

Llufrio smiled nervously. "We aren't the only ones in Mahrae who can use it, but we seem to have the, er… strongest affinity for them. And Aidan is something else completely," he said, ruffling his son's ears. Aidan waved his arms in protest and pulled his ears to the safety of his forehead, scrunching his nose.

Aidan still studied the staff intently. "How does it work?" he asked, leaning on the table to get a closer look.

"Would you like to try it?" Osiris ventured, more to Freya than to him.

Aidan nodded shyly, his eyes still glued to the tool.

"As long as you feel safe to permit, however," Osiris said, bowing his head to Freya and Llufrio. "You know his capabilities and temperament; I have no intent to overstep my bounds."

Freya scratched her neck, watching her son as he sat, politely impatient, as he waited for the outcome of the conversation to coalesce. "To be honest I'm not sure if we *do* know his capabilities yet. He's consistently surprised us. But…" she clasped her paws together in front of her and leant towards Aidan. "You can try it, but we'll be right behind you. Please, be *very* gentle."

"Promise, Mum" he replied quickly.

Osiris rose from his seat, gave a bow to the others at the table, and beckoned Aidan to follow. His parents followed suit, and together they walked to the buildings that the young fox had marked with his creativity a short while earlier.

The gryphon turned to face Aidan as they arrived. Aidan felt the brush of air from his wings and blinked away the sand that flew into his eyes.

"Why not start by making these walls neat and flat again?" Osiris suggested, kneeling to present Aidan with the rod. The cub took it gingerly, and the instant his small paw clutched the metal, he felt the crystal veins blossom into life beneath his fingers. It was like a pipe with water cascading through it, a constant, pulsating presence. Unlike anything he'd ever felt, but still part of him.

He walked to the wall, and hesitated. "Do I just… use it as normal?"

Freya nodded. "Hold it to the stone like you did before, but this will happen a lot faster, so be careful not to push too hard. Think of it like trying to pour water very, very slowly from a bucket with a wide mouth."

Aidan pulled at his waistcoat's shoulders for a second and then circled his hind paws in the sand to ground himself, as he'd been taught by his parents. Then, slowly, he pressed the prism's tip to the building's edge, took a deep breath, and tightened his grip on the staff.

A ripple thundered from the contact point, coursing around the walls, eliminating in moments the drawings and relief Aidan had put there, so quick that dust shook from the surface and sand pushed away from the foundations. Aidan stumbled back in surprise and fell on his tail, clutching the staff in both paws.

Osiris, Llufrio, and Freya all walked forwards to inspect the wall, and each carefully stroked its surface. It was as smooth as a pebble from a river; clean and precise.

Aidan rolled onto his haunches. "Is… is it okay?"

"This, young Arc'hantael," Osiris breathed, "is incredible. You may be the most promising resonator we have ever come across."

Aidan grinned and ran to his mother. "Can I help you now?"

Llufrio shook his head. "As I long suspected, I think we're going to be the ones helping *you*, Aidan."

Osiris knelt to the fox's height, who stood smartly and rested the spear by his side. "Aidan, if you could do anything with your resonance, what would it be?"

Aidan looked around cautiously. "Can it be lots of things?" he asked slowly.

"Anything," Osiris replied. "What do you want to do?"

"I like making things. Like buildings, for people to live and play in. And I want to fly!"

Osiris smiled, an expression that looked like it came rarely, but was of the highest calibre when received. "If you practice well, and stay honest and kind, I will help you do those things. One day, I would like you to visit Arete and learn from our scholars. When you are ready."

Aidan beamed. "Yes!" he whirled round to his parents. "Can we go now?"

Llufrio laughed. "Your mother and I need to stay here and look after Mahrae for a while. Let's wait till you're a little older before sending you away. You have a lot of practice to do."

Aidan frowned, not counting on the idea that he'd be going by himself. He edged closer to his parents, nestling between them. Osiris stood to his full height, still keeping his focus on Aidan. "We will be back regularly to provide resources to your village, so you are safe to focus as you need. I will check on you every time I pass through until you feel ready. Does that sound all right?"

Aidan nodded, and looked to the building next to him. "Can I go and practice?" he asked. Freya nodded, and Llufrio gave his son a pat on the shoulder as he darted to the next defaced building, eliminating the designs in clouds of dust.

Osiris stepped over to the fox's parents, his expression a little more sombre. "I promise you will be protected. You are remarkably fortunate to have fostered such ability, and we are fortunate that you nurtured him with kindness. The dangers of the world cannot always be fought against, but together, we will try. And maybe Aidan will be a cornerstone of setting things right."

Freya folded her arms. "He's not to become a pawn in any prideful wars against the Dhraka."

Osiris stiffened. "If things get worse, we may all be embroiled in this, but I will do what I can. It is the exact reason I am here, to assure you and other outlying communities that we are not seeking extinction or weaponisation, but co-operation. Arete has existed in fanciful pride for too long, and it has been killing us for generations."

"We turned away other tribes seeking alliances because we couldn't trust them," Llufrio said in a low voice. "Were it not for you personally, Venedreus wouldn't have convinced us. The gryphons have a history of indifference or outright derision for anyone they consider below them. She's little different to those who promised much and delivered nothing. What we lack in faith for others, we make up for in work for ourselves. Please keep trying to change Arete. Not even for you or me, but for Aidan."

Osiris bowed his head. "I promise. Even if nothing else survives, he will."

Chapter Four

"The shadow of war never leaves, does it?"

"For as long as I have been alive, there has been conflict. It is... hard not to draw a correlation, but the truth is we have not yet brought everyone to a place they can live peacefully. That was, and still is, my intent."

The following years harboured a slowly-creeping tension as the village grew. The gryphons visited every four to six weeks, sometimes with resources, sometimes with stories, but always with tired reservation, and a hesitance to discuss how the outside world was faring. Mahrae tried not to push too far out so as not to raise scrutiny from errant neighbours, but elders would increasingly report who had been seen at the forest's edge or what movements had been sighted from the watch towers on the cliff. It rarely affected daily routine, but still coloured it. On the whole, things actually became easier for many villagers and the population grew by a considerable amount. But with prosperity came a sinking uneasiness that it could easily turn dangerous later down the line, whether through direct misdeeds by the Aretians or an escalation of fortune or tension that would paint them as a target. Some villagers refused to leave their houses when the Aretians arrived, such had their apprehension grown.

Aidan had been far from the only child when he was born, but now there were more every year, and the meals became bigger and more varied. Desert cultivation resulted in tolerable conditions for crops and livestock, eventually silencing the argument that the whole settlement should move somewhere more temperate, though it was not without setbacks along the way. Fertile land was in great competition, and Mahrae had survived peacefully so far simply for having the resourcefulness to survive where nobody else wanted to live.

But these resources were under growing concern of being raided, and while Mahrae's growth and successes could subdue the worry for short moments, it was something the elders, and Aidan's parents, knew too well, and regularly reminded him of as he trained his way through resonance tools. It was never to have him live in fear, but rather as a prompt to exercise caution, and focus on benevolent construction projects and means of defence. If Osiris was going to be true to his word, they intended to make Aidan as indispensible and diplomatic as possible. And, true to expectations, he excelled at consistently expanding the horizons of his ability.

Now sixteen, Aidan had managed to focus his behaviour

considerably in the last few years. He still nurtured a mischievous streak with light practical jokes, but being able to completely focus on training had helped to eliminate the more argumentative habits of his childhood.

He had shaped numerous crystals for specific purposes and elements, allowing them to be used right away without any additional modification, and had hewn great chambers into the cliffs for cool, secure food storage. He'd formed glass from sand and reflected natural light into hidden caves to discover more living areas and underground resources. Part of the cultivation's success had been down to his location of an aquifer nearby, which the gryphons helped to tap. His buildings became more intricate and sturdier, even without the assistance of the Aretian stave. So protective of these tools were the gryphons that Aidan could only use them upon the Aretian visits, but he quickly came to understand their characteristics. The crystal forks around the shaft accelerated resonance impulses in the same way a pendulum swung round a claw will increase in speed as its chain shortens. It took far less energy to impart a much greater physical effect, and thus the energy influenced a far wider area. Once Aidan's knowledge of the acceleration was basic enough, he could apply the changes to crystals in their raw form, although it degraded the crystal to reshape it multiple times for different purposes unless attached to the stave.

After a time, he took over his parents' role in fulfilling tasks that required resonance, and he taught his methods to others where they had the affinity for it. Many chose not to because prolonged use resulted in numbness, aches, pains, and other afflictions, but he was able to bear it for the most part. Freya and Llufrio could not sustain their abilities for as long as Aidan could now; even with his improved methods and refined crystal structure, they became exhausted quickly. It worried him, but he saw it as greater precedence to learn and practice as much as possible, and find new means of supporting the village to allow them peace and stability.

Osiris' previous visit came with another offer for Aidan to embark on a trip to Arete; no matter how often he was asked or how long he considered it, he couldn't determine if he was ready. There was always more to *do*. The young fox felt a duty of care to his home and his parents, but his knowledge was still limited. Poring over the ancient books Osiris brought him, he realised many were philosophical rather than practical, and the meditation he was encouraged to perform only brought him so far into developing new techniques. But then, leaving Mahrae brought promise of seeing how he could benefit more than just his home, and bring the opportunities he'd been granted to other villages who needed them. It was obvious that any good person with an ability could be of use anywhere, but he knew it was short-sighted to grow complacent. Each place had its own needs, rules, and traditions that needed adhering to. To Aidan's mind, he existed through the generosities of others; not just the patience of Osiris and his parents, but the village as a whole, and by extension anyone who had yet passed Mahrae over as being unworthy of invasion or ransacking. The choice by a faction to not ravage them wasn't true generosity so much as a temporary lapse of malice, though.

Osiris was returning today. Aidan had thrown himself fervidly into the projects that needed finishing, and currently there was little that needed the crystals' intervention. It was as good a position as any to be in, but he grew anxious whenever he considered that the minute he stepped out of the village, something catastrophic could happen, and he wouldn't be nearby.

His parents insisted they would be safe; that things would continue as they always had. His concern was a testament to his kindness, but also a potential limitation. He could only grow so far within Mahrae.

He rested on the edge of the short cliff that overlooked the village, letting the breeze run through his fur. Below him lay the stairs, hand-carved into the rock by generations before him, which he had smoothed over and levelled. Even though it was ultimately safer, there was something sad about losing the stones' rough, historic nature. It took an enormous amount of focus to create in front of him what he saw in his mind, and tiny fluctuations could alter something permanently and unintentionally. Striking a balance between natural and functional didn't always work, either. Age was impossible to create artificially, at least as far as he'd tried, and although geometry was natural on a smaller scale, the bigger it became, the starker it looked. Aidan preferred twisting shapes out of existing forms, keeping their character. He hoped this would be something Osiris, and the other Aretians, would understand as he began his training.

He adjusted the thick belt around his waist, an intricate plate of leather and cord, with a spiral at its widening centre. For a long time, it had been believed that their powers came from inner energies, so many of the patterns on resonators' clothing were made to channel focus to various parts of the body, always outwards, from the core, to the limbs and head. Some villagers had shaved patterns into their fur for greater effect. Aidan found this interesting and attractive, but never considered the benefit anything other than motivational. More pertinently, he never settled on a design.

Leaning his head back and closing his eyes, he let the sun warm his face. He gently rolled over the small piece of crystal in his right paw, feeling its clean edges against his palm. This was his meditation, refining his connection to the crystals to work out more ways of using them. He wondered whether the Aretian device's shaft or its crystal had been constructed first, or whether they had to be wrought simultaneously. He was excited to find out. He'd tried emulating it with a wooden base, but often the energy from the crystals desiccated the branch, or burnt it, or warped it to a point where the delicate veins snapped.

A light, sharp horn split the air. Aidan's eyes flared open. A familiar shape swept across the sky, golden wings reflecting bright in the sun. Aidan leapt to his feet and sprinted down the stairs. The instant his feet hit the sand, he knelt and planted the crystal into it. A disc of sand whirled beneath him, whisking him along the village streets like a wave.

Osiris landed; a second later Aidan drifted to a halt before him, dividing the crowd that was forming to greet the eminent guest. Aidan looked to his mentor, resolute.

"I could fly into this village a thousand different ways and you would still find a way to outdo me," the gryphon chided with a wry smile.

Aidan stood smartly to attention. "Complement you,

Osiris. I would never attempt to overshadow you. Flight's not something I expect to master as gracefully. You were born for it."

"One could say the same for you and your abilities," Osiris responded. "Do you mean to tell me you are ready?"

The fox scooped his tail into his hand and grasped it, somewhat fretfully. "I was until you asked," he said, with a nervous laugh. "But I'll go where you need me," he said.

"Aidan," Osiris said, in a low, soft voice. "This is not about what *I* need. This is *your* journey. I cannot make you come to Arete. Your achievements would mean nothing if drawn under force."

Aidan let out a whistling sigh. The promise, the fantastical ideas of what he could achieve ran through his head constantly, but – he kicked the red sand, pushing his pawpad into it to leave an imprint – this would always be home.

"I'll come back, right?" he asked timidly.

Osiris lent out a talon to him. "There is no world in which I could deny you a path to where you belonged," he said.

Aidan clasped his paw around the gryphon's claw and shook it, a short sigh belying the confidence in his grip. "Let me get my things." He turned and began the walk home, feeling the buildings' closeness much more now than a few moments prior. By the time he reached his door, Osiris his shadow, his arms felt like heavy, hollow tubes, and his head buzzed. His tail flicked from side to side with nervous energy. As he reached for the handle, the door swung away and just inside were his parents, with Tennax. He swayed backwards a little, and almost turned directly into Osiris' breastplate.

"Ah, our young prodigy," Tennax creaked, in his inscrutable way that sounded both reverent and patronising. The coyote had developed a twist in his spine that bent him to the right, so his walking, talking, and movement were laboured, but through pure tenacity he conducted himself as powerfully as his body would allow. Apparently that meant racing to Aidan's parents at the first sign of development.

"Captain Tallon," he continued. "As always, a privilege. I assume you are about to conduct our young Arc'hantael's exodus?"

Osiris bowed his head. "If he so wishes, then yes, it will be a punctuated visit from me." He looked to Aidan. "But I believe this is the moment for him to make that decision."

Tennax clasped his paw on his cudgel-like cane and hobbled over the threshold. "Then we shall wait outside." In agreement, Osiris stepped back to allow room for the elder to leave, while Aidan slipped inside and quietly shut the door behind him. His parents watched him expectantly as he laced and unlaced his paws together, trying to find words that vanished deep within his chest.

"Do you have everything you need?" his father asked quietly.

Aidan nodded. "There's a… sack in my room."

While Llufrio went to retrieve it, Freya smiled at her son. "You'll do incredible things, you know."

He sighed. "I… I'll try, anyway. So I can bring them back here."

His father descended the steps. Perhaps his trepidation at leaving was inventing reasons to stay, but Aidan could swear his movements were stiffer than even a week ago.

Llufrio passed the bag to his son.

"Here or there, we will be thinking of you always."

Once he took the bag, Aidan cast his arms around his father in a tight hug. Freya stepped up and embraced them both.

"We'll be fine, Aidan," she said. "We're proud of you."

After a second more, Aidan backed away, and gave a deep, controlled exhale. He swung the sack over his shoulder and looked to his parents one last time. "See you soon. I love you."

"Love you too," they returned, taking each other's paws.

Aidan turned to the door and pushed it open, letting the light spill onto his body, and took his first step towards Arete.

Outside, Osiris was finishing his debrief to Tennax.

"The Castije have suffered in the recent drought to the north, too. They are an outlier to our diplomacy, so this may be an opportunity."

Tennax scratched the underside of his muzzle. "You've really been having that little luck against Dhraka? They're hardly the most charismatic nation."

Osiris' feathers puffed slightly. "Their tool is coercion, not charm. Where resistance is not enough to repel them, they redouble with territorial encroachment or resource strangling. I believe they sabotaged the river. It is my hope that an offer of reconstruction will sway them to our favour."

Tennax noticed Aidan's exit from his homestead and gave an approving wave of his paw as a signal to approach.

"Safety be with you, Arc'hantael. Make us proud, and good luck."

He bowed his head and left.

"Are you ready?" Osiris asked.

"By the time I *feel* ready, I'll probably be too late," Aidan said, his voice an unsteady mix of determination and resignation. "I need to go, and…" he gave a sigh, "despite my fears, I *do* want to. And maybe… if I do everything right… it won't be long before I can come back."

His guardian swelled. "You do yourself justice with a mind and heart so honest," he preened. "It will be my pleasure to guide you through your time in Arete."

Osiris spun round and strode to the gathering space at the village's centre. Aidan almost had to run to keep up with the wide, powerful strides. "Will you need me to follow on foot?" he asked quickly.

Osiris spread wide his wings, giving a wry look over his shoulder. "You wanted to fly, correct?"

After a moment of bewilderment, Aidan carefully clambered onto the gryphon's back, and clasped his arms around his thick, feathery neck. Just as he began to doubt whether this was a good idea, he felt himself lurch backwards, and before him was a rush of wind and blue. He tensed, burying his head in Osiris' feathers, closing his eyes.

It may have been the wind, but he swore he heard the gryphon laugh.

After what seemed like minutes, he rocked forwards. Osiris had stopped ascending and had levelled out. After a brief scrabble to reposition himself, Aidan caught his first glimpse of the land below.

Far below.

A dizzying spread of sand and high stone lay beneath him, with a silvery river cascading through it. In the distance was the gentle haze of the trees. He glanced around to see other horizons, different plateaus of desert and trees stretched in all directions.

"I never realised it was this big," he shouted, half-gasping for the force of the wind against his face.

Osiris kept his steely gaze forward. "From your village, you would have no idea what the rest of this world is," he replied. "I have seen it, far and wide, and I still discover things anew."

"Will we fly over any villages?" Aidan called back. Osiris glanced over his shoulder.

"The path to Arete is mostly desert," he replied, "but there are some settlements. We fly predominantly over unpopulated areas to avoid unnecessary conflict. The air is typically safe, except near Dhraka."

At the mention of the dragons, a chill swept over Aidan, and not from the wind. The sky may be safe from any warriors on the ground, but dragons could match them with ease. He prayed there would be no scouts.

They flew for another hour before Osiris took them to the shade of a large menhir in the middle of otherwise abandoned scrubland, where they ate and rested. Aidan dug around in his sack for a map and rolled it out over his knees. Mahrae was labelled, and he traced a claw over the path he estimated they took.

The land, traced in dark ink on the thick parchment, was a single, uneven continent, known as Vu-ori. It had stubby but defined peninsulas, making it not unlike a squashed, ancient starfish, and a spiralling archipelago to the north-east. That was Skyria, legendary for lush green landscapes and rich forests. Dotted around were other tribal territories, nations, or settlements, but there were many undocumented thanks to constant moving, annexing, and a distinct lack of extraneous exploration from Mahrae. Most of their knowledge of the land came from the sparse trade meetings, ceremonies of truce, and the few travellers who crossed them in the central south desert. Within minutes, Arete had demonstrated knowledge of a greater world than Mahrae had developed in decades. Although he had a vague idea of where it was on the map when Osiris had mentioned it previously, Aidan hadn't yet placed a mark on Arete.

"Your village is in the wrong place," Osiris said, tearing into a mouthful of dried fish. "It is further East than that."

"Oh. Well, I suppose you'd know, seeing it from above," Aidan mused, casting his eye around the map's coastline. "Most settlements are on the peninsulas, aren't they?"

Osiris nodded. "It's where the resources are. This landmass is too wide to sustain anything at its heart unless you have abilities like yours. And it is often too harsh for many to traverse. This is why competition for space and capabilities has become so desperate among the other settlements. It is becoming crowded."

Aidan frowned. "And the Dhrakans, where are they?"

"South-west, almost exactly opposite us from you. They control much of the lands over there, and have a tight grip on metal mines for weaponry and armour. We had a… fragile peace agreement, which has all but dissolved in recent decades."

"What happened?"

Osiris shifted uncomfortably. "That will be for your tutor to impart."

Aidan shot him a suspicious glance. Osiris returned it with a look of similar misgiving. "It is not for want of omission. Our achievements are numerous and illustrious, but I… have reservations about our direction. The agreement to your staying was that I would not be in charge of your political and historical education, for fear I may… misrepresent us." He looked at the sky. "However, you asked for transparency and I will give it. We are a flawed nation, and too often we flatter our history with accomplishments and conquests instead of humility at losses or hubris. If our future is to mean anything, we must learn from our mistakes. Ignoring them places us on a precipice to commit them again, and again, until we are nothing but dust and regrets."

He sniffed sharply and shook his shoulders, ruffling his feathers. "Time, currently, is of essential consideration. I wish to arrive by twilight. While they would be unwise to venture this far south in numbers that would do us harm, Dhrakan eyes see better in the darkness, and in red environments."

Smartly finishing their provisions, once again Aidan clambered onto Osiris' back and they soared into the brilliant blue.

Flying exhilarated the young fox. Although his arms tired, he dared not ask for a break. He watched the land pass serenely below, marvelling at natural patterns so vast and sweeping he never could have grasped their scope from the ground. It immediately put him in mind of ways to change the crystal formations. The desire to explore even further overtook his apprehension.

Much of the journey he spent in silent contemplation or reverent wonder at the expanse below them. Despite never having been closer to the sky, he could not wait to once again touch the land of Vu-ori, and converse with it to uncover new, enticing secrets.

They chased the sky as it darkened, until in the distance a coastline split the landscape, and the ground beneath them grew more populated with trees and grasslands. Settlements, visible before only for the clearings of trees surrounding them, began to light torches as the sun dipped in the sky. Tiny orange flickers shimmered below them.

Ahead, a blazing beacon flashed into view. The closer they drew, the brighter it blazed, forming a sparking, roiling flame that licked the night sky. It sat atop the silhouette of a massive cylindrical tower, the largest of a network connected by bridges in a geometric web. Further out from them was a wide circle of smaller watchtowers.

"Is that Arete?" Aidan stammered.

Osiris couldn't help but swell at the fox's reaction. "It is. The culmination of our sovereign nation so far. A testament to our survival and quest for knowledge, and soon, it will be worth even more for what we are yet to bring to the world, and the direction you may take us. Our towers are a conduit between the sky, where our dreams and spirits take flight, and the ground, on which we walk and depend for survival and growth." He paused for a moment, then spoke more quietly. "I hope the mark we leave will be worth everything preceding."

Torches illuminated the unblemished walls of the silver-white towers and bridges. Spiral walkways painted with gold railings laced their way up the outer edges of the buildings with immaculate precision. The largest towers, in a line perpendicular to the shore, were tiered, with flying buttresses resting on each layer below. On the roof of each tower a series of spires encircled a central, larger belfry. It was in the belfry of the largest tower that the beacon Aidan first saw roared and billowed.

Aidan barely registered that they were descending, and tensed when he noticed the tree line encircling them on their landing approach. Osiris' wings spread wide, and with a graceful, powerful swoop, came to a rest immediately in front of the gatehouse at the shore's edge: the head of the bridge leading to the massive towers themselves. Either side of them, and further into the forest, were more watch towers. Arete was intimidating not only for its unforgiving promise of constant vigilance, but also its sheer eminence over the landscape. The precision of its construction was on a scale unlike anything Aidan had ever seen. Gigantic natural formations were one thing, but it was another to hone accuracy and detail on grand entities such as these.

"I… have a lot to learn," he murmured, sliding from Osiris' back to his wobbly legs. He staggered for a second, then braced his paws on his thighs and looked up at the shining tower.

"That is, of course, why you came here." Osiris pulled at the feathers on his neck with a smug grin. "I think you can manage."

Aidan gripped his knees tightly. "It'll take more than a few nights to reach this standard, that's for sure."

Osiris clapped the fox on the shoulder and, once Aidan felt confident he wouldn't collapse just for looking up at the gargantuan citadels, they traversed the bridge. It led directly from the height of the cliff to the tower, looming above the sea. The undulating froth of waves crashed against the rocks below, and the breeze that whipped through the parapet gaps was fierce. Aidan could tell why wings would be useful here; the wind sheer would enable you to take flight in moments.

Arete wasn't so much a city as a network of palaces. Everything gave the impression of eternity. From the immaculate, unworn stonework to the stalwart guards standing at intervals along the bridge, Aidan felt his journey to a whole other world begin. This was the land of the ancients. Above him, golden wings glided between towers, illuminated by the brilliant torches below.

Partway across he pressed his muzzle through the parapet to study the base of the tower. Waves crashed around it; the huge tapering foundation was the widest structure he'd ever seen, and looked completely smooth from this distance. Light from window slits trembled with flickering flame. At varying levels from the tower's midpoint to the sea were large, open platforms populated with awnings, arenas, amphitheatres, gardens; all manner of open-air leisure grounds. Aidan thought he could see a modest port to the rear of the furthest tower, but it was mostly obscured, and there were no boats in his narrow angle of view.

"I'm surprised you need boats when you can fly," he said idly.

Osiris gave him a look askance. "Individual flight is far

from useful when you have goods to trade or several hundred aeries' worth of mouths to fill with fish," he retorted. "One day I hope for something different, but until then we find ourselves confined to sea vessels for those purposes. We even have wheeled carts for transporting stone, if that is not too much of a stretch for your imagination." He flicked some sea spray from his pauldron. "I would wager, however, that our boats are the best engineered of any in this world for speed and efficiency."

Aidan nodded blankly, not assuming anything to the contrary but ascertaining this may be a source of future interest from his guardian.

The gates at the end of the walkway were about ten times taller than he was, golden, and bore enormous casts of gryphons holding what looked like the sun and moon, represented as duos of fish chasing each other within an egg. Through the open door lay a semi-circular courtyard in front of the tower's base. Aidan could see more gryphons talking, milling around, closing marketplace stalls. White and gold plumage seemed to be the most common, but he saw gryphons of silver, charcoal, slate blue, and russet as well; he didn't doubt there may be even more colourful creatures within the city proper.

"You have a market!" he said incredulously.

Osiris shrugged. "Of sorts; considering we are more or less self-sufficient here, within the walls we trade services and agreements for what we need. We have hunters, builders, crafters, physicians and entertainers much like any other place you should see. Highest esteem belongs to the engineers, scholars, and philosophers, however. They reside in this tower, in the upper levels."

Osiris walked Aidan through the plaza, where he was given curious glances by the other Aretians. Under the ostentatiousness of the buildings and their stature, Aidan could see familiar strata of village roles playing out in the plaza, and it was heartening to see something more down-to-earth as part of the intimidating magnificence he was walking into. But the comfort of normality was fleeting, as he felt the pressing gaze of the citizens, as if expectation of his performance was already carved into the steps of a library dais somewhere, with some grand plan to fulfil that they already knew far more about than he did.

He watched the dizzying ceiling of the entranceway pass over his head, and he could only look at the mosaic tiles for a few seconds before his vision began to swim. They traipsed through gilded marble halls and immense corridors until they exited the rear of the first tower. They passed many other gryphons on the way, to whom Aidan found himself bowing his head as each went by. By the time they reached the central tower, his eyes were wide and his fur on end.

"Are you all right, Aidan?"

Aidan nodded, barely. "Yeah... I'm just a little, er... this place is so big. You're all so big. Arete is huge and it's... you can *feel* it. It's, um... it's a lot to live up to."

Osiris took in a deep breath, and held it for a few seconds, chewing his answer into shape. "Our past is less important than our future, even though it brought us here," he breathed eventually, as they climbed a wide spiral stair. "Whether our futures entwine for a week or a lifetime, we honour those around us at this moment. Our race is likely not long for this world, so it is our duty to pass on what we can to those who will make best use of it. The world is to be lived in by those who protect it in the time they are given." He laid a claw on Aidan's shoulder. "Our history is not your history. Do not let it intimidate you. You have knowledge and experiences we have never seen, and will bring light to shadows where we did not even know there was darkness. Do not get caught up in the arrogance of our hereditary privilege. You have a purer truth than one learnt from books written about ourselves."

Aidan sighed, and managed a tired smile. "Thanks. I'll do my best."

They came to a landing lined with rows of dark oak doors of incredible finish. They made their way to the furthest room to the right. Even with Osiris' visible strength pushing against it, the wood's weight was apparent, as it drifted open with the same energy as one expected a tectonic plate to have. Inside lay a bedroom about as large as Aidan's old house, with a spiral staircase leading to a balcony-mezzanine, and a large bed nestled in an arched window nook. The floors were smooth, cool stone. Aidan immediately pressed against the window, the firm, rich cushion barely registering the drop of his satchel. He could see three towers from here – two watchtowers from the outer circle, and the final large tower of the central line. The sea rolled gently below them, turning purple in the cascading twilight.

"I know this room is grander than what you have known," Osiris said, "but I hope it will provide a space of comfort and serenity all the same."

"Thank you," Aidan said quietly, staring at the waves.

Osiris turned over an apple from a bowl of fruit which

had been left for Aidan's arrival, checking that a blemish was not, in fact, an insect of some kind. "Please help yourself to anything in here. I will be back to call on you after sunrise. There should be an attendant at the end of the landing if you need anything during the night." He rested his claw on his rapier pommel. "Is there anything else you need of me?"

Aidan half-turned to the gryphon, and shook his head.

Osiris paused for a second. The fox's tail was curled tightly around him, and his ears angled back.

"It is… very different here," Osiris said quietly. "But your bravery in venturing so far from home does you credit. You will be a great asset, not only to us, but to yourself, your family, and the world which we are humbled to share together." He crossed the room to a wooden bureau, adorned with tall candles in bronze dishes. "If you would find it a therapy, on the desk here is parchment, to write to your parents."

Aidan gave a quick, weak smile, and nodded. "Thank you. I'll probably just eat and then get some sleep."

"Till morning, then. Rest well." Osiris bowed politely and made a quiet exit.

Aidan knelt on the bed, gathering the sheets around his shoulders. He gazed through the glass at the darkening sea, and the ghostly reflection of the rising moon playing across the waves like a pale white flame. Slipping it from his belt, he tightly gripped the crystal he brought from home, and held it to his chest.

Chapter Five

"We... we both left our homes at such similar ages."
"Under very different circumstances, Faria."
"It doesn't make an unknown future any less intimidating."

Aidan awoke to a pounding on his door. He hauled himself upright, and with a breathy grumble threw his arm over his face to shield himself from the beaming sunlight. After a few seconds of strained squinting he pulled the sheet over his head like a shroud and stumbled out of the bed. Whispered curses rattled in his throat as he staggered to the door. With about as much effort as he expected, which was considerable, he pulled it just open enough to see who summoned him.

Osiris was vaguely sympathetic, perhaps; Aidan couldn't focus properly, trying to blink away the fog that slid over his eyes.

"I apologise for the disturbance, but I am glad at least to see we can survive a premature awakening."

Aidan groaned. "S'fine. Hi Osiris."

"Was your comfort adequate?"

Aidan looked wistfully back at the bed and shrugged. "I slept. I think. A little. Not enough."

Osiris frowned. "If you require different bedding, we can supply—"

Aidan shook his head. "No, it's – it's fine. Thank you." He managed a brief, polite smile and hugged the sheets around his shoulders. Osiris cleared his throat.

"Well, when you are fit to do so, I will take you to our halls for breakfast."

Aidan nodded, and quietly shut the door to get ready.

A few minutes later he emerged, no longer a phantom of sleep, but his flattened ears betrayed his uneasiness. He barely talked to Osiris as they traversed the chambers and corridors to the dining hall, the energy to converse lost somewhere in the back of his mind.

Osiris suffered no such impediment, however, continuing his tour of Arete as they navigated past benches and stone tables. "We provide food enough for all who need it, including guests and soldiers, and give supplies to those who wish to cook for themselves later. We ensure none of our number go hungry."

It was impressive, but Aidan could immediately see the difficulties of working with wings in a kitchen environment. The pinions were covered in cape-like sheets that tied around the waist and under the thigh to keep them close to the body, reducing the risk of them swinging into co-workers or shelves. The cooks and servers wore hoods over their crests and held utensils with leather sheaths over their claws. It was remarkable attention to detail and hygiene; Aidan had never seen anything so organised. A line of gryphons passed the railing where the food selections were: huge dishes of meat and vegetables laid over ice to preserve freshness, and trays of individual servings above them.

Osiris exchanged salutes with friends and soldiers as he passed. Aidan shrank behind him to avoid looking conspicuous, but seemed to attract attention regardless. He sensed it was on the side of kindness or indifference, but he was too tired and self-conscious to maintain more than an instant's eye contact, and even then it was often accidental. He turned his gaze immediately to Osiris' back as soon as he saw two younger gryphons talking animatedly with eyes focused on him. He felt his face flush. Following Osiris around like a surrogate father was unsettling, and he was already a diminutive unknown in a land of giants. Once he reached the food he snatched a few things that looked familiar and kept to his guardian's heel like a shadow.

"If you would rather go somewhere private, I can arrange for food to be brought to you," Osiris said, his brow furrowed with concern at the fox's flicking tail and tapping foot. Aidan cracked his paw knuckles.

"I don't mind being here, I'm just… I was expecting more… you're all gryphons."

Osiris returned him with a blank look. "We *are* gryphons."

Aidan cleared his throat. "Yes, I mean, but there are so many of you. From the way Arete was talked about, I had thought to see something more…"

"Intersectional? Dead?"

Aidan clicked his tongue. "No… maybe. I'm not sure. I don't even know what I thought this place would be like. I'm not used to standing out as a fox. There are so many of us at home."

Osiris chuckled. "There are worlds of infinite scale, from the one we walk, to the ones that walk within us. You will be a curio for those who never see anything but our walls and the ocean. I will marshal them away from you when appropriate, but there is a limit to how much I can diminish your presence. After all, you are here to learn and be celebrated for that." He leant in. "I will, however, always guarantee your absolute safety."

Aidan finished his meal in silence, wary of the scrutiny he may be receiving at a distance. For the excursion here to have been on his terms, he suddenly felt very little was actually in his control.

Sensing his discomfort, Osiris took Aidan swiftly into the rearmost tower of Arete, to what felt like an incredibly high level. They ascended past a massive theatre, adorned with all manner of ancient and classical artistry and reliefs. Above this, the staircase widened on a sweeping ascent to its final level. Sunlight streamed through towering windows. Laid out before them was a library taking up the entire breadth of the tower. Staircases at its edges led to sprawling upper levels laden with monumental racks of books and scrolls. At the centre of this floor was a spiralling, gently rumbling orrery of Eeres, their world, encircled by the sun and moon, and a platform of the seasons rotating beneath it.

Aidan's jaw and tail dropped.

Waiting by the orrery was Venedreus, and an even older gryphon, who nudged a set of glasses up her beak upon sighting Osiris and his charge. The two stood smartly, and bowed to them upon their meeting.

"It is an honour to see you again, young master," Venedreus declared. "I am glad you are safe arrived, and look to be in good health."

Aidan bowed in kind. "It's been an incredible trip," he said quickly, suddenly remembering he had no clue what the formal address was for a creature of such standing. Thankfully, Venedreus was politely impassive enough to not give away if he had made a mistake in not saying anything at all, and turned to the elder gryphon. Her plumage was mottled grey, and her eyes a shade of ashen yellow. Despite her glasses, her gaze was acute and discerning. Aidan suspected the lenses were for reading, as she still looked capable of sighting prey at great distances. Aidan hoped he didn't present himself the same way.

"This is Gygel, one of our most esteemed scholars," Venedreus said. "She is an expert on history, and on resonance behaviours and techniques. Along with Osiris as your supervisory companion, Gygel will be instructing you on deeper knowledge that will prove invaluable for exploring the secrets of crystal divination and their appropriate use, given the way of the world."

Aidan looked to Osiris, then back to Gygel, and gave a quick bow. "It's a pleasure," he said quickly, talking to a sudden stop. He glanced around for a second. "Forgive me… if I sound rude; I thought gryphons weren't resonators?"

"We are not," the wizened Gygel muttered. "But there are theories of matter, element, history, substance, and morality that will be vital to your understanding of resonance as a part of nature and a tool for communication. You must have a sound mind in order to have a thorough grasp of the implications of power."

The fox gave a nervous grin. "Well, I did explode a desert rat once, so that's probably no bad thing…"

He froze at the stony expressions that greeted him. From their countenance he might as well have started blowing porridge through his nose. Suddenly he felt out of his depth again, instantly transported to any of the various times in his youth when an idea he'd posited was met with viable criticism or warnings of danger. He had not anticipated being further evaluated on his morality given what he ventured here to do in the first place, and this set a foreboding shadow over him as he considered what the lessons may entail. He looked down for a moment to recompose himself, clasping his paws. "There's a lot for me to learn."

"We wish you swift and healthy progression," the Archon replied, more formally than she needed to. "Should you be in need of anything, it shall be provided."

She gave a curt nod to her colleagues and marched away.

Gygel turned almost immediately and began walking towards the right-hand staircase. After a few steps she cast her head back to Aidan.

"Our journey to enlightenment commences, unless you have any objections."

Aidan obviously looked a little more distressed than he intended, as Osiris gave a sort of apologetic head tilt before gesturing for the fox to follow the scholar on a brisk, unwavering path to education.

The study room was as grand and ornate as the library's main chamber, albeit on a smaller scale. There were a dozen of these lecture rooms around the upper level, each one with its own immaculate window and wall-to-wall metal shelves covered in books and scrolls. This one appeared to have been set up with Aidan in mind, as at its centre was a single gilded stool, and a writing desk before it. The seat of the stool was at about the height of Aidan's head, so he had to vault himself onto it. At his full arms' stretch he grabbed the desk and scraped it across the floor towards him, almost unbalancing it in the process. Gygel stared at him with a single raised eyebrow, not even paying attention to the book she was leafing through. She seemed to know the pages by feel alone. She stopped suddenly and placed a claw at the top of a new chapter.

"What do you know of our world, Master Aidan?"

Aidan shuffled in his chair. He would need to smuggle a cushion from his room, as the cold, hard seat was not made to accommodate creatures as small as him. He tried to hide his awkward shifting as much as possible, but he quickly determined from Gygel's deepening stare that nothing would ever escape her vigilance.

"Well, Eeres is a world with a mostly singular landmass, Vu-ori. There are three major nations; yours, Skyria, and Dhraka. The rest are settlements, tribes, or small independent cities."

"And of the land?"

Gygel began a slow, wide circle around the room. Aidan glanced to Osiris, who was reading by the window. "Mostly desert, in the centre, and forests towards the edge and on the peninsulas. Mountains are relatively common in all landscapes."

Gygel nodded. "A perfunctory introduction. We will build on this, as the land is key to all types of resonance, their variance, application, and history. You are here to learn about resonance, are you not?"

"Yes," Aidan said firmly. That was one matter about which he was resolute.

"Very decisive," she preened, a glint in her eye. "Then you must be willing to understand all there is about the crystals, including all that came before. What do you know of them?"

Aidan clicked his claws on the desk. "They're… malleable, but only by those with a power to—"

"Where are they from?" Gygel commanded, her voice suddenly amplified.

"I, er…"

"We have established a baseline," she sighed, shifting her glasses up her beak with a stiff claw. She paced further around him. "They are from the moon," she began, raising her talon animatedly. Her voice echoed around the chamber; it was like being addressed by a chorus of her as the acoustics reflected the words back to him from all directions. "Long ago, a meteor of indeterminate metallic composition struck the moon in a glancing blow, sending debris – and the majority of its own body – hurtling towards Eeres. As it entered the atmosphere, it heated tremendously, but did not burn up or vaporise. It struck our surface with incredible strength, forming many craters, sending ash into the skies, darkening and cooling our planet for some time afterwards. The desert which your village of Mahrae resides in, is the result of the impact."

Aidan gripped the edge of the table. "But that's… that desert is most of the continent."

Gygel peered at him over her glasses. "Indeed. Such was their impact, and so must your respect for their power match that capacity for destruction. At the very centre of Vu-ori is the widest known resonance crater, where the largest concentration of debris fell. The land here is strange, uninhabitable to normal, unprepared creatures. Many of the native settlements believe it to be cursed by spirits or home to a demon monster, so we have typically needed to intervene little to keep villages away from its resources. Dhraka, on the other hand…"

She tapped a claw on the edge of her book, before taking in a sharp breath to continue. "The crystals themselves, do you know how many types there are?"

Aidan shook his head.

"We have documented eight distinct colours, with varying purity and crystalline structure in each, and several sub-types of these. We believe this was due to the speed at which they cooled, their density, the absorption of impurities from the surrounding area and materials from impact with the moon, and henceforth alterations in their elemental composition. Those which cooled more rapidly have a tighter structure and tend to be smaller, so have less flexibility in their output."

Aidan nodded, rolling his blue prism between his fingers. Gygel raised her eyebrows and loosened a sly smile. "I see you already investigating this knowledge as an application," she mused. "We will not be conducting practical experiments in a room such as this, however."

"Oh, of course," Aidan sputtered. He dreaded to think

how long it would take him to repair any damage to a room so intricate. "I was just getting a feel for this type of crystal."

"Yours is common, but one of the most versatile. These are located mostly around the impact site. They cooled slowly, so their structure contains larger striations in the…"

Aidan's mind wandered as he turned the crystal over in his paw. With a stroke of his thumb pad he could imbue it with a soft glow, and a swipe in the reverse exterminated it. He suddenly realised Gygel was still talking.

"…as we studied it over time, we have found it similar to a vibration, a natural energy that flows like breath or blood. There is a quality of sound to it, a pulse or tremor, when it is used." She paused for a moment. "Have you noticed that?"

Aidan looked at his paws. "Yes. When I use them, I feel the buzzing in my pads. The harder I push, the more it pushes back. It travels up my arms too, and I have to put my paws in cold water. Sometimes I can feel it in my ears, if I let the energy flow further."

She nodded. "Good. Then you have a greater affinity for resonance than many we have seen before. It will be of utmost interest to follow your experiences," she said, a certain anticipation in her voice. She snapped her claws together. "But first, you must learn our histories."

She dropped the book onto the desk, which rattled with its impact.

"I will talk; you will answer my questions by supplementing information from the book. Is that adequate?"

He had no choice.

The lessons continued almost daily in much the same way for about a year; lectures on the histories of different species, settlements, and geographic formations common to the crystals, broken up by presentations of his research on aspects such as physiology and architecture (which Aidan excelled at – he seldom received any corrections during these). He rose every day and collected his food, becoming less apprehensive about involving himself with the Aretians, even striking up friendships with some over breakfast. There was only one sticking point so far, and that was in discussing the Dhraka with Gygel. Aidan felt a vital thread was missing from his lectures, especially where Arete's history was concerned. There would be mention of 'a battle' or 'a disaster' or 'over time', accompanied by a distinct lack of extrapolation from Gygel, who normally obsessed over minutiae. It was stark even to Aidan as a relative beginner to anthropology and her manner of teaching. Aidan's earnest questions or subtle attempts to edge knowledge about them into his presentations consistently ruffled his tutor's feathers. Osiris had stepped in to quiet a potential disciplinary action more than once.

It took some time for him to muster confidence enough to challenge Gygel directly, but eventually Aidan protested that he should learn about the Dhraka as much as any other race. Gygel stalwartly refused, threatening that Aidan would amount to little if he kept venturing on 'irresponsible tangents' until he was 'fully prepared'. Aidan wondered whether she distrusted his youth, believing him impressionable enough to sympathise with their ideals. Osiris assured him this wasn't the case, but stopped short of giving an explicit justification. Aidan could see Osiris' struggles against Arete's odd, almost ascetic dedication to instructions, especially from their elders.

Aidan decided he would need to inspire something a little more rebellious.

"How do you feel you are progressing?" Gygel sniffed in her following lecture, tapping aged claws on an equally aged walking staff.

"As well as can be expected," Aidan replied. "Given my restrictions." He glanced surreptitiously to Osiris; the gryphon's eyes narrowed with wary regard.

Gygel stroked the silvery feather tips under her beak. "Restrictions?" she said dimly. "I do not believe you suffer from those at present. In your pacing, perhaps, but that is a matter of age and unfamiliarity with such extensive history."

Ignoring the slight to his intellectual capability, the fox shifted in his chair, leaning forward onto his books. "If you agree that I should be fully informed and educated, then yes, I am restricted. How do I incorporate morality into my learning by never discussing something that makes you uncomfortable?"

Gygel's feathers puffed around her neck. "I know to what you are referring, and you will not sway me. It is through shared debate and communicative reasoning that we achieve enlightenment and the furthering of our purpose. But one cannot have debate when one still has such a childlike view of the world. That is why you were brought here, Young Master, to be taught not only what you are capable of, but to ensure your capabilities are used optimally to keep the world on the correct, furthering path. We have seen firsthand the destruction caused by those with purposes unfettered by conscience."

"You mean the Dhraka, right? Do you really think you're in a better position to guide me when you're still stuck in an emotional war and refuse to acknowledge the reasons your battles occurred in the first place?"

Gygel's beak tightened shut; she rapped her claws on the walking stick with increased rapidity. "We are both old species," she clipped. "We grew up on Vu-ori in a tumultuous rivalry for resources and space. We plundered from each other, murdered, conducted savage attacks on each other and villages like yours for food."

"You ate... us?"

"When we were at our darkest and most desperate, yes. After we suffered exhausting battles not only from Dhraka, but also from other land-bound nations, we withdrew to the sea, and began our journey towards an enlightened, peaceful, knowledge-based means of survival."

Aidan rubbed his forehead. "But you're still at war."

Gygel thumped her stick on the ground. "We are in *defence*. A halt, in fact. And we no longer aggress even if conflict were to arise."

"But you still want them gone."

"They have not yet learnt to listen. Do not patronise me by suggesting we have not tried. They are dangerous, brutal, unforgiving, and greedy."

Aidan locked her with determined, fiery eyes. "Do they have resonance capabilities? Is that what this is about?"

The gryphon fluttered her wings, feathers bristling. "Your questioning is simplistic, reductive, and insulting. This is a complex matter long past definition by absolutes." She let out a gruff sigh. "To answer your bludgeoning query, the dragons are, unlike us, able to use resonance in small numbers. They have in the past tried to forcefully imbue each other with its power, with minimal success. It is not a system that can be harnessed to its full potential by coercion. Until they are able to learn that you cannot force evolution or intellectual progress, that it must come from both within and without in the truest of senses, with all willingly striving towards a single goal, we will always find ourselves in fundamental opposition."

"Do you believe they can change?" Aidan continued, flicking the corners of the closest book. "Or is it your aim that they're *made* to change, one way or another?"

"They will not change without guidance. Their failings will likely become a disaster for everyone, especially us."

"Where do they get this guidance from, if the only other option is extermination?"

There was a deafening pause. Neither Gygel nor Aidan shifted their gaze from one another, caught in a deadlock. Eventually, the gryphon broke the silence.

"We were much like you, at the beginning of our exile, trying to engage in pleasantries and understanding with a race that was absolutely content with brutality, who first mocked and then capitalized on our deference. Progress does not always come at the price of reason. This war is centuries old; do not believe that you have a solution just because you are benevolent and new. Some struggles require greater degrees of intervention than others, but we will always strive to use the path most beneficial to all."

Aidan's whiskers bristled. "So you aren't trying to wipe them out?"

Gygel did not move, but a stony look met Aidan's defiance. "That would be avoided in ideal circumstances," she said slowly.

"Good," Aidan snapped. "Because if I find out I'm being used as a means of racing to the top of some technological weapons tree then I won't help any of you. I came here to move the world forwards and learn to provide for it, with no exceptions."

"The means by which you may help the world are vast and complex, Young Master," Gygel rumbled. "It can be both difficult and cruel, and has to be met with equal regard if you are to survive it. There is much you do not understand."

"You're right!" he retorted. "Why haven't I seen any other resonators? Why did it take so long for you to reach out to us? If the Dhrakans are doing something so world-threateningly evil, why won't you tell me what it is?"

Osiris caught a fiery glare from the older gryphon as her beak opened and closed in disarmed irritation. "This is *your* doing," she fumed. "The lesson is over. You are dismissed!"

She whirled back to the shelves and began violently sorting scrolls from various sections onto a trolley.

Aidan picked up his array of tattered books and swept out of the room, slamming the door with a decisive crash.

Chapter Six

"Osiris, are you all right?"

"I am. Despite such time passing, the reminder of what was lost can still feel so fresh when detailed in such a way."

"I'm sorry…"

"Grieve only briefly, Faria. Although a sadder past has made us, we belong to the future to spite it."

Aidan wandered Arete for the rest of the day, circling the massive sea turrets' grand walkways, climbing all the way to the tallest belfry, as high as he was allowed before being warded off by guards. He found a beautiful stasis between the heat of the sun and the cool, strong breeze: a place of complete focus and balance. The noise of the wind and crashing waves soothed him, washing him in an empowering stability. The bright walls mirrored the gleam of the sun's rays. The city looked celestial, the only tethers to a sensation of reality were felt in the spray from the sea and the peaceful, rising sway of the forest to the west. As Aidan hadn't been assigned any additional tasks by Gygel in her haste to evict him from the library, he enjoyed the luxury of the landscape's natural harmony and rhythmic white noise. He travelled to the lowest platform above the docks and watched the fisher gryphons adding to the stockpiles for the tower kitchens.

Osiris said there was a freedom of choice over roles in Arete to an extent, but there were evidently tasks better suited to some than others. Divers for shallow sea fishing seemed smaller, their svelte bodies making it easier to crash through the water's surface and re-emerge with little weight hindrance. He wondered if these were adolescent gryphons, such that they were. Osiris had said even *he* was considered adolescent by some standards, so this was a much grander scale of experience and age than Aidan would ever witness. He assumed Aretians considered graduation past a certain age beholden to some great academic or athletic achievement, or an otherwise unsurpassable milestone in comparison to other species. At his most cynical, Aidan believed their traditional sense of enlightenment wasn't about contentment but achievement. While that was fine for those with purpose and ambition, it made Aidan wonder if it permanently exiled some individuals from satisfaction. Maybe that was the idea – that every level of existence brought on the need to find something better; that you can be both satisfied with who you are *and* moving forward. That was what Aidan hoped; that everyone could set their own goals and not be held ransom by some arcane academia or expectation.

He ran his paws over his head and hung them around his neck, a low groan in his throat. He let the bracing wind push against him for a time, trying to keep mindful when arguments of philosophy bounced around his head like tadpoles in a bucket. He had been close to finding out what Dhraka actually did. The guessing and double-guessing as to whether he should take Arete's warnings as genuine or whether they were obfuscating their own atrocities was difficult to resolve. He didn't want to be patronised, safeguarded from the real histories. In order to truly help, he needed to know everything, even if it was revelational. He gave a short, sharp sigh, and continued to watch the athletic fisher-gryphons win their catches.

As evening bled into the sky he returned to his room, where he intended to write more letters to his parents, or study some of the reading material he'd been assigned. The tomes about the crystals were intriguing, but written in such a dry manner that the book functioned as a pillow more often than it did as reference material.

He had barely sunk his teeth into a mouthful of seeds and dried fruits when the door resounded with an imposing knock.

He chewed his food as swiftly as he could, but couldn't manage a response before there came a second knock, accompanied by discontented rumblings.

He wrenched open the door, clearing his throat while trying to shift the food that was stuck to his teeth. He closed his mouth immediately when met with the grave expressions of Venedreus, Osiris, and Gygel. He half-hid behind the door as they stood before him in stony silence, and in a few awkward seconds it became clear they weren't entering. He clasped his paws together with the sinking feeling that he should have already started packing his belongings for the journey home. Or prepare himself to be eaten, if they fancied a re-enactment of Gygel's history lesson.

He emerged from behind the door and took a deep breath.

"No, we are not sending you back," Venedreus pre-empted, anchoring him with a steely look. "Your protestations have not been ignored, and we have come to a decision that this must be addressed. If you would kindly join us, we have something to show you."

Venedreus spun round; Gygel and Osiris parted for Aidan to follow. Carefully looking between his mentoring duo, he kept pace behind the Archon and heard his bedroom door shut with an ominous *boom*.

They led him along a different pathway, back underneath the main tower, and this time downwards. The stairs narrowed, and the walls appeared more aged. Still well-kept, but with considerable weathering that could not be hidden with polish and paint alone. They passed armouries and storehouses. The stone beneath his pads grew colder and he could feel the rhythmic pulsing of the waves against the walls. With the tightening corridors and gentle vibrations of the sea, the atmosphere became almost urgent, inescapable, a building tension that pressed into his ears and along his nose. His fur pricked on end. He found himself instinctively glancing around each new bend or doorway as if something were to loom out at him, or to catch a glimpse of something meant to remain hidden.

The torches began appearing at further intervals, leaving longer stretches bathed in darkness. After a time, when the rumbling of the waves vanished and a quiet, low vibration was left in its place, the burning lights were replaced with something completely different. Crystals jutted out from the walls on twisted metal sconces, glowing warm white. The sea's pulsing hum harmonised with an increasing, palpable sensation from within the building itself. Aidan had not passed a door in some distance, but the narrowing corridor wound in a wider and wider circle, as if skirting around a broadening column in the centre of the tower base. When he ran his hand along the inner wall, he felt undulations of cold and warm. If he pushed the stone hard enough, he felt like he would be swept away by the current beneath, into whatever cavernous space existed beyond it.

The wall ended, replaced by a stone railing, and finally Aidan saw what lay beyond.

A high, round chamber with a domed roof yawned before him. At its apex were six enormous prismatic crystals, each several times bigger than he was. The staircase expanded to a sweeping, waterfall-like crescent washing against a mosaic floor of blue, white, and black. The wall-mounted crystals' light mixed with the hue of aquamarine that wove around the room between and across the bricks. A spiralling web of crystalline dust and stonework curled to a low platform at the room's centre.

Aidan's fur stood on end. Electric tingles danced over his skin. The resonance-washed room seemed to stare at him from all directions, reaching towards him with long, invisible arms and static fingers. He swayed slightly, but a steadying hand on his shoulder kept him grounded. He glanced quickly back at Osiris.

"This…" Aidan began, leaning forward to peer around the room without taking another step. "This is terrifying."

"That is the correct response," Venedreus enounced,

stepping past them both. "Welcome to the resonance chamber, Master Arc'hantael. Please, attend."

He felt Osiris' talon lift free from his shoulder, and cautiously continued his descent. The stones below glittered with specs of blue dust. With each step he took, a glowing pawprint was left for a moment, then dissolved.

When he reached the floor, his heart was racing. Whispers of electric cold breathed over him, and he had to keep his feet moving as they began to itch and prick if he stayed in one place for too long.

"What is this?" he murmured, feeling his voice fill the room even at a breath's volume.

"This," Gygel said quietly, "is where our most powerful research is conducted."

Aidan's eyes narrowed. "You don't have resonators in Arete."

"Does this look like a recent construction?" she responded flatly. "But you are correct. Aside from you, there are none with resonance within Arete's walls. And the reason for that is… not of particular favour to our history."

Aidan scoffed. "Wasn't hard to anticipate."

Venedreus stepped forwards before Gygel could ruffle her feathers at the fox again, and led Aidan towards the plinth in the centre. "I understand the atmosphere is uncomfortable, but the assistance of the chamber will accelerate your progress by a significant order. This dome amplifies the harmony between you and the crystals so you can discover your talents without burning through your body in the process. Most resonators that suffer heavy use of their powers and do not have supplementary assistance either lose their affinity, or die early."

Aidan stopped walking, flashing back to his parents' increasing lethargy and inability to use their resonance. He dug his claws into his belt. He would write to them again tonight, without fail.

Taking a second to regain himself, he examined the intricate twists and corners of the crystal veins in the ceiling. "So the resonators who built this died too?"

"They have now, yes. Some… more directly than others."

He recoiled slightly. "Are we… are we just tools to you?"

"Not to us," she said firmly, with a touch of regret. "Not any more, at least. We had long been slaves to our arrogance, and in some manners yet we may still be." She looked to him imploringly, the first time he had ever seen her even remotely vulnerable. "I cannot ask you to trust me given what we have done, and what I will tell you shortly. But please know that we have changed. Listen for now, at least, and then make your decision under full disclosure."

He nodded, hesitantly at first, then resolutely.

She gave a thankful, if apologetic smile, and produced a black crystal from her robe. Gingerly, with her long black claws, she placed it on a divot in the platform. The humming in the room lessened slightly, and from one of the crystal's smooth edges came a beam of light, projecting onto the wall a whitewashed image of a bulky dragon, his body and face cratered and torn with scars.

"This is Sarr Crawn, leader of Dhraka. He is the one with whom we have been at war for endless decades. Our most recent treaty has thus far lasted longer than most, but we fear it may soon lapse."

Aidan knelt down to the black crystal. "These store pictures?"

"They interact with light; but one of their facets is the ability to store images within their structure and project them when the angle and energy input is correct. Those crystals mounted on the wall are of the same variety."

Aidan gazed at it for a second more, then shook his head. His ears were ringing. "Sorry, I'm a little unfocused. Please go on."

Venedreus bowed her head respectfully. "You are not impertinent, but I appreciate your sincerity. The crystals have long been a source of conflict and this entire space is no different. This chamber is also a means of protecting Arete from a Dhrakan assault. Several centuries ago, we were researching means of protecting settlements from geological instabilities, and this chamber counter-balances the movements of the waves and stone around it to keep our towers standing. Much of the region to the West, including Dhraka, is on volcanic ground. We recruited resonators from these areas to assist us, but as Dhraka was unerringly protective of any assets it could get hold of, most came from Skyria. Crawn saw this as an alliance against him, and began subjugating our allied villages. After we developed the chamber, we shared it firstly with Skyria, as their enormous trees are both their life source, home, and defence. Once word escaped that they had access to our development, Crawn issued an all-out invasion of our city, and tried to assault Skyria. Unfortunately, they did considerable damage to their capital, and captured a few dozen resonators in the process."

Venedreus fell silent for a second, tapping her claws

together. She looked sad, almost.

"We had not intended to omit Dhraka from our discovery," she continued eventually. "We hoped this would bring some form of conciliation between us, but they preempted our research as being armaments, and militarised against us. And sadly, resonators were treated as commodities in this struggle."

Venedreus rotated the crystal; another image beamed onto the wall. In washed-out red and white was a strange sort of siege engine of a mostly conical shape, on struts, mounted on a low, wide wagon. It was being pulled by rows of dragons alongside creatures of burden. Beside it were legions of soldiers; the image blurred too much at the edges to tell how far back they went, but the numbers appeared monstrous.

"The culmination of their ire was this, the earthquake machine. They intended to use it to flatten Arete, and anyone else who may attempt to overpower them. However, in working their captured resonators under duress to complete it, it malfunctioned, and ended up burying itself and most of their army, along with all those who had been extorted into its construction."

Aidan grimaced. He pressed his arms against his abdomen to try and curtail the swirling energies of the room and sickening dread at the Archon's story. "We were used as weapons," he scowled.

Venedreus nodded. "Sadly so. We had no consciousness of our mistreatment until that day, and it was a tragic awakening. We both stepped away from the world and sought to guarantee your protection. I will not lie that a… benevolent utility, of sorts, has been a priority to us. But no longer at your expense, where once we saw it as inevitable, and to the arrogance of transposing our will as your benefit."

Aidan sat on his haunches, rubbing his muzzle. "I can see why you fear including them," Aidan discerned, scanning the image. "They really hate you."

"Indeed, we are not blameless," Osiris interjected, stepping to the crystal. "At times this was nothing but a war of pride that did nothing but deepen the scars we wrought on each other. Now, it is a matter of survival to give them no quarter in defence."

Venedreus concurred, flexing her claws. "Regardless of our transgressions, we cannot let their repeated incursions on innocent territories stand. Not least of all for this reason."

She rotated the black crystal again. A projection of a massive, rocky obelisk at the heart of a strange landscape dominated the wall.

"At the core of Vu-Ori is the Zenith, the monumental epicentre of the impact that brought the crystals to our world. It is the biggest single deposit of crystal we have ever found. It was the focus of our disagreements for a time, but with neither of us in a position to take control or use it, it has been declared a demilitarised zone. Even the slightest threat to it puts us all in dire jeopardy."

Aidan stood slowly, wordlessly. She continued, her voice severe. "While we have shadows in our own history, we are trying to move past them, while others yet stoke the fires of war and hate. Do not be mistaken in thinking we are aiming for mutual destruction, and do not think naiveté will benefit anyone with its false politeness. We are the only ones who can keep Dhraka in check. And we can no longer do this alone."

The air stung Aidan's nostrils. He paced around the centre plinth, breathing deeply, pushing his hands down his stomach and thighs to work out the unsettling cold that was creeping up his body.

"You told me that if I came here," he began slowly, "it would be on my terms. I will hold you to that. Those conditions must stand for anything I'm involved with, even indirectly. If this war is to end then it won't happen by genocide. We need to work for peace and reparations from all parties. A war for you means a war for us, and you already know we won't survive it." He looked between the gryphons, his next sentence halting in his chest. He could already anticipate Gygel's horrified response. "If this is as dangerous as you say, then we should ask them to stand down, and show that you're willing to do the same. And if they won't trust you enough not to kill you on sight, then… I'll meet with Dhraka as an ambassador."

Three sets of feathers bristled before him; Osiris more in anticipation of his seniors' response than his own shock. Gygel's eyes looked like they were about to fall out of her skull.

"Absurd!" she blared.

Venedreus cleared her throat. "That will not be conducive to your safety. They will either kill you or capture you."

"Then it's lucky I have such prominent guardians," he shot back. "But if I prove myself adept enough to be seen as equal, or at least valuable, that shouldn't be their first choice," Aidan replied.

Gygel frowned. "You have conjured some bold assumptions in this fanciful plan."

Aidan pointed at the shimmering projection of the Zenith. "That's a lot of crystal. Would you prefer it to be fought over, or protected?" He paced, his tail flicking in consternation. "If harbouring me, or any resonator, is enough for Dhraka to initiate a war, then we're past a tipping point regardless of what they may be doing already. And if nobody else has even the slightest ability to do *anything* with this," he gestured at the Zenith again, "massive lump of power, it has to be me."

He gave an exasperated sigh, pulling at his whiskers. "The world is huge and terrifying, and I know I'm young, but I'm a part of it as much as anyone else… I can't just walk away." He turned to his guardians. "I'll work as hard as I can to master resonance completely. I promise that whatever benefit I can bring, it will be for all of us."

Gygel stared at him over her glasses. "And if diplomacy fails?"

"Then… there's nothing left to fight over."

Venedreus lifted the crystal; the projected light faded from its prismatic arc. She placed it roughly among her robes and gestured for Aidan to lead the way to the staircase. Gygel bridled away and marched up the stairs ahead. Osiris gave him a furtive glance as he walked beside him.

"You have asked for a lot. But by some grace, you were granted it. While I am not above scepticism for their generosity, in truth, I will be glad the future should fall to one driven by his conscience instead of his reputation."

The fox rubbed his palms. "I hope to do it justice. I might not have your history, but we all deserve a future. And with luck… we won't be relegated to its footnotes."

Chapter Seven

"I ... A lot must have happened to change his mind about Dhraka, from how he described them to me before he left... and all that happened after."

"Our misfortune was long, remarkable, and sadly, permanent. But he was not the only one whose trust was lost."

"Could they be saved yet?"

"Be careful with your language, Faria. 'Saving' implies they are without responsibility for their atrocities. It is the same pretentious language Arete used to revel in. We must be aware of all of our choices, and those of others."

To begin with, Aidan ventured to the resonance chamber only once a week to hone his skills. True to Venedreus' promise, he could conjure strength and abilities far more easily when at the centre of the enormous dome. Similar to how mirrors in the correct array could reflect sound to shatter a glass tankard, so did the composition of the carvings in the walls and floor, and the inverted spire of crystals above him. In fact, it took a very short time for Aidan to notice discrepancies in the flow, and asked permission to alter their patterns to make them more efficient, reduce his nausea, and heighten the room's blue ambience for more visibility. Within days of changing it, he felt steady enough to come down twice a week, and by the passing of several months he was here as often as he was in the libraries. He broke from both forms of study to explore Arete's workshops, shadowing blacksmiths, sailors, builders, surgeons, and biologists. He wanted to know everything about the way they worked, what they knew, how they trained themselves and worked materials, what broke, what slowed them down. He kept a thick journal of his observations, endless scrawls and diagrams of tools, rooms, materials, joins, and on the pages opposite were his adaptations or affirmations with his own experiences working with the crystals. Anywhere he felt he could make a difference by making a tool sharper, harder, mixing materials or adjusting them for malleability, he inked it onto the parchment.

He met Teratai, a female engineer gryphon currently designing mechanical wings to augment gryphons who had lost or broken theirs, or bring flight to landlocked creatures. She had designed the lightning conductors that pierced the skies above Arete, and boasted about the things she had made explode trying to harness the power that came down them. She talked with him at length about the property of metals and their lightness and flexibility, how trying to construct them to mimic feathers was almost impossible, and that if he was ever able to create something with both strength, lightness and flexibility, that she would be the first in line to experiment with it further.

Teratai was a gryphon of grey-blue plumage, with a white chest, neck, and face markings, and brown streaks running down her shoulders and wings. Her eyes were piercing green, and her beak faded from grey to black at its tip. She was nicknamed 'Kingfisher', not only for her amazing diving skills, but also her perfect strikes with a javelin from the air. Despite her intimidating reputation, she met Aidan with kindness and as an equal intellect. She was a welcome reprieve from Gygel's austere, often snide attitude of intellectual superiority and condescension.

Gygel and Aidan came to a tacit accord that further debate around Dhraka was not to be considered. They did continue to speak at length about other things, however. They had some argument about his dietary requirements, as she insisted she had the optimal food plan for him, but Osiris thankfully supported Aidan's protestations that reducing all of his meals to nutritionally-boosted fish-oat paste would kill him more quickly than any resonance disaster.

Teratai confessed that she had been kicked out of Gygel's mentoring after increasing division between the two, and had studied her own way into mechanics. She had built the orrery in the library over several years, and that seemed to seal an unspoken accord between the two, but not enough for them to actually communicate again.

Aidan's first experiments in the chamber were party only to him, Osiris, and Gygel. As their friendship grew, Teratai snuck in when Gygel was absent. Whomever was present observed Aidan closely and stepped in if he seemed about to falter with exhaustion or nausea. Upon the visits back to his parents in Mahrae, and in most of his letters, he told wondrous stories of the chamber and promised to bring them to see it one day. They were elated with his progress.

The further his skills developed over two and a half years, and the more Aidan networked, the more observers would creep in, and further word spread. Some were by invitation, others seemed to appear spontaneously. Aidan wondered at points whether Gygel was secretly boasting about his progress, or Teratai subversively encouraging others to cheer him on.

Thus, of late Aidan's training had become quite the spectacle, and Gygel was beset with commission requests for Aidan to experiment with new materials or specific circumstances. To her fortitude, she was strict about how Aidan should progress, and did not give him anything he was not explicitly ready for, but kept a list of each consultation regardless.

Aidan took to wielding resonance in a way that was almost supernaturally refined. At one particularly crowded venture, he widened the staircase to allow more onlookers to comfortably see, and joked about adding a gallery. Gygel protested initially, but no more than a week later Aidan had hollowed out a smooth, solid corridor around the upper level of the chamber, at no sacrifice to its efficacy as an amplifier. He found creating spaces, like the buildings he played with in his youth, to be most satisfying; a place for something new to exist where there had once been solid rock.

He had been planning for today since he first met Osiris, and it happened to coincide with his nineteenth birthday. Strewn about the floor around him were pages from his journal about metallurgy and blacksmithing. He finished reading from one and let it float to the floor beside him. Teratai clasped her claws excitedly; he gave her and Osiris an anxious smile as they stood and watched by the edge of the circular stone floor. He closed his eyes and took in a deep, hesitant breath.

Before Aidan sat a stone dais, atop which was a hollow silver shaft about four feet long, resting on a sheet of gold. At both ends of it were several resonance crystals, all thrumming in harmony with the vibrations of the room, now significantly less audible than before. In slow, steady movements Aidan nested two carved crystals into the ends of the shaft, balancing it between his palms. He twisted his hands slightly, and with a soft glow, the crystals began to funnel into the tube. His eyes flashed with the coursing energy. Slowly, steadily, he kept pushing his palms to the ends of the shaft to sink more crystal into the reservoir.

After about a minute, with two large sections of crystal still protruding from the tube, Aidan stopped twisting and pinched his hands against the outcrops. They began to spread and flatten, forming into spear-like points at both ends. With another quick flash, tiny blue fissures crept and twisted across the shaft, as the metal tube split and shrank inwards, forming perfect veins of crystal between the plates. Carefully, though a little shakily, he placed the staff on the gold, laying his hands on the flat of the crystal spearheads. The golden sheet bent and folded up and over the centre of the staff, curling and tightening to an immaculate seal. With a stroke of his fingers, Aidan laid more gaps in the gold, and the blue resurfaced in its twirling, cascading pattern. He held it still for a few seconds, watching as the light ebbed to a soft glow, then let out a long, relieved sigh.

He turned it over a few times, blew across the edges of the spearhead, then touched it gently to the top of the dais. The stone vanished into the ground, leaving no trace of it ever having existed.

A sudden rumble of applause burst above him. He jumped back. The gallery was full, and all eyes were on him. He glanced around and gave a shy, nervous wave. With every movement of his stave, the ends shone brightly, in harmony with the cavern.

"Congratulations, you have put our meagre tools to shame," Osiris mused, folding his arms. Gygel was scrawling fervidly on her parchment, and Teratai was alight with excitement, tapping her feet in anticipation.

Aidan gave a bashful laugh. "Well, I wouldn't have succeeded without the chamber, or the knowledge of everyone here. It's only my first try." He knelt and gently ran his paws over the area into which the plinth had vanished. "Still needs a little refinement. Seams should only be visible if they're a feature. Reconnecting something without leaving a scar takes more control than speed."

"Both would be an asset in the immediacy," came a booming voice. Upstairs, the crowd began to dissipate; Aidan turned to see Venedreus marching her way from the stairway. "Will you be able to heal the seams of our nations, and make us indivisible?"

Aidan stood to attention; something in the Archon's stiff, stern nature alarmed him immediately.

"I mean... I'll try, but stone is a little more passive than the people who live on it," he replied cautiously. "Has... something happened?"

Venedreus shook her head, finishing her approach to the fox in a few determined steps. "There has been a development. Your wish to become an ambassador may be approaching sooner, and be more difficult, than anticipated. Osiris, are you in good stead to fly?"

The Captain nodded, his wings bristling.

"Dhraka?" Aidan called, as the two gryphons turned and began an impossibly fast pace to the exit, pursued by Teratai.

The older gryphon didn't look back as she answered. "I do not doubt they had a hand in it, but they have not yet appeared," she muttered. "Two groups have apparently drawn battle lines over the Zenith – the ruling Gauros clan, and the nomadic city Kitaia. If, as I suspect, there are resonators among them, they may disturb the crystals. That in turn would destroy them all and have serious consequences for the rest of us."

"Except us and Dhraka, perhaps," Osiris growled.

"That is a distinct possibility, and the primary reason I believe Dhraka may be involved. It would not surprise me if this front was constructed by Dhrakan meddling as an excuse to infiltrate and control the Zenith. We *must* act swiftly to ensure this does not happen."

"What do you want me to do?" Aidan juddered, almost tripping over himself as they ascended the central spire and broke onto its belfry platform.

The Archon stopped, taking scope of the landscape beyond. She knew exactly in which direction the Zenith lay. Aidan skidded to a halt; Osiris held out his claw just in time to stop him from crashing into their commander.

"Master Aidan, bold as you are, you are not a combatant. We need you to observe the crystal, check for signs of trauma, damage, or excavation. Osiris and his guards will try to extricate the battle lines; your job is to watch and report."

"And if the battle's already started?"

Venedreus' claw tightened. "Despite our arrangement, it saddens me to ask you to alter your discretion and prevent a greater disaster."

Aidan looked at his staff. "This wasn't made as a weapon."

"You may learn your ideals are far from practical," Venedreus' voice rumbled, even overpowering the winds that swept through the belfry and the beacon's rippling flame. She tossed a satchel, packed with rations, to him. "I pray, however, that today is not the time you are subjected to such a lesson. The decision is yours, but the land is volatile and the Dhrakans brutal. Neither may give you a second chance. Do what you can to quell the situation, but understand your options may rapidly diminish."

Aidan nodded and clambered onto Osiris' back. Teratai and numerous guards stood to attention behind them.

"I will follow shortly with another company," Venedreus called. "Fly safely."

Osiris gave a determined salute, then spread wide his wings and charged off the edge of the belfry platform.

The flight took most of the day, and they travelled in grim silence. Aidan was wary to criticise the gryphons' tactics while several heavily armed soldiers were flying within earshot. He knew Osiris and Teratai would be fine and open to his misgivings, but political or military criticism was still a touchy subject among traditionalist structures, and many soldiers were proud of their duty, raised to know very clearly who their enemy was and the destruction they wrought. Aidan felt his stomach grow tighter and deeper as they swept across the sky, unsure of what conflict they might encounter, or whether Venedreus' concerns would be met and he'd come face to face with a dragon. And, even if no conflict came to pass, whether he'd start a war merely by existing in the gryphons' company. He gripped the staff tightly. The luminescent blue thrummed constantly, mirroring his own heightening anxiety.

The sky dimmed and the horizon faded to a fiery red as they surveyed the lands near the crystal.

"Do you see it?" Teratai called sombrely. Aidan craned forwards. His ears flattened; he felt a chill course down his spine and tail.

"Yeah…"

In one of the widest expanses of land Aidan had ever witnessed lay the immense mountainous rings encircling the crater where the crystals landed. They were wide enough that even from this height Aidan couldn't spy the exact impact zone. Between and among the rings at irregular intervals stood mesas of random size and shape, reaching up like the fingers of buried giants. Just looking at the pattern from above, Aidan felt the familiarity of the raw crystals' unstable nature; this was undoubtedly a side-effect of enormous energies being discharged by the debris' impact. The strength of it, laid out over such a wide area, set his stomach churning.

Approaching the inner circle of mountains, the ground colour shifted. Where the outer rings were desert and rocks, twists of green crept out from the centre, snaking from gaps in the ridges. Aidan caught waves of undulating energy, washing him with faint electric sensations. The closer they came and the lower they descended, the more frequently they hit. A growing nausea swelled in him. He gripped Osiris' backplate and steadied his breaths.

"If you vomit, I will make you polish it out," the gryphon warned.

Aidan chuckled through gritted teeth. "It's fine, I have it. I can't afford that kind of mistake. Just… no sudden dives, okay?"

Osiris' eyes narrowed, spotting two fiery glows in the distance. "No promises."

They swept overhead in a wide arch, banking to get a view of the preparing camps. They were both within the innermost ring of mountains, on almost polar opposites of the crater wall. Aidan couldn't make out individuals, but the torches illuminated enough of the ground to show the relative sizes of their encampments. One was considerably larger than the other, and from there he could hear tumultuous roars. He couldn't tell if they were of threat, anticipation, or sheer boisterousness, but they were big, and unafraid. The smaller camp was considerably more muted, but there was an unfamiliar energy about it that set Aidan on edge, distinct from the ambience that permeated the air.

"Osiris… Venedreus was right; I think they're resonators."

"Do you know what resources they have?"

"I can't tell."

Osiris signalled to the gryphons behind. Together they careened downwards to come to an abrupt halt behind an outcrop, landing deftly on the grass. Aidan managed to hold his stomach, barely, sliding from Osiris' back to hold his abdomen in the shelter of the rock for a few moments.

"Are you all right?" Teratai asked quietly. Aidan half-shook his head.

"The crystals in Arete are stabilised; these aren't. It's a wonder anything else can withstand it." He looked at the grass beneath them, glistening with a gentle blue iridescence. He brushed his paw over it, and tiny, almost imperceptible sparks fizzed across his claws.

"This whole area is saturated. Even the plants have absorbed it."

Osiris ruminated, checking over the outcrop for sentries from either camp. "That's why it must not fall under hostile control. We have to stop this skirmish before it becomes something greater."

"Do we know when the battle will start?" Teratai cautioned, screwing the wooden hafts of her javelins together to form a deadly, double ended spear.

Osiris frowned. "These are not ordinary combatants. I imagine they are each aware of that, and would not risk underestimating their chances by attacking at night. We should be safe, but maintain a watch nonetheless." He turned to Aidan. "Can you identify anything about the crystals from here?"

Aidan peered around the rock. At the centre of the crater lay a large, uneven mound of blue-grey ore, a calcified cloud with jagged blue spires erupting from it at random. Deep gouges spread from its base along the ground like a web, rippling with the iridescent grass and undergrowth. He planted his feet firmly and closed his eyes, gripping his paws together. His brow furrowed and his ears flattened as he tried to gain a sense of the landscape and the catalyst within it. The unrefined nature of the imbued land made it difficult to traverse. He would find gaps, surges, undulations that disrupted his ability to detect the size of the crystal formation. Finally he found a navigable channel and reached down through it. The energy took him, faster, accelerating towards the central mass. His heart raced. His eyes, even closed, were glowing.

It was *huge*. It extended deep below the surface, at least twice again the size of what was visible. He felt it pulse, a sleeping monster. Carefully, already brimming with charge, he withdrew his presence and snaked back to his body. Except…

He could sense the camps and their weight on the grass. Cautiously, but swiftly, he moved again. If he could ascertain their numbers, maybe they could make up a more definitive plan, or work out if any Dhrakans were indeed present.

Creeping closer, he found a web of energy being drawn and siphoned into something in the larger camp. He edged forwards.

Suddenly, a burst of power from the source of the drain. A voice pierced his mind, shook his being.

"*Who goes there?*"

His eyes snapped open and he collapsed against the rock. Osiris and Teratai jumped to his aid; he waved them back, scrambling over the rock to view the crystal.

It was quiet.

"Who was that?" Aidan breathed, rubbing his forehead.

"What do you mean?" Osiris murmured. "Is someone approaching?"

"No, to our fortune," Teratai responded, quickly scanning the area from behind the stone.

Aidan pulled at his shoulder. "I... I may have been seen."

Osiris shot him a glare. "What do you mean? How?"

"While I was exploring the resonance fields, I came across something... well, *someone*, in the big camp. They were drawing on the resonance energy, and I think they sensed I was there. I cut myself off; hopefully they won't know where we are."

The gryphon gripped the hilt of his rapier tightly. "I would prefer a more concrete assertion than 'hopefully'. Are they able to search as you do?"

"I don't know," Aidan protested. "They seemed to... be absorbing energy, not reaching out. But I... I'm not sure." He shrank back as he saw Osiris' demeanour shift from grim distraction to savage discontent. The looming soldier whirled round to brief his guards, and when he turned back to the fox his expression had lessened only enough that Aidan felt he wouldn't *instantly* be flayed for potentially uncovering their presence, but that it could still be a possibility if things went awry.

He took a deep breath and stretched against the rock, welcoming its cool surface against his back. "The crystal seems safe. Nobody is nearer to it than we are, at least," he said, sliding down to sit.

"Good. Get some rest," Osiris ordered.

Teratai gave him a sympathetic grimace, then took her position as sentry.

Aidan nodded and huddled as close to the rock as he could. The grass pricked and fuzzed with energy as he settled down to rest. Any comfort he found was short-lived, however, as creeping restlessness and sharp aches jabbed into his limbs. He could shift position, but each movement sent faint current rippling across the area around him, and he feared raising another alarm, so he forced himself still. An inescapable drone, a surreal harmony of low hum and high whine, beat the air. Every time Aidan felt himself drifting to rest he became aware of it again and jerked back to alertness. It was tempting to turn the whole area to dust just for some peace and quiet. Any slight noise above the ethereal murmur pierced his consciousness, sending him into a frozen dread that someone was approaching. Even glancing over at Teratai or the other guards provided him no relief, as masking sound or visibility would be easy to a resonator of particular skills, and he had no clue what these were capable of.

Eventually, as clouds splintered the sky above, he drifted into a fitful sleep.

Chapter Eight

"*You look worried, Faria.*"
"*I just... we went through so much of the same. Yet... he had so much less. Thank you for being with him.*"
"*Until you, it was my greatest honour.*"

A claw gripped Aidan's shoulder. He started awake, instinctively clutching his staff to his chest. He glanced round, blinking hard to rid the blurriness from his eyes.

Osiris stood over him.

"They're stirring," he said quietly. "Time to parlay."

Aidan sat up unsteadily and poked at the rations in the sack. He had no appetite for it, and instead brushed himself down and stood ready behind Osiris as they faced the smaller encampment and began their deputation while the others remained at their landing spot.

A low, shimmering mist drifted across the crater's border. Where a normal mist would spill downwards, this fog clung to the sides and appeared, very steadily, to spread upwards instead, following the energy currents in the ground. It swirled and crackled as they strode through, sometimes spiralling into vortices that drilled through the air for metres at a time, then dissipated in a sudden burst. It was easy to see how this was considered a cursed land by anyone unfamiliar with resonance. It would take a group either determined or ignorant to willingly venture so far inside.

As they approached the first camp, they could tell immediately which these soldiers embodied. The moment Osiris and Aidan were noticed, three sprang up, brandishing daggers and swords. Aidan had expected intimidation at Osiris' size, but these soldiers did not flinch.

From behind the guards, a wolf emerged. Taller than Aidan, but slender, with well-defined musculature. He wore metal half-armour, covering his outer arms and legs, on every surface of which lay rows of metal shards cut into rough blades. A short sleeveless coat, padded with sheepskin, had needle-like blades around the collar like a mane. Around his head was a metal band, again adorned with metal shards. Sweeping down his face, and the rest of his visible body, were swirling purple markings. The ones on his face surrounded his eyes in crescents, heightening the impact of his indigo eyes, locked in a hunter's focus.

"Has Gauros sent their lunch as a peace offering?" he growled.

Osiris did not falter. "We are not from Gauros. I am Osiris Tallon of Arete. You cannot fight here."

The wolf licked his teeth. "You do not decide our battles."

"This involves more than you know," Osiris said grimly. "Those crystals may not be disturbed. What are you here for?"

The wolf shook his head and chuckled. He looked over his shoulder. "Oakhe, we have a third party for our skirmish." Behind him, a lynx scoffed, shouldering a spear. The wolf turned back to Osiris. "We heard Gauros was attempting to take hold of a great power at the heart of the continent. We set out to take it from under their noses, distribute it among their enemies, and eliminate as many of them as possible." He gestured to the two of them placidly. "Why do *you* object? You have no love for Gauros, nor any of us desert folk. There's nothing you can gain from the outcome of our struggles except some haughty philosophy lesson. Arete is a city of ignorance, decadence, and separation. Nothing in the lesser world has ever held value to you." He flicked a claw to his forehead, in which was embedded a shimmering, purple crystal. "No doubt you want these as baubles for your self congratulating feats; a most extravagant waste."

Aidan glanced quickly to Osiris. He could see the tension bristling in his wings, but the gryphon remained steady.

"There is little we can gain from your conflict, but a lot that we all could lose," Osiris pressed. "Where did you receive information that Gauros was attending here?"

"Our secrets are sacred. You get no claim to them."

"If this battle takes place, secrets will be all that remains of any of us." Osiris retorted. "We know well of Kitaia and the city you carry on your backs. We've tracked your movements around the continent for some years. I applaud your confidence and evident resilience, but that does not extend you the right to claim territory and risk the balance of lives on our continent. I insist you move elsewhere."

The wolf let out a short, low laugh. "You at least respect our reputation. Perhaps you should ask your friends in Gauros first; I'm sure your luck will be similar. If they rescind, we will consider. But I can tell you, they will not. So it seems our path is already chosen."

He scanned Aidan briefly. His eyes narrowed on sight of the staff, and he stepped forwards. "What is that?"

Aidan's eyes widened. Just as Osiris went to hold out his arm, the fox stepped forwards. "It's a resonance tool," he said firmly. "I made it."

"You use the same power as the Gauros Queen."

Aidan shrugged. "I've not met her, so I wouldn't know. I hope my presence isn't all the more alarming for that."

The wolf smiled. "Hah, you're definitely not one of them – far too small, and fatally polite. Ordinarily we would have strung you up on sight for holding their crystals." He stepped forwards again, now on the other side of the guards whose blades were at the delegation's necks. "Can I see it?"

Aidan gripped it tightly for a second, then held it out. The wolf gestured for the guards to move as he took it and turned it over. They retracted their blades and guarded their leader on either side.

"Feels powerful. Is it a weapon?"

"It could be," Aidan replied, not taking his eyes from the rugged claws playing over the staff's crystal blades, eager to have it return to him. "That's not what I intend to use it for."

"Then why are you here, at an impending battle, with a sometimes-weapon, if not to use it as such?"

Aidan looked towards the crater. "To be honest I'm

very new to this, especially war. I'd experienced nothing outside of my village until travelling to Arete. I hadn't realised the state of the world and the struggles of those around it." He looked back to the camp behind the wolf. It was minimal, with many improvised canvas shelters. The inhabitants were packing away what little they'd carried, concealing it under rocks, while others sharpened weapons. The creatures were all predators; Aidan recognised coyotes, wolves, hyenas, and lynxes most prominently. Their armour was a mismatched tapestry of bamboo, wood, metal, and leather. Their unifying feature was the same intricate purple tattoos as their leader. They held a glittering, lustrous quality.

"I assumed my village was faring as well as any other," he continued. "But evidently... there's more out here than I ever anticipated."

He looked squarely back at the wolf, suddenly. "It's not a weapon. It's a shield."

The wolf looked thoughtfully at the staff for a few more seconds, then held it back out to Aidan. "Wise words. Use them to teach these gryphons a lesson, will you?"

"I have been trying," he replied, uneasily but quickly taking the staff back. Upon lifting it, he saw the wolf's palm remained outstretched. Carefully, Aidan reached out, and shook it.

The wolf bowed his head. "Dhalan Rook, joint leader of the Kitaia."

"I'm Aidan Arc'hantael, from Mahrae."

"When we win, come and find me. We'll talk more."

He bowed his head and whirled round to return to camp, rolling the lustrous dust with his tail. The guards motioned with their blades for Aidan and Osiris to leave, and kept watch until they were some distance away.

The gryphon's stern expression was fixed on the next camp. His paws fell heavily on the grass, his tail flicked stiffly, and his ear tufts were angled back almost flat. This was the soldier Osiris, the hunter. The negotiator in him pushed further back.

"Are you all right?" Aidan chanced.

Osiris kept his eyes forward. "I do not anticipate success. The stench of glory and manipulation was all over them. Gauros will only be worse."

All the questions flooding Aidan's mind felt so childish in such severity. "Gauros... are they like Dhraka?"

"Somewhat," Osiris growled. "Albeit with fewer mistakes thus far. That makes them reckless and prideful, a dangerous combination in a burgeoning fire such as this. We may be laughed out of their encampment, and in the death that follows they will howl with fury at their righteous cause."

The Gauros camp was several times bigger than the first. The large canvas tents were set up in strict formation. The tents were not the only imposing presence, however – immediately Aidan saw the bulk of the warriors. Lions, all large and powerful, with at least one close to rivalling Osiris for sheer mass. Huge axes and claw blades glinted in dawn's spreading light. Fires smouldered from the night before, and blades clashed against shields in training for the battle ahead.

The Gauros sensed their approach much as the Kitaia had, but instead of leaping to them with unfurled blades, the first to see them let out a roar:

"Queen Raikali!"

The call echoed through the camp, passed from soldier

to soldier. From the grand circular tent at the camp's heart the cover flew open and a lioness decked in blue-black armour stalked outside, marching immediately for Aidan.

Osiris instinctively reached for his blade.

"That would be unwise," Raikali barked. Aidan froze upon seeing her eyes, the same bold blue shade as his. She regarded him suspiciously, but not with an inch of fear. "What are you here for?"

Osiris straightened. "You know this place is dangerous," Osiris boomed. "What claim are you trying to lay stake to here?"

Raikali shifted her right vambrace to reveal a shard of resonance crystal stitched to her forearm. "These crystals are my lifeblood. My family has been connected to them for generations, so we have a right to our heritage. You have no cause to stop what we are destined to become."

"I might," Aidan said, brandishing his staff. He whirled it round, creating a trail of vivid blue light that spun around the stave's tips, then receded back into the crystal. The Queen's eyes narrowed.

"You were the one I sensed last night," she rumbled.

"Well, I kind of ran into you," Aidan replied with a wry smile. Raikali did not return the attempt at humour.

"One fox does not have an equal share to an entire tribe," she hissed.

"My ancestors are also resonators," he replied. "Several in my village are."

She snarled, teeth glistening. "Don't insult me, whelp. I know well the indoctrination these gryphons ply you with to exploit your powers. We will never be influenced by their impotent greed. Not one of them has ever been a resonator themselves."

"And where would you hear such information?" Osiris thundered. "Where are the Dhrakan consorts who guided you here? This was declared a demilitarised zone under the danger it posed, and the destruction it may yet wreak."

Raikali spread her arms wide. "Do you see us in peril or servitude?" she growled, looking back at her tribe, who responded with laughter and grins. "We are not weak, and nor do we run from that which promises us glory. We answer only to our conquests." She shot him a warning glare. "And besides, we are under no such contract. Your wars are aged, boring, and pointless. *You're* the one under violation of such a pitiful agreement. You didn't even have the bravery to kill each other off and leave the world to those who could use it to its full potential."

Osiris' beak clenched; his neck feathers brimmed with tension. "You expect me to believe you ventured away from your lands to lay claim to a piece of land nobody had set foot in for decades, and nothing prompted this except divine coalescence of your destiny?"

The lioness sneered. "This power runs in my veins. We fought all who ran against us, and if you desire to join them, we'll be only happy to oblige. We will not move." She eyed Aidan with wild ferocity. "I am unchallenged."

He locked eyes with her for a few seconds, discerning her expression. Her energy wasn't ringing as true as she intoned. He could feel it in the way she stood, still drawing upon the ground around her. Her confidence relied on stealing strength from her surroundings, probably storing it in the crystal to expend later. She displayed abundant fervour, and was undoubtedly vicious, but he wondered on how narrow a precipice that hung if he was to interrupt her supply. Surreptitiously he laid the tip of his staff on the ground, and gently began changing the direction of the energy currents which swirled underneath them like a whirlpool. The grass shimmered in waves, all circling around him. He kept his focus on her as he spread the energy currents outwards, widening the spiral. Her eyes shifted from brazen self-satisfaction to something darker. Anger shadowed her face. Blue ripples coursed through the grass; the air began to hum. The other lions recoiled as the energy sparked and spat between the grass blades brushing against each other. Her claws flexed, her body tensed, and instantly he withdrew the stave. The energy vanished with a rumble like thunder, plummeting into the ground beneath.

"If that is your decision," Aidan said softly, before bowing his head and turning to leave. Osiris took two steps back and followed on, leaving the lioness fuming with indignation.

"You dare provoke me?" she roared. "I will tear you to *pieces!*"

They kept their course, returning to the soldiers behind the rock.

"I know her weakness," Aidan said quietly, shakily, as they strode. "But I don't think I deterred her."

"It is a step more than we had," Osiris replied. "Can you exploit it?"

"Probably. But I can't stop the Kitaia resonators in the same way."

Osiris glanced around, and in the distance sighted a tall figure with a long, spiny tail and lizardlike wings vanishing over the rise.

He drew his sword.

"Find your plan quickly. We are out of time."

Chapter Nine

"*Do you need to stop for a moment, Faria?*"
"*No, keep going.*"

Osiris and Aidan ran back to the relative shelter of the rock; the other gryphons' weapons were already drawn.

"Did you see?" Osiris hurried.

Teratai nodded. "There are several Dhraka on patrol. More are undoubtedly near. No indication of who they support or their number."

Osiris shook his head. "They will exploit the winners and destroy the rest. I wager support will go to Gauros as their powers and Raikali's mentality are more in line with their own ideals."

"So we back Kitaia?" Aidan asked.

"No," Osiris barked. "We cannot have *any* stake in this battle, or our war starts all over again, and that is exactly what the Dhraka want. We must prevent it, not join it."

"They have already made clear *their* interference,"

Teratai warned, gripping her javelin fiercely.

Aidan looked back at the camps they'd left. Kitaia was moving already, and he could hear the battle roars of Gauros echoing across the crater. He looked to the towering crystal ore in the centre, its uneven, shimmering protrusions gleaming in the emerging light. The sky was a deep, unsettling orange.

He turned to Osiris.

"I'm going to the crater. I'll cut off the crystal's energy supply to the field and divide the two armies."

Osiris nodded at his guards. "We'll protect you. Go, now."

Aidan broke into a run; the gryphons took to the air behind him. To the right, circling ahead, was Kitaia. As Aidan reached the crater's edge, he saw one stop, catching sight of him. He clambered over the edge and half-ran-half-slid down its side, keeping the crystal tower in sight.

A grey blur darted from where the Kitaia had been – within seconds, Dhalen appeared in front of him, purple markings glowing fiercely. Aidan was a moment too slow, and a lightning punch to his chest sent him crashing to the ground several feet away. Osiris swooped down, barging into Dhalen with his full weight onto his shoulder.

The wolf didn't fall.

Dhalen braced against him, and for a second they appeared locked together with Osiris suspended in the air held up by Dhalen's grip, but a moment later the wolf twisted, hurling Osiris clean over his head. While picking himself up, Aidan saw the gryphon writhe in the air and land, barely, on his feet. Two other gryphons descended on Dhalen to restrain him; with incredible speed he leapt between them and launched a devastating tear to the male's wing. He faltered and crashed to the ground.

Aidan renewed his sprint to the crystal. Another blur from the right, this time Dhalen's lynx companion, Oakhe. Aidan jammed his staff into the ground to shift the earth away from Oakhe's terrifying kick. Osiris grabbed the lynx from behind. The markings on Oakhe's fur flashed, and he wrenched himself free.

Dhalen chased after Aidan. "Hold now or be held!" he barked.

Aidan didn't dare look; he heard the wolf gaining at blistering speed. He used the ground to create a moving platform under his feet that morphed its way around the crater. The wind rushed through his fur; he was nearing the crystal when something wrenched the platform from beneath him. He was sent reeling forwards, hitting the ground and rolling over and over, twisting his body to keep hold of the staff.

Raikali lifted her claws from the earth she'd summoned to dislodge his platform, and charged. He staggered up, but disorientated, tripped again. She rounded on him, fangs bared, and suddenly vanished as a heavy object crashed into her side. Dhalen pounded at her chestplate. She roared with fury and returned punches and claw swipes at him, landing a blow on his jaw. He careened back. More soldiers from both sides began spilling over the crater walls. Aidan stood upright, took a deep breath, and plunged his staff into the ground.

A deep rumble shook the crater. His eyes flashed a brilliant blue, and beneath him a wall rose, lifting high and fast, spreading around the crater in a wide circle. Uneven ridges burst from the rapidly-growing base of the wall, breaking apart the battlefront. Raikali fumed, throwing Dhalen aside, and drove her claws into Aidan's barrier. A large section disintegrated, but he replaced it just as quickly. She gnarled her teeth, then began a rapid climb, shifting her handholds with resonance energy to propel herself upwards. Dhalen surged with power and in one enormous bound sank a clawhold almost halfway up the wall. His increased strength crushed the wall in his grasp as he clambered up at breakneck speed.

Aidan saw them approach. Behind him the circle closed around the tower and began to seal over the top of it. He jabbed the staff again; fingers of rock exploded from the wall, aiming to displace his pursuers. One struck Raikali square in the chest; she latched onto it and began twisting it back round to the wall, raising it higher as her own platform. Dhalen dodged the first and smashed the second with his fist, still climbing.

They were almost on him now. With one final burst Aidan twisted the staff and two massive hands of rock spiralled from the wall, taking hold of them both and suspending them in the air, restraining them so they couldn't move their claws to attack. A few seconds later he closed the stone over the tower. The blue glimmer from the grassland shrank back behind the walls, drawn into the main prism by his staff. The hum in the air deadened, replaced by a whistling, blustering wind.

He collapsed at the mound's apex, the bruise in his chest pounding with the intensity of his resonance power's exertion. He dropped the staff, arm trembling. Osiris landed by his side.

"Aidan, are you alive?"

He gave a weak smile. "Heck of a question. Guess I am."

From below they heard a deep laugh. Aidan hauled himself to the tower's edge to see Dhalen shaking his head. "Impressive!" he called. "You use your powers far more effectively than Gauros."

"How dare you!" Raikali roared. "Release me or my warriors will rip you to shreds!"

"They will not," Dhalen scoffed. "Look where you are." He motioned to Aidan with his head. "You don't stand a chance against him. You're obsolete."

Raikali wrenched against the rock that pinned her, straining and fuming. Osiris stood tall, helping Aidan to his feet.

"Are we now in a position to negotiate?" Osiris boomed.

"I think not," came another voice.

A hulking, red scaled dragon came to rest opposite them, his armour black as coal, his eyes deep, green, and hungry. His face held deep scars displayed with pride, and he was missing two claws on his right talon. His tail was lined with missing or split spines and had a slight inflexibility to it, as if it had been broken and reset several times over.

The Dhrakan General, Sarr Crawn.

"Crawn," Osiris snarled. Aidan leant down to pick up the staff.

"Hold it!" Sarr growled, his voice bearing the same roughness of his battered scales. "If you touch that, we will take action. You are already in trespass."

Osiris glowered at the dragon. "You dare accuse me of

invasion when you were in violation first?"

Sarr gave a rumbling laugh. "Your bias is rivalled only by your ignorance. You are the one wielding illegal alliances and technology."

"I am not a weapon," Aidan croaked.

The dragon's eyes flashed with affront. "Impudent brat. You should learn your place, for your own sake. You are nothing but a device to them, and you are playing into their hands with such a dangerous toy."

Osiris stiffened. "Is that what you told the resonators who died inside your defective earthquake machine?" he spat.

Sarr's defiant grin soured. He raised his fist and within moments a second dragon appeared, hugely muscular, with great wingspan. His amaranth scales gleamed under a hardened suit of charcoal steel, and his yellow eyes scanned both Osiris and Aidan diligently, perhaps even with hunger. He was slightly taller than Sarr, with a longer trail of spikes down his back and around his head, but undoubtedly similar.

"Take them, Fulkore. We will conduct a thorough, painful interrogation."

"With pleasure," Fulkore gloated. He raised his left arm and more dragons took to the sky from behind the crater wall. Just as Fulkore stepped towards Osiris, a call rang out from the Dhrakan flight.

"Arete approaches!"

Osiris whirled round. Leagues of gryphons swept through the skies in numbers rivalling the Dhraka, perhaps even exceeding them, with Venedreus at the fore. She descended upon the massive stone tower beside Osiris, and bent to hand Aidan his staff. Aidan took it, eyeing the venomous looks from the Dhrakan commanders.

"There is explaining to be done," Venedreus growled.

"Yours is the transgression," Sarr retorted, flicking an accusatory claw at Venedreus. "You send armed soldiers into the demilitarised zone *and* equip them with resonance weapons – how is this not an act of war?"

"*We* responded to reports of an already-occurring disturbance and sought to quell it before the crystals were damaged," the Archon retorted. "We are well aware of their instability. Failure to intervene could have brought great disaster to all of us. We assumed you would have felt the same given your previously disastrous experiments."

The fire shifted from Sarr's eyes to his teeth. As his claws rattled over the handle of his handaxe, Aidan spoke.

"They're stabilised now. At least, as far as I was able. So…" He paused as a wave of pain passed over his chest. "There isn't any immediate danger from our presence anymore. Everyone can withdraw."

The dragons and gryphons exchanged determined, silent refusals. Aidan gave a low growl.

"Or I can destroy everything and solve this immediately and permanently."

All eyes turned to him. He scraped the tip of the staff in front of him and readied it above the tower. He looked to them all in turn.

"Thought so. None of you are ready to let go of this power. You've depended on its existence for the promise of some future you don't even know you can achieve. What good will this do if you turn yourselves to dust just to stop someone else from having it?"

Fulkore grunted a half-laugh. "If you destroyed the Zenith, would you then remove the chambers beneath Arete and Skyria as well?"

Aidan locked him in a fierce glare. "I would. Then maybe you'll all see what you really are without the lure of unreasonable power fogging your eyes. Or will that reveal weaknesses you're too afraid to confront?"

"Dhraka has never been weak!" Fulkore spat. "We rise to any challenge and conquer it with a ferocity unmatched in this world."

"So you agree it should be destroyed?" Aidan retorted.

Venedreus stepped forwards. "That is hyperbolic. Our race is dying. We need these if we are to have a chance to survival. If we cannot be wardens of protection, this world may fall to darkness that we have never seen."

Fulkore reared his head back with a callous laugh. "Such arrogance!" he taunted. "As if the world existed solely for your dependence. It is a poor excuse for your own mortal fear that you insist the rest of the world is indebted to your mere presence."

Osiris lunged forwards. "Better a protector than an oppressor! What have you done for the world except divide and subjugate?"

"Our resources were stolen from us by invaders, thieves, and natural disasters," Fulkore goaded. "And you, in your *exceeding* love for the world denied us any access to other lands. This has always been about your desire for supremacy and refusal to grant us a right to exist!"

Osiris' wings flashed open; he gestured widely to the other dragons about and below them, all red-scaled. "What of your dragon brethren? The other clans, the other dragon races once in Dhraka? The ones who refused to take arms in your name? Were those natural disasters selective or have they rescinded their identity from your barbarism?"

Fulkore took a step closer, cracking his shoulders and pulling himself to his full height. Osiris readied his claw over his rapier.

A tremor shook the tower; they stepped back in alarm. Aidan removed the staff from the ground, sparks flaring from its blade, glaring fiery warnings at them both. "Don't test me. I can walk away from here and leave you all with nothing but your ridiculous squabbling."

"Hey!"

Aidan glanced over the edge to see Dhalen. Now joining him, having climbed up the side of the tower, was Oakhe. He was clawing at the stone that bound his comrade, trying to wrest him free.

"While we argue validity," Dhalen continued, "would you mind including us in your impromptu war summit? We were fighting here first."

Raikali let out a spiteful scoff. "This humiliation will not stand," she rasped. "Release me instantly."

Aidan rubbed his forehead. "What do you want from this place?" he called to Dhalen.

"If you discover a tyrannical despot is attempting to control a source of astronomical power and potential subjugation, would you not at least attempt to show resistance?"

"Apparently we were right to make a move, seeing as you would have arrived too late," Oakhe shrugged, regarding the strange and tenuous scene about them. Aidan moved to Raikali.

"What about you? Is supremacy your ultimate goal?"

She grimaced. "I will not speak while entombed in your puerile parlour trick."

"This is a dangerous bloody farce," he muttered under his breath. He sighed, and slowly raised the two stone prisons to his artificial mesa. Carefully, with enough manipulation that they could anticipate how to land, he released their bonds. Dhalen, Oakhe, and Raikali stepped swiftly away to separate spaces, joining the tense and disparate congregation at the Zenith's summit.

Osiris looked about. "Do you want to summon Skyria as well? They are the only party missing."

"Might as well," Aidan groaned. "I doubt this will resolve anytime soon, and if this is going to decide the fate of these crystals, they at least deserve to know what's going on."

Osiris flicked his claws to beckon another gryphon. He gave them the orders, and they swept into the sky to the north-east.

"How many injured do you have?" Aidan asked Raikali.

"We don't need your charity."

He turned to Dhalen, who raised a dismissive hand.

"Thank you, we can handle it. You don't look like *you* can, though."

Aidan still clutched the right side of his chest, where Dhalen's monstrous punch had landed. He was about to protest when Oakhe stepped forwards.

"May I?"

Aidan lowered his hand and nodded. Oakhe held his palm to Aidan's chest for a few seconds, moving it in small circles up to his collarbone, down to his diaphragm, and then back to the centre of impact. He pressed into it. Aidan winced. Harder he pressed, then jerked his hand backwards. There was a sickening *crack* and Aidan let out a gurgling rasp, arching his head back. Osiris jumped to his side. Quickly, Aidan raised his arm to stop him. He breathed deeply for a few seconds, hissing out the pain through his teeth, then lowered his head. Oakhe stepped back, giving a short, polite bow to his patient. Aidan smiled in joint relief and discomfort, as the pain of his cracked rib rippled between existing and not existing and the adrenaline of such an adjustment rocked his body.

"That's… impressive," he whistled.

Oakhe nodded. His armour was much less formidable than Dhalen's, mostly of leather and woven braid, with metal plates across his chest and back. His bob tail had its own leather and metal slip, and chains linked from crystal rings at the tips of his ears to the fur around his jawline. He gave Aidan a warm smile.

"I'll discuss it with you once we have less intrusive company, if you so wish,"

Aidan smiled nervously. "Let's make sure we survive this first."

Chapter Ten

"*Diplomacy sounds more terrifying than war.*"
"*In some ways, it is far more complicated. War is a constant shadow, the consequence of failure. And... we failed.*"

Two days later, four camps surrounded the tower: Dhraka, Arete, Kitaia, and Gauros. Mostly, things had been quiet. The uneasy silence was not a lack of hostility or suspicion, however, as periodically jeers or yells rang out from one camp or another, or sentries passing too close would provoke a spat that needed to be broken apart. Most of these came between Arete and Dhraka, but occasionally Gauros as well. Kitaia was the most subdued. Aidan surmised this was their means of conserving energy by letting the other groups fight and do their work for them. He had staunchly remained atop the tower and forbade any other group from approaching except to bring him supplies until Skyria had arrived. This in itself had caused argument, so he periodically requested representatives from all four camps to ascend simultaneously and provide updates.

He'd even trapped his staff on a makeshift plinth, visible from the entire crater, to avoid accusations of sabotaging the mound before any diplomatic consultation began. It felt childish, but seemed to outwardly (and begrudgingly) appease everyone, at least insofar as nobody could reasonably object to such a simple system. Yet impatience and resentment were high, and several times Aidan caught sight of Gauros and Dhrakan troops conversing well away from the main encampments. From their introductory demeanour, it unsettled him. While he had to remain nominally impartial, believing no species to be born evil, he feared Osiris and Venedreus' warnings may have been justified about the Crawn dynasty at the very least, even if the strength of their prejudice still cast doubt on the merit of their accusations. Reminders of his naïveté swept back into his head like a bad smell. Thinking like that again could risk everyone's safety.

The weather had been kind, at least insofar as it hadn't rained. The wind atop the tower was strong, but was disrupted somewhat by waves of energy that occasionally seeped from the rock. Dhalen had donated a bivouac that sheltered Aidan to some degree, but given the unpredictable demeanour of the wind and its tendency to come from many directions at once, he retreated to a mound of blankets for warmth, and spent most of his time watching the clouds sweep overhead. Were it not such a tense situation below him, it would be a beautiful place for meditation. He found himself thinking back to the relative simplicity of Mahrae, and whether a place like that could ever exist again, knowing what he knew of the ancient wars and Vu-ori's bloody histories. But it would be his aim: to create a place of sanctuary and discovery.

After what seemed an interminable period of tension pacing the tower, awkward delegations from visitors, and arguments sparked over supply drops from each nation's respective cities, a new faction appeared in the distance. A flight of gryphons coursed through the clouds, bearing figures on their backs.

The arrival spurred activity from all areas; troops took to arms, shifting towards supplies, and Aidan caught sight of the leaders reappearing from tents or shelters, gravitating towards the tower. As the gryphons carrying the Skyrian delegation swept to the tower's summit, simultaneously Fulkore and Sarr arrived, and shortly afterwards Osiris, Venedreus, Raikali, Dhalen and Oakhe. Aidan rose and withdrew his staff from the plinth, standing at the edge of the gathering circle. The two Skyrian delegates stood politely to attention: a sloth bear and a greater glider. The glider appeared stalwart, with tight gold bracelets on her wrists and upper arms, and a gold and black robe which rose to a high collar around her neck. The sloth bear looked more apprehensive, clinging to his claws, every now and again reaching for a pendant of smooth green stone around his neck and rubbing it into his palm.

"Some new faces," the glider mused. "Skyria appreciates the chance to meet you. I am Virvel, Chief Representative of Skyria, and this is Nidjimes, my advisor."

Nidjimes waved cautiously to the circle, rescinding the gesture quickly when he caught Fulkore's stern (and potentially hungry) countenance. Aidan gave them both a short bow in return.

"So... what now?" he posited, glancing around.

Wary looks.

"Do we destroy the crystal, move it, split it, barricade it off; does anyone have any thoughts moving forwards?"

Oakhe frowned. "Moving it would provoke the same issues as before – maybe more so. Every potential direction will encroach on another's territory and gives no guarantee of protection or shared ownership."

Dhalen agreed. "It would make us vulnerable wherever we travelled, and even after. Trying to somehow divide it could lead us all to turn to ashes."

"You only wanted it because we did," Raikali sighed. "You can't even use it."

Dhalen shrugged. "We don't know that. We can change our bodies – we may find a way of making ourselves receptive to these crystals as well. Without it, we'll never know, but taking an entire menhir with us would be impractical to say the least."

"So you would refuse those with the power and right to use them just because you *may* want to toy around with them?" she scoffed. "This is ludicrous."

"Nobody has a 'right' to use them, or everyone does," Virvel retorted. "Experimentation and research isn't trivial, either. Skyria has found vital means of survival through their use."

"Of course you did," Sarr growled, leering at Venedreus, who shook her head in disdain.

"We will not tolerate moving this further from our lands," Fulkore echoed. "We have already been disadvantaged, and demand fair treatment."

Osiris stiffened. "You will get fair treatment when your

neighbours are offered the same guarantee. Your history precedes you."

"Because of your slanderous bloviating," Fulkore seethed.

"Is it inaccurate to recant historical events?" the gryphon replied, his voice brimming with derision. "I could just as easily talk of the whispers *you* spread to paint us as egomaniacal demons."

"Pretending you're without an agenda is absolute pomposity," Fulkore spoke in a poisonous scoff.

"This is not about *reasons*," Venedreus scathed. "This is about *reputation*. We have tried to help those around us–"

"When not subjugating their most powerful resonators to build your towers." Raikali jabbed.

Venedreus rustled her wings. "We are *now* set about rebuilding our connections to *all* creatures of Vu-ori; knowledge doesn't belong to one nation alone. Nor do our violent histories."

Aidan gestured with his staff. "That has to include Dhraka, though."

Her beak tightened. "You have only just arrived in this theatre, do not be so quick to surrender our future."

"*Our* future is a shared future; they'll exist whether you like it or not," he replied. "I'm not asking for old wars to be forgotten, just to end. Now. Especially around something that could destroy all of us."

"Why exactly are we answering to you, in any case?" Fulkore rounded on Aidan now. "You're an Aretian plaything."

"I'm just mediating," Aidan returned, with an exasperated shrug. "And as of right now I'm the only one with the means to change what physically happens to the Zenith, so if you want it, I have to be satisfied everyone gets a share they can use, and that we're not going to turn around and kill each other five paces out."

"Sounds more agreeable than arguing at this point," Dhalen muttered.

Raikali was next to cast her focus at Aidan. "You are *not* the only one capable of using these crystals," she barked. "There are several resonators in my clan – do we each get an equal vote as well?"

"Are you all separate nations?" Virvel asked.

Raikali tutted.

Aidan exerted supernatural effort to not roll his eyes. "For my part I'll represent Mahrae, my home village." He looked to Sarr and Fulkore. "Independently. If that helps assuage any doubts about possible prejudice."

Fulkore gave a short laugh. "Polite, but meaningless." He flicked a claw over Aidan, the Skyrians, and the two gryphons. "You already have your traitor's alliance."

Venedreus' face flared. "What of you?" she shrilled. "You cajoled these tribes into battle in the first place – what are we to think of *your* machinations here? We may have an alliance, but we use it for benefit, not to tear others to pieces."

The boiling pot of tension spilled into the fire. Hissing insults and roaring voices charged across the tower. Aidan, Nidjimes and Oakhe all stepped back, while Dhalen shook his head, then sat down facing the crater.

Aidan looked to Nidjimes, who kept trying to get Virvel's attention, but seemed afraid to interrupt her arguing so just bashed his claws together and looked about with great anxiety. Aidan walked over to him, paw extended.

"My name is Aidan; it's good to meet you."

Nidjimes smiled bashfully and gently took his paw. "Nidjimes. Oh, but you knew that, I'm sorry."

"You're fine," Aidan said, half-laughing, half-sighing. "Some consideration here wouldn't go amiss to be honest. Was there something you wanted to address to the group?"

Nidjimes nodded. "I-I was just thinking, there may be another option."

Aidan pulled him away from the spat's epicentre; when massive creatures with wings were involved it was easy to be sideswiped by someone else's ire. "What do you have in mind?"

The sloth bear gave him a polite, shy smile. "It... er... seemingly if everyone wanted to do research on the crystal then, we could... set up a research station here m-manned by representatives from a-all nations. Th-that way it's n-not moving and we all get to see where the re-research goes."

Aidan laid a hand on Nidjimes' shoulder. "I think that's the best idea, if we can get them all to agree. Let's see."

He held the tip of the staff to his mouth. It glowed softly; the air at the point shimmered just before his snout. He took a sharp breath, then gave a short, sharp bark:

"Hey."

The abrupt utterance was amplified by the tip of the staff, cannoning out over the argument and stopping it dead in its tracks. The delegates winced. Dhalen stood to attention and rubbed his ears. All eyes turned to Aidan, who edged Nidjimes forward.

"Nidjimes has a proposal. Would you like to share?"

The sloth-bear bashed his claws together with increasing

rapidity. "We, um, we could set up a-a joint settlement around the crystal with all n-nations sending scholars to co-contribute or conduct their own research and exp-periments."

"I think it's a sound idea," Aidan asserted. "We all get access and the chance to learn, nothing gets confiscated by another nation, we don't risk destabilising the crystal by moving it, and we all get accountability and supervision. All in favour?"

Virvel nodded and raised her hand. Oakhe and Dhalen did too. Osiris looked to Venedreus.

"You know my feelings about Dhraka, but we cannot claim to be of the world while acting as if we are above it," he said quietly.

The Archon frowned. "Peace is one thing; collaboration? I cannot stomach the idea of it."

"This isn't collaboration, at least not yet," Aidan continued. "We all exist here independently. You know your war is no longer sustainable, even if you always find each other's existence intolerable."

Osiris sighed. "We are dying, and we will only die faster while our war sputters in embers. Either they kill us, or we kill ourselves." His claw tightened around his sword, staring at the Dhrakan delegation before them. "Even if we never have a true peace, I would have us survive in a world to ensure its continuous protection from them."

Venedreus gave them a doubtful, disappointed look. "I may one day be feeble enough to live and let live, but I will never, ever call a Dhrakan our equal." She turned away. "Osiris, what we do will be your decision, and your responsibility. We will station soldiers here to protect you and the Zenith, but I will have no part in any governance here. I simply cannot endorse a forgiveness of Dhrakan militancy."

She spread her wings and turned to take flight.

Sarr let out a snide puff of breath as she left. "They never change. They would rather drive themselves to extinction than admit they have a single fault."

Osiris remained before him, his arms folded. "We accept the proposal. May it lead to a longer future for all of us," he said pointedly, glaring at the crimson-scaled reptile.

Sarr flicked his tongue dismissively.

"Very well. *One* among them has some humility. We will see how long it lasts. As it seems our claw is forced, we acquiesce. But believe me, Dhraka will not be subject to a single moment of further humiliation or refusal."

Raikali's claws, still firmly at her side, flexed and cracked. She glowered at Aidan.

"Your arrogance is disgraceful," she seethed. "You appear from nowhere, ransom a league of powerful nations by stealing their most precious resource, pretending it's all in the name of civility and fair distribution. This is manipulation, pure and simple. How do you expect any of us to believe you won't leverage dominance further down the line for greater control?"

The words "*I'm not you*" were on the tip of Aidan's tongue, but he swallowed them down. "I have no hostility towards you. I never did. I never even *knew* you. I came here expecting an understanding to be reached far more effectively, but my introduction to you was essentially a war council."

He rapped the staff on the tower's surface. "You were

ready to *die* for the chance to access this. That's your fanaticism, not mine. You'll always be inventing your next threat, your next perceived persecution, when everyone who *is* suffering wants the chance at the life we all deserve. I consider you part of that, believe it or not. This benefits us all. But that comes at the price of laying down arms."

Her face tightened, glancing at the other representatives, all eyes on her.

"The world is not as innocent as you believe," she growled. "It is not magnanimous to hold hostage our birthright stone and offer us a meagre portion of it in exchange for some weak morality."

Aidan folded his arms. His tail tensed. "Compassion is not weak. Where any of us has privilege and skills in excess of those who are struggling to live, it becomes our responsibility to aid those who need it. An unfeeling world becomes a self-fulfilling prophecy when you pre-empt it with violence and oppression."

She snorted. "We have fundamental disagreements, it seems." She looked to Fulkore, who had been watching her keenly. After a second, she broke from his gaze. "We have no opportunity to refuse; much like Dhraka, this is dangled over our heads like a guillotine. Go build your precious city. We will be here to see it turn to chaos."

"Which brings me to my question:" Virvel interjected, "how do we secure the city?" She looked between the other delegates, all of whom were taller, and all carnivores. "Skyria isn't a military or predatory nation so we have a disadvantage here, if we're to be kept safe from conflict." She shot a pointed look to each other delegate. "From within or without."

Just as Raikali seemed about to speak, Aidan turned demonstratively to Dhalen and Oakhe. "I volunteer the Kitaia to take charge of that, if they have no objections. You seem to be the most neutral here."

Raikali's nostrils flared. "They were about to go to war with us."

Oakhe shrugged. "We rescind our declaration. The resources we sought weren't what we believed, and if we're being offered sanctuary it feels only appropriate to protect it. But if our presence is contentious, we can leave."

"You are welcome here," Osiris said firmly. "As much as I would prefer it overall, it would create more conflict to have Arete solely in charge of protection." He rested his talon on the hilt of his rapier, watching Fulkore. "We will each of us stand in total defence of it at all times, however."

The dragon gave a derisive snort. "Do what you will. We need no babysitting."

"The rest we can work out once we have the city's foundations set." Aidan turned back to Nidjimes. "It seems we have a tenuous agreement. Did you have a name for this place?"

"W-well, in the very first language, 'Nazer-e-al' meant 'vow to others'; I-I think that may be a symbolic conjugation of a joint venture."

Dhalen frowned. "Poetic, but a little clumsy. What if it was truncated to Nazreal?"

Nidjimes nodded, and although Aidan couldn't tell whether it was through sincere agreement or polite intimidation, he would take the first signs of co-operation before the moment passed.

The fox gave a sigh and craned his head back to the sky

overhead. "All right. Now we've settled that, it's time to stabilise this place and give us a more practical means of living instead of camping in tents and under sheets. If you all wouldn't mind, I need space."

The delegates retreated to the ground, and the camps began to withdraw.

Osiris was last to leave the Zenith's peak. He stood next to his companion, looking over the receding encampments. "You have created quite an adventure here," he mused. "I hope you are ready for what may happen."

Aidan cracked his knuckles. "I intend to give nobody reason to object to their treatment. But… I'd be lying if I wasn't intimidated. We just need to subdue these immortal grudges." He gave Osiris an imploring look. "I need you with me. Please tell me how I can keep us safe, and… protect me."

The gryphon took a knee before him. "I have already made my promise, but now more than ever, I renew it. For what you displayed today, and the power you have within you – not only in your resonance but in the way you communicate with the world and those to whom it belongs – I am proud to stand by your side as a guardian, and a friend."

He offered his talon, which Aidan took gratefully and heartily.

"Thank you, Osiris."

The gryphon bowed his head, then took to the sky, leaving Aidan alone on the tower. The winds shifted, sending a cold through him that he'd never experienced before. The clouds coursed by, swirling distally, and for a second he was filled with a sunken dread that somehow they were trying to escape.

"Let this be the right choice," he whispered.

He took a deep breath to release the tension of the parlay, and looked down. Holding the staff in front of him, he circled his hind paws to ground himself and brace his body for his imminent task. He had strayed from his ritual somewhat for casual or small resonance feats, but this would require his total concentration.

After a few seconds of deep, meditative breathing, he raised the staff, then plunged it into the stony summit.

A brilliant light shone from the tower's peak. The ground rumbled, shook, and shifted. The tower began to sink downwards, slowly at first, but accelerated quickly, until it completely disappeared below the ground. The rumbling grew and spread; some onlookers lost their footing, reached out to one another for support, or sprinted away from the vanished Zenith in fear. The rumbling ebbed and rose in strange rhythms, then from the edge of the hole rose fingers of blue-hued stone, swirling together to form a tall, narrow pyramid. It ascended higher than the old Zenith, a needle piercing the sky. Two pincer-like spires grew from the tower's apex like the tines of a trident. As the rock solidified, rivulets of iridescent blue cascaded up the tower, and another blue light burst from between the twin spires, a brilliant, shimmering beacon. Windows blossomed open over the tower's walls, and at its base four arched doors twisted into place. Dust and sand drifted into the air as the rumbling slowly rescinded and the craterous valley was left in awed silence.

One of the stone doors boomed open. Aidan strode through, his eyes glowing almost as brightly as the beacon above him. He tapped the staff to the tower's threshold and a web of paved streets shook into place from the ground beneath them, displacing the iridescent grass to border the neat walkways.

He steadied himself with his staff, trying not to collapse. His body rocked and quaked, but after a second he quelled his painful, electric tremors and spread wide his arms to the audience.

"Welcome to our new beginning," he called. "Welcome to Nazreal."

Chapter Eleven

"*I know you were all from that time; you, my father, Fulkore and Raikali... but hearing it is still so surreal.*"

"*It is my regret that I lack a better story to tell you. I hope, soon, that we reach a full and prosperous conclusion together.*"

Nazreal grew quickly, in bursts. Aidan was the main architect, talking with leaders about what each nation needed to begin their research, then forming a building to suit their needs, and logging all of it within his ever-growing journal. He levelled the crater's edges in places to form pathways through the mountains. Where the grass would have obstructed further developments, he shifted it to outside the city borders, which altered on an almost daily basis. The walls of each structure were thick and smooth. All the stone plucked from the Zenith's ground held a blue-purple hue thanks to the unique mixture of rocks combined with crystal residue. As other resonators arrived, mainly from Gauros but also from Skyria and Kitaia, construction began on larger buildings and living areas, and sometimes expanding the ones already in place. Some areas were constructed traditionally to avoid exhausting the limited supply of resonators, particularly Aidan, but now he'd committed to his plan, he was intent on being available at any moment to improve their resources and curtail potential conflict.

Skyria volunteered to irrigate the city using nearby aquifers, of which there seemed to be several thanks to the craterous mountain rings, with long-term plans for an aqueduct from a major river to the northwest. Until the supply was steady, however, they were still reliant on deliveries, and had to prioritise drinking water over anything used for research. It limited the number of people that could immediately reside in Nazreal, so maintaining the balance of new voices against the probability of forcing people out due to diminishing provisions was delicate.

The tower at the centre was dubbed the Tor, or the Beacon, depending who you spoke to. It was designed not only as a centrepiece but also as a provisional answer to stabilising as much of the enormous crystal shard below it as possible. Aidan had reformed a portion of the ore into the Tor's walls and constructed a resonance chamber underneath it like the one in Arete. This reduced the amount of raw crystal in one place, but Aidan didn't have the power to transform it all at once and, to his frustration, had to leave a large chunk of potentially unstable material directly underneath them. The energy channelled through the Tor was expelled as light and heat, and any geological instabilities were negated with a burst of energy from here. It also provided interior light for scholars to work, and heated the city streets to a comfortable degree, to negate the chill of the winds that blew across them. Several times he'd seen Dhrakans asleep on the ground during times the power surged and the temperature rose to a cosiness that mimicked the volcanoes they left in their own lands.

Aidan's constant activity had not been met without consternation. Raikali, a persistent shadow over his work, frequently remonstrated what she saw as interference and opportunism, but refused any offer of his training or direct calls to her for help. More questionable to him was the Dhrakan presence, which seemed at times to be literally only Fulkore, until massive troop deliveries offloaded huge sheets of black metal for experiments he had no knowledge of, or for plating their buildings.

Other individuals and nations had been much more accepting of the arrangements. Skyria set about ferrying researchers to the growing city almost immediately, and brought with them years of horticultural research that flourished remarkably quickly. The Kitaian emissaries moved between camps, usually offering medical advice, but several had set up a permanent base for improving their own crystal affinity, and had sent foragers back to the regions they'd travelled through to find more purple crystals.

While Aidan hadn't intended to become the arbitrator of the city's governance, the responsibility of convening meetings often fell to him. They were typically tense, staccato affairs where each nation laid out their goals, progress, and grievances in the Tor's central chamber. Where Raikali and Fulkore were present, things moved even more slowly, and stressfully. The first few gatherings hadn't been eventful, but as the city grew, so did potential infractions and supply issues.

After a particularly gruelling encounter, Aidan sloped in his palanquin-esque chair and rubbed his forehead. Osiris leant his folded arms against the long, oval table, and silently commiserated.

"How did I go from resonance training to city management?" Aidan groaned.

"Fate rarely hands us predictability."

He sighed. "So much of this feels unnecessary."

"Do you mean the conflict, or the process?" Osiris chimed. "You have begun a path that will take your aims higher than you imagined. You summoned a city from the ground, and it will help the world to grow. It is… undoubtedly a big step very quickly, but if you keep your authenticity in focus then this should not deter you. In fact, I would advise you to find empowerment in this opportunity."

Aidan steepled his claws and leant forwards on the table. "I just… I *know* so many prospects are left unsaid for being too provocative, either directly or by objection. In many heads, there's still a war going on."

Osiris nodded. "I sensed the same. You cannot fool yourself into expecting centuries of ire to revert within a few months. Keep moving forward, but always with one hand on your hilt. The peace you wish for will likely not come from benevolence alone."

Aidan ran his paw over his ears, grimacing. "It's been over a year and we've barely moved at all, have we?"

Osiris plucked a broken feather from his upper arm and twirled it between his claws. "I would not say that. You have taken the first step to offering a better future, and a display like that does not go unnoticed by other sovereigns."

"Sovereigns?"

"Nations, or any coalesced group with a unifying ethic. Not all of them have borders on a map, but their identity and autonomy is still distinct. I believe it to be a more inclusive term."

Aidan pouted. "Ah. Well… we'll get to the naming pedantics later. Have we heard from any other nations, tribes, or settlements about our offer to join?"

Osiris blinked at him.

"What?"

Long pause.

"Yes, I know I could have just said 'sovereign'."

"Just making sure you understand the inefficiency."

Aidan gave him a blank look. "I have about six hundred different hills to die on here and you're picking that one right now?"

Osiris broke into a rare, wry smile. "You would not die if you did not battle," he oozed.

The fox groaned, leaning heavily back in his chair to smack the headboard with his crown.

"But to answer your question," Osiris continued, "We have had several replies of interest. I believe a caravan or two have already begun their journeys."

Aidan rubbed his eyes. "I hope they're nice."

"I believe the power dynamic between individuals and a collective should be very different to manage."

Aidan paused. "They'll still need seats on the council, won't they?"

Osiris gave a thoughtful whistle. "That would depend on their contribution, I daresay. Giving everyone a unique facility will become untenable very quickly. We are already pushing our current limits. Have them stay and observe for a time, adjoin whomever they desire, then confer about accommodating them within the means we already have."

"That... seems fair." Aidan breathed, resting his muzzle on his paws. "Thank you for being here," he said after a time. "I am very much in over my head."

"I do not believe that," Osiris replied kindly, "but I am here for you all the same."

Over the next few weeks, caravans, travellers, and other assorted groups of resonators and researchers filtered into the city. Most were immediately awestruck by the city's construction and the various schools of resonance. Crystal lamps lined the city streets and shone into the night. Strips of gentle luminance marked pathways and doors against the stone ground, which itself amplified the light with its crystal iridescence. The buildings themselves were varied, but all grand and unique. Aside from the Tor, Aidan had summoned other tall structures, and stretched existing ones upwards or outwards when they were found to be inadequate, or shuffled buildings' positions where they were too cramped to be practical. It was his playground, albeit one that he hoped others would find the most fulfilment in. Despite his introductory grievances with Raikali he did not deliberately shy away from any Gauros he encountered. He wondered if their wariness of him resulted from Raikali giving them a tacit order of avoidance or whether he genuinely intimidated them. It left him with a bitter hesitancy to fully unwind, the constant fluctuation that he was either contributing too much or too little to try and win their favour, all while the city grew and others began their flourishing research.

Other newcomers, however, were horrified. The sheer scope of the crystals' use seemed to terrify a few, who turned away before even setting foot within the city gates. Aidan tried to chase one bear that he saw retreating but was rebuked with vehement cursing of the 'brazen disrespect for the natural resources' and their deficiency in other lands, that this was a 'decadent atrocity of self-fulfilment'. She laid into him with savage chiding for lack of responsibility and forethought, alongside fears of extinguishing these same crystals within too short a time if growth on this scale continued at such a rate. She had come to see what potential it may have had, but was left with nothing but disappointment and fear.

The bear had mauled him without even touching him.

Aidan took all of these concerns to heart, and met with the council several more times to ask their opinion. Meanwhile, Arete was distressingly silent with sending resources other than soldiers and books. Teratai, Dhalen and Oakhe, who had quickly become good companions to Aidan, were unable to offer much support except sympathetic pragmatism.

The grand council chamber echoed with quiet sounds of the city below, while Aidan sat alone again, as he often did, scratching at a parchment with a quill.

"I'm so fed up of this room," he sighed, drawing a long, curved line across the paper's soft, uneven surface. It was a crude ship design at Osiris' commission, with notes about materials and construction scrawled along the page's edge. The Aretians had a staunch fleet of elegant ships, but Teratai and Osiris wanted to take it further and make a craft, like the gryphons themselves, that could master both the air and the sea. He wished to bridge the gap between Nazreal and Arete, and create a symbol that would convince his nation that a cooperative future did not mean sacrificing their identity or history. It was a great deal of pressure for Aidan's first mechanically mobile project, having not made much more than a kite in his youth.

Aidan's ears flicked as he heard a figure shift behind him.

"I'm not very interesting right now," he called.

"Company does not have to be interesting, merely pleasant," Osiris tutted. "Do not discredit yourself; you are more pleasant than most in this city."

Aidan tapped the quill repeatedly on the paper, his brow furrowed. "I'm glad you think so. I don't feel like I'm the best example right now."

The gryphon looked at the designs, scratching the feathers at his neck. "Will it fly?"

"I'll be relying on Teratai to tell me that; she's got the expertise here."

"Then I have news," Osiris replied. "She has been granted leave to stay here permanently. Arete has acquiesced to send a small team of scholars and some research materials for her. And… she is now my breeding partner."

Aidan's whiskers twitched. "Breeding partner? I thought your race was sterile?"

"A talonful of us are lucky."

The fox circled his claw on the table's smooth surface.

"Oh, right. Well, congratulations! I had no idea."

"It takes some time to determine our fertility, and even longer to be paired. There is something… while I am hesitant to call it artificial, I believe all of us would prefer the freedom to make our own choices were we not nearing complete genetic exhaustion." Osiris fell quiet for a second. "However, she is a worthy partner with an amazing intellect, and I am lucky to be her compatriot. I will endeavour to live up to such an honour."

Aidan watched his friend for a few seconds. Osiris seemed to be aware of it, and shifted his focus to outside the wide, arched window.

"You don't sound honoured."

"It is… complicated, and not up for discussion," the gryphon snipped. "I would rather talk about other things for the moment."

Aidan nodded, bending forward to stare down at the table for a while. He hadn't considered when he would have children. He presumed it was an inevitability, but if it were the only thing left to keep his race going, the pressure would be so much greater. There was so much to do in the world, would they even be safe? Was it fair that the fate of his world, and the survival of a unique ancestry, fell solely to someone with no choice over their lineage? Maybe those weren't Osiris' concerns. He had been alive for years longer than Aidan, and would be alive a long time after he was gone. Decades of experiences were written in his voice and body. Many times, Aidan felt naive to even be talking with him so openly, but was grateful for his company, stern as it often could be.

Just as he was about to offer up some words to break

the silence, Osiris craned his neck to view something outside. He unfolded his arms and marched to the balcony.

"We have a new caravan. Would you like to greet them?"

Aidan paused, staring at the drawing that seemed fatally crude for the plans Osiris had for this flying ship. With a disdainful huff he flicked the quill onto the paper. It tumbled, leaving a small trail of diminishing ink spots across its path.

"Sure, let's go down."

Well into their routine, Aidan clambered onto Osiris' back and the two glided down to the walled gate that the travellers were approaching. Between the seven of them rumbled a small cart loaded with provisions and shelters, pulled by a small breed of Theriasaur, a quadrupedal burden lizard. They halted at Osiris' majestic landing, some shying cautiously away. Aidan slid from his back, and together they gave a polite, humble bow.

"Welcome to Nazreal," Aidan said brightly, pushing the frustration of the council chamber as far behind him as he could manage. "Have you travelled far?"

"Far enough," came a weary but not weak voice from the right of the cart. The owner of the voice wore a deep hood of light green that covered tall ears. Aidan could see some of their face, but not all of it. "You're not screening us, are you?"

Aidan held up his paws. "No, no. I just like greeting people before they get into the gates, so we can show you where to go, depending on what you need."

"Well, that's a relief. We feared a place such as this would be stolen by elitism under poor leadership."

Aidan laced his digits together smartly in front of him, over his staff. "It's my greatest hope that doesn't happen," he said hopefully. He stepped forwards to the hooded figure and held out his paw. "My name is Aidan Arc'hantael. I am from Mahrae."

The figure watched his staff. They took his paw, and with the other swept back their hood. The long ears belonged to a slender fennec with fur the colour of desert sands. Their eyes shone blue, just like his.

"Elysser," they replied. "We're from a few different regions, mostly along the southern coast." They glanced again at his staff. "Do you make these here?"

Aidan's mouth moved, but no words came out for a second. He realised he'd been staring at them for longer than he should have, and laughed, taking a small step back. "We can. I mean, I made this, but it wasn't here, although I could. Would you like to hold it?"

Elysser smiled and took it gently in their paws. The crystal glowed warmly, smoothly. They tapped the tip of the crystal to the cart's metal front axle, and the cart gently shifted upwards at the nearest end.

"I ignored it for too long, it was driving me spare," Elysser sighed. They spun the staff round and ran their digits over the edges of the leaf-like blades at either end. "This is remarkable crystal work."

Aidan's face lit up at the effortlessness with which they used his device. The process seemed almost cleaner, more efficient than his own energy expenditure. His tail swept back and forth excitedly. "Your skill is incredible," he marvelled, eyes wide as he bent down to inspect the fixed axle. He couldn't see even the remotest seam or distortion.

He stood back up and was almost bouncing in front of them. "We have numerous places inside where you can study or practice, but if that's your level of experience I dare say we'll be learning from you." He froze suddenly. "I mean, if you decide to stay, or even want to work with us at all, that is. Mainly right now we're expanding on cultivation and material strengthening."

Elysser nodded, once, but then looked to the cart as they handed him back the staff. "We should settle first, but an introduction would be most welcome when you have time. Can you direct us to a tavern, or... just a place to rest?"

Osiris stepped forwards. "Absolutely," he boomed, taking the lead at the head of the cart, in front of the burden lizard pulling it. "If you would all follow." He gave a distinct glance to the rest of the crew that Aidan had somewhat ignored, and the fox winced slightly, nodding apologetically back.

He then gave Elysser a quick bow and jumped to Osiris's side to match his pace. The gryphon gave him a sideways glance.

"Your focus is a somewhat compromised," he said in a low voice.

Aidan rubbed a paw over his ears. "Sorry; I'm a mess, I'm tired, and I'm just... happy not to get torn to pieces again."

Osiris paused. "You are still young. Many of these experiences will be new. If you are to represent a city in earnest, however, you will need decorum. Getting personal comes later, if appropriate. Control now can strengthen an impression later."

"Yes..." Aidan replied immediately, before trailing off, resisting the urge to look back at Elysser. "I just... I never thought I'd see another fox resonator. Especially one who could use my staff so perfectly without any kind of instruction."

Osiris bobbed his head, a sort of half-nod. "There have been resonators in other parts of the continent for many years, honing their skills as you have; some with infinitely fewer resources. There may be many more yet to come. It is important you do not show undue bias."

They passed under the thick stone archway, into which had been hewn corridors and walkways to allow protected travel around the city's circumference. The stone's blue imbuement shimmered in waves as they walked by. There was no gate as such; instead the stone would be folded into place by a resonator to close the city at night or if there was ever a threat. Theoretically, the whole city could be encased in a dome, but it would turn defence efforts into little more than a waiting game or forging an escape tunnel. Ideally Nazreal would be kept from ever falling into that kind of conflict anyway, so Aidan had not put much consideration into the city's defences aside from the impenetrability of the walls themselves. He was more concerned about what might happen from within.

"I feel positive bias is less damaging than negative bias," he murmured pointedly, making sure not to catch the ear of the Gauros guard flanking the archway.

"It means the same to poisoned eyes," Osiris muttered darkly back.

A quick look over his shoulder made sure their conversation was not given away to the newcomers, who seemed adequately distracted by the architecture. Softly glowing spires reached to the dimming sky, and the radiating beacon at the city's heart cast the streets in a rich, light hue. Directly ahead of them sat a wide building with sloped walls and a garden on its uppermost floor, with vines and flowers climbing up and over a slatted rooftop trellis.

Aidan dropped behind Osiris to address the travellers. "This is… well, for want of a better term, a welcoming hall. We have food and lodging available, and a growing catalogue of the projects each sov– er, nation is undertaking. We try to allocate space evenly, but our resources are fairly limited right now."

"It wouldn't appear so," Elysser mused, admiring the intricacies of the structures around them.

Aidan clicked his tongue and paused for a second, trying to dispel the immediate rush of criticisms that flooded his mind. "We… are trying to be sensible, but admittedly we grew very quickly. There are some very talented resonators here."

Elysser gave him a keen look. "So I gather."

Aidan's tail went rigid for a second, then he gestured quickly to the Tor. "That's the Tor, or the Beacon, our biggest resource library and council chamber. We're still working on how to govern things so it's a little chaotic, but you are welcome to observe."

A small rumble reverberated from their right; all heads turned to the sound's origin and the train stopped in caution.

"Some experiments are loud…" Aidan began. A thin wisp of smoke loomed from a few streets away. "Excuse me."

He leapt sideways, and with his staff summoned a stone disc from the ground, skating immediately away.

Osiris motioned to the building ahead. "He will return. For now, please make yourselves comfortable."

An hour or so later, Aidan returned to find Osiris was waiting for him in the gathering centre's lobby. Pillars of crystal rock arched over the ground to form an angular web-like pattern on the ceiling, defined by curves and sweeping pointed lines travelling from pillar to pillar. The smooth floor was almost reflective; as Aidan returned his pawpads slipped a little against the surface with each step.

"Knew this was a mistake," he muttered, exerting twice as much effort to walk as usual.

"I warned you," Osiris called.

"Looks nice, though."

"I recommend perhaps confining your shiny habit to a centrepiece, so at least the walkways are usable."

Aidan nodded, somewhat defeated.

"Is everyone safe?" Osiris asked, leading his friend to a seating area with a bar to the side.

A dry laugh escaped the fox as they traversed the impractical flooring.

"A crystal overheated and exploded in the Skyrian lab. There must have been a fault in it."

Osiris chewed his thoughts for a second. "This will become more frequent. That is the danger of rapidly expansive progress."

"They aren't inexperienced," Aidan replied, a little stern. "We should be careful, though. We can only afford so many mistakes, and not a single disaster. Exhaustion could undermine us in ways we don't realise until it's too late."

"Gygel would have said the same," Osiris returned, knowingly.

Aidan's face descended to a tight frown. "I'm sure she would."

His dark countenance evaporated when he saw who was waiting for them on the benches. Elysser had removed their cape and hood, and sat in a neat, tight robe of dark green with cut out shoulders, wide bell sleeves and a russet sash, draped over trousers that tapered outwards from their waist but stopped above their ankle. Their sandy beige tail blended to a dark tip, which flicked slowly with thoughtful countenance. On their feet were dark brown open-toed boots and leg bindings of dark grey. The sash was pinned at their left hip with a large gold medallion, hooked onto which was a sizeable handaxe. Its blade was lined with shining blue, connected to a large gem at its haft. A chain ran around their back to their right side, at the end of which was a metal buckler, ringed with a sharp crystal edge. They had their hands in their lap as Aidan approached, watching him expectantly.

"We aren't about to explode, then?" they cajoled, raising a gentle, sly smile. Aidan shook his head, another smile breaking his command to keep sincere.

"Not all of us, no. But a faulty crystal did." He regarded their weapon set and his eyes widened. "That looks incredible."

"My own design," they replied, picking up the axe and twirling it in their left paw. They held it out to Aidan, who gently took it and turned it over, watching the crystal play in the light. There was very little used, but it was spread masterfully thin; thinner than he'd ever managed and still have it retain strength and function.

"How did you do that?" he breathed.

"Patience," Elysser said flatly. "And a certain amount of pre-conditioning to the crystal before laying it. It helps to have a blacksmith for a mother."

"Remarkable," he said, handing it back to them. His whiskers flicked as he watched the light play off the delicate metalwork. Elysser's craftwork was some of the most meticulous he'd seen – this excited him far more than anything in Arete's libraries except the orrery. He tried not to let his energy overcome him, however, and withdrew his paw quickly as soon as the axe had been safely handed over.

Elysser slid the axe back into their belt ring. "We're all remarkable in some way or another. It just takes time to find out how, and some are more willing to embrace the search than others."

Aidan looked at his paws. He had been squeezing and rubbing them unconsciously, and had thinned a patch of his fur on one of his digits. He tucked it away in his paw, and gave them a small bow.

"I admire that," he beamed. "A very admirable way to see the world. I hope this will be a place where you can continue looking for whatever you seek."

They straightened, tilting their head slightly to give Aidan quizzical address. "What of you?" they asked. "What are you here to discover?"

Words caught in his throat and the sentence he intended to utter died in a sigh through his nose. "I'm not sure yet," he said candidly. "This city wasn't really part of my plan.

Initially I just wanted to find out more about myself and my abilities. I think I've learnt more about everything *but* me so far."

"How you react to the world is as much a part of you as anything you do consciously," Elysser continued, with a kind smile. "I'm sure you'll come to find you've learnt a lot when you find a point to reflect."

Aidan lost himself for a moment. Their features were elegant, distinct, yet inscrutable. Their eyes were some of the brightest Aidan had ever seen; not only in sheer colour, but for the intensity of thought behind them. He would have to force himself to look away, and the more he did it the more conscious he grew that they already knew his efforts to avoid contact were failing, but his descent into their beguiling, open confidence was inspiring him in a way he'd never felt before.

He stroked back his ears, which returned upright instantly. "You're welcome to a proper tour of the city anytime you want. Even tomorrow. With your group, of course."

The fennec reached into their sleeves and held their wrists, bringing the cuffs together like a tunnel in front of them. "I wouldn't miss it," they replied, before giving a light bow, and turning to the lodgings. As Aidan spun on his paw to give his friend a wide, mooning smile, Osiris caught his arm.

He said nothing, but pointed to the distance, where Gauros and Dhrakan troops were marching in joint patrols, and at their head were Raikali and Fulkore.

Osiris kept his eyes targeted on the archway. "They are making their presence known, and they will have eyes on us in no uncertain terms. Be wary. Displays like this are made to draw attention from an uninformed audience, but the moment you speak out, they will twist it against you to cry discrimination. Let the council meetings show your impartiality and fairness, but give no undue advantage. They will take it, and we will be the worse for it. We must be ready."

Aidan gripped his staff tightly.

"Just… for one evening, I would like to sleep in peace."

Chapter Twelve

"*Do you think it's wrong to give so much to the world?*"

"*There is always balance to be found. Too little, and nobody will aid you. Too much, and you cannot aid yourself. But for me, seeing how both you and Aidan live, I would always err on the side of too much than too little. Kindness is an infinite asset more valuable than anything dug from the ground. Never underestimate it.*"

The next day, Aidan waited in the seating area, opposite the stairs from which he expected Elysser to arrive. His leg twitched, jerking up and down while he kept cracking his paw knuckles in anticipation. Every now and again he'd wave to passers-by, trying not to look inordinately focused on anything in particular. He knew Osiris would have no problem discerning his intent, however.

So focused was he on the stairwell that he lost awareness of anyone approaching from behind, and the smooth floor made pawpads the perfect stealth tool. As he gnawed at one of his claws, a quiet voice sent him almost leaping off his stool.

"Good morning, Aidan."

He whipped off his stool to a standing position, face to face with Elysser. He froze for a moment, then clasped his paws together and gave a smart yet rushed bow.

"Elysser! It's a pleasure. I, er, hope you had a good first night here."

They scratched their left ear. "Sleep isn't easy for me, sadly, no matter the comfort of the room or promise of company. This city… definitely has an energy, doesn't it?"

He pouted in agreement. "For all of the building we do, it won't change the amount of crystal gathered here. I tried to capture as much of it within the stone as possible but is still ekes out. Anyone receptive is going to feel it no matter what, I think."

He gestured for them to pull up a stool, they politely declined with a raise of their hand. "If I might," they began, "I wondered if I could view the city first. I wandered some of it last night, but did not want to overstep my bounds."

"Of course!" he replied. "Will… would you want to wake the rest of your group?"

They shook their head. "They don't tend to rise early, and we travelled a long way; I'll be glad to brief them once I've seen what there is to offer. We came from Irara, on the northernmost peninsula, after an envoy from Arete told us about the crystal city. We can't all use them, but we've studied them for years."

"That sounds like my village," Aidan mused. "We were in the desert though. Most of our work was in cultivation, solidifying sand, and wind protection."

Elysser tilted their head. "A red fox from the desert and

a fennec from the northern forests," they said, with a slight smile. "It normally works the other way around."

He shrugged. "This is barely normal by any stretch of the imagination." He looked idly into the distance, as if plotting a course in his head, then turned back to his companion. "If you feel ready, shall we go?"

They circled outside of the Tor first, then Aidan took Elysser in a circuitous route through Nazreal, first to Skyria's horticultural and hydroponics stations, then clockwise round to the small Aretian stronghold, and the Kitaian medical centres and living areas. When they approached the Dhrakan segment he took a wider berth. The air smelt of heat and something vaguely sulphurous. The noise of forges and clattering metal rang through their narrow windows and towering chimneys, from which rose steady, rhythmic plumes of smoke.

Aidan's stride stiffened as they skirted the edges of the complex, watching the Dhrakan guards on the rooftops and in the streets. He tried a few times to acknowledge them, but they seemed aloof, and he couldn't decide whether they didn't think anything of him, or they were reacting to his apprehension. Either way, he spent a short amount of time telling Elysser what he knew of the Dhrakan areas of study, from metallurgy to seismic and volcanic control, and how they were perhaps more reliant on other resonance users than anyone else except Arete, who reciprocated with supplies and materials in payment for shared knowledge and technological advancements. Dhraka appeared to be working most closely with Gauros, which was their final part of the city to skirt around, or through, before returning to the Tor. For how bombastic the Gauros were in displaying might and physical presence, their skill at tapestry and textile artwork particularly garnered attention. Had Aidan not been so averse to risking a reaction from entering their jurisdiction, he would have loved to see it up close.

Elysser glanced at Aidan drawing the staff closer to his body. "Is something amiss?"

"No," he said quickly. Before Elysser could ask anything further, Raikali stood before them both, with a stare that could slice a fly's wings off at ten paces. Aidan straightened and tried to relax his shoulders, but the stiffness of his tail belied his attempts to be open. He was determined, however, not to be undone by the lioness' acerbity.

"Queen Raikali, a pleasant surprise. Is there something you need?"

"I could ask you the same, as you are entering the Gauros compound. I am on my way to Dhraka."

She flicked her eyes to Elysser. "A guest?"

"A new party to the city, potentially," Aidan replied, firmly.

"Elysser Remine," the fennec said sharply, quick to interrupt any potential second-hand introductions or the ignoring of them altogether. "I represent Irara in the North."

"Never heard of it," Raikali said flatly. "I see we stretch ourselves ever further in the name of 'inclusion'."

Aidan dug his thumbs into his belt. "We can afford it," he replied, to which she gave a dour look askance. "How are you finding it here?"

She gave a sharp, curt intake of breath, and tugged at the shoulders of her thick, armoured robe of leather and feathers. "The city is gaudy and indulgent, but our focus is strong. There may be *some* merit to the way things are conducted here, so long as we do not sabotage ourselves with compassionate overreach," she said, shooting a pointed look at Elysser.

Elysser folded their hands into their sleeves. "You mean, offering too much to those who need it?"

"That is a reductively naive counter. Nations are made on their ability to prepare, and you destroy its foundations when you give away excessively. Gauros did not become the strongest land tribe by continually splitting our resources."

"We never heard of you," Elysser said bluntly. "And you obviously never conquered us, so unfortunately there's still some comparison to be made about how you measure your strength."

Raikali's expression darkened. "Let me be clear, I have no time for charity or provocation. Ignoring one and challenging the other is the path to dominance."

"This isn't a place for dominance, Raikali. This is a place for coexistence. We all have something to give, and a right to survive" Aidan replied. "A hoard goes to waste gathering dust in a vault."

Raikali shook her head. "You sound like a cub's parable," she scoffed. "Attitudes like that will run you into impoverishment."

Aidan smiled, not a friendly expression, but one born of frustration. "You really don't believe in this city, do you?"

She scowled. "I believed in it when it was a pile of crystal. It had potential as a raw resource, not a playground for daydreamers. You waste it and call it generosity. You're a trickster, promising the world yet delivering nothing but a facade."

She didn't even attempt to hide her disgust. "A city is an empty vessel, determined by its leadership. Strength and ability are two different characteristics that alone may make a warrior great, but together makes them unstoppable."

"We are not warriors," Aidan replied stiffly. "This is not a city for war. What you think of as waste is giving homes to creatures without shelter, finding ways to grow food in barren wastelands, cure diseases, to live with more freedom than ever before. Why do you insist compassion is weakness?"

Her jowls tensed with anger. "You think those you help will stop at what you deign to give them? The world is hungry and desperate. You will be left no choice very soon but to turn to war, I guarantee it."

"Are you volunteering as the arbiter of that guarantee?" Elysser asked.

Raikali drew up to her full height, glowering down at the fennec. "I laid claim to this land before it was invaded. If this city turns to war, it will be defended, and things *will* change thereafter."

Aidan stepped forwards. "That's why I'm extending invitations so widely. Nobody should have need to conquer if they're here freely."

"We will see."

She swept past them, throwing one last glare to Elysser.

As she disappeared into the Dhrakan complex, Aidan let out a long, stiff sigh. "One of our council members. She's been... averse to some of our ethics."

Elysser gave him a flat look. "She's dangerous. And afraid her supremacy will be erased. Which it should be, if she's to make threats like that against you."

"I… can't argue with you. We don't deserve to be a world living in fear. But we're trying to calm tempers. This was very contested land, so the more stable we can keep our voices, the easier I hope it will become in the future."

The fennec looked back to the Tor. "You said that was where you held the council meetings?"

Aidan nodded.

"I look forward to seeing it often, if you would accept Irara's formal request to join."

He blinked. "I mean, we haven't even—"

"I'm decided," they replied. "In this world, nothing stops if we just watch it happen. We need to do better, all of us. No indecision."

Aidan bowed his head, then held out his paw. "Thank you, it is my great honour to have you."

Elysser took his paw in theirs, and after shaking it firmly, let their digits slide slowly from his.

His cheek fur stood on end. "There, erm, there is some documentation to sign."

"Of course," they replied, with a smile.

Elysser swiftly took an affirmative presence in the council meetings to discuss new resonance techniques. Raikali was belligerently uninspired by their presence. She made no effort to hide her disdain whenever they and Aidan were together, not least of all because Elysser demonstrated a great deal more finesse with the same powers she held, and quickly harnessed a greater rapport with the remaining council, except for Dhraka.

Fulkore's attendance eventually dwindled to perhaps half, but the others came diligently, and with Elysser's help even more joined to represent coalesced groups from other regions.

As the council grew, so too did the city. The walls expanded again, the grass and farmland outside spread further, and travel routes led in six directions from the city gates, wearing more and more cleanly as greater traffic passed along them.

Finally, after almost a year and a half surviving off aquifer siphoning, the Skyrians completed their aqueduct, bringing water from the northwest, and with it, a reservoir and slow but steady barge travel to the coast. They set up the flora and fauna, allowing the reservoir to stay clean and provide a supply of fish. It quickly became a popular route for walking, such that Aidan and others designed a trail around it.

Further from here, in a separate artificial bay, lay a large flat structure on which had begun the framework of something extraordinary.

"The Coriolis," Teratai said proudly, laying out her most detailed schematic yet on the table in the softly-lit warehouse containing her stockpiled materials. "Our ship will harness the force of the winds to master the skies."

Elysser leant over the section at the bow. "These are… turbines?"

"In a sense," she replied, stroking her beak. "This should be the only point that needs ignition by resonance energy. They're engines to provide the initial thrust for take-off and maintain speed in the air. That amount of power couldn't come from natural or mechanical means without sailing in a straight line for about a week."

Aidan rested his muzzle on a closed fist. "I wonder how the rest of the council will react to it," he murmured.

Teratai didn't glance up from her papers. "I am not optimistic. I expect Dhraka will claim it is a weapon, and Gauros will make more comments about being disadvantaged by the rest of us."

Elysser twirled a metallic ribbon through their paw. "If they actually made it clear what they needed and didn't end every conversation with a door slam, they'd probably get a lot more help. But as it appears they specifically don't want assistance from me or Aidan, and they effectively ignore Skyria. That only leaves Kitaia, who seem content to pick up the jobs nobody else wants, and they don't have our resonance abilities anyway."

The female gryphon shrugged. "It works, in a strange way. I would not complain as long as they remain impotently belligerent, at any rate. I have neither seen nor heard any pushback of late, and I am glad of it."

Aidan looked to Osiris, who slowly tapped his beak. "This lack of communication is exactly what worries me," he said in a low voice. "Dhraka do not take slights quietly, and neither Sarr nor Fulkore have been attending lately, where they held far too much bluster in the first months. Their presence has faded, and that brings me concern that their focus may be elsewhere."

"Arete, you mean?" Aidan asked.

Osiris shook his head. "I could not say. The less we know, the worse it may yet be."

They gathered up their materials for presenting, and trod the path to the Tor. The long journey often resulted in drawn-out conversations into the emotional and speculative. Elysser and Aidan shared stories of their ambitions or exchanged experiences from their homes, or talked about resonance. Today, however, was more muted. Clouds hung over the city like a shroud, low, passing almost interminably. There was no feel of rain, but heaviness that filled the air all the same.

Partway through the walk, Teratai and Osiris dropped back, and from a few brief glances over his shoulder, Aidan saw them deep in conversation.

Eventually they ascended the Tor's wide, segmented stairwells to the council chamber at its heart. They convened at the door, at which stood a pair of gryphons and two lions from Gauros; the current rotation. Elysser and Osiris pushed the wooden slab open, and all eyes turned to them.

Sarr Crawn's bulky form sat at the head of the table directly opposite the door, his wings swelling with anticipation of their entry. Next to him stood Fulkore, with an inscrutable expression that inferred immense satisfaction and impending severity, without giving it away in a smile. He knew his power, and succeeded in displaying it by doing nothing at all.

"You deign to join us," Sarr rolled, clicking his claws on the smooth marbled surface. "I don't know whether to be relieved or disappointed."

"I have no doubt either would be an insult to your satisfaction," Osiris countered, striding to the table to land his leather scroll caddy heavily on the table. Fulkore's nostrils flared. His claws hung close to a large axe at his belt, with a specially-fashioned blade of crescent serrations, perfect for tearing through feathers where smooth blades may slide free.

Dhalen and Oakhe exchanged knowing, awkward, looks. Raikali stood at Sarr's other side, arms folded.

Aidan eyed the setup suspiciously. "We have a full complement today, it seems. Sorry to have kept you all, we were returning from our current project."

Sarr sucked in a preparatory breath. "Yes, this… project has interested me, as my soldiers have reported on it from their patrols of the reservoir. I am concerned it circumvents some of our civil agreements outside of the walls."

Osiris stiffened, and Teratai gave an impolite huff. She unfurled her parchments.

"This is no weapon," she said firmly. "The agreement within the walls of Nazreal was that if disclosure was given, research would be put to a vote as to whether it was deemed safe and appropriate. So far our project has been nothing but research. Now that we have shaped the groundwork, it is in a fitting place to show you what we intend."

Sarr leaned back in his chair, gave a quick glance to Fulkore, then gestured lazily with his claw to begin. Teratai took a breath, but as she did, he opened his mouth again.

"Just so we are clear, it is also an agreement that any advancements made within these walls are subject to sharing with all other nations, am I correct?"

Osiris clenched his claws. "That is correct. Once we have it in a stable form to do so, subject to the assertion that this technology may not be misused, and on the condition that the nations in commune are in good standing."

Fulkore rolled his neck, letting out a loud crack. "I'm

sure the definition of 'good standing' will be subject to its own interpretation," he muttered.

Aidan raised his arms. "Please. We're here to be transparent."

Sarr vaguely waved his claw again, looking aside.

Teratai held up the schematic to the room, rotating so all could see. "This is the Coriolis, a ship we're designing to be fast in the water, light, and made of metal."

"We already have metal ships," Sarr remarked.

She continued. "The primary difference with this will be its speed, and, we hope, the ability to engage in flight."

Sarr snapped back to attention. "Flight?"

Aidan watched Osiris' expression. He was on high alert, eyes wide.

"We have studied aerofoil dynamics and believe it will be possible," Teratai explained, firmly yet cautiously. "We ask the council for permission to advance to the next stage of our research, which will be building the structure, experimenting with thrust using resonance energies, meaning tests both in the air and in water. We may require the bay and dock to be expanded for this purpose to act as a runway, to avoid damage to the city."

There were some murmurs around the table. Raikali looked dour and said nothing, but listened to the deliberation between Fulkore and Sarr. Dhalen shrugged.

"We have no issue with it, as long as these experiments are contained safely."

Virvel nodded. "And if it doesn't create undue noise or disruption to the air quality. A working mechanism like this could be useful for our research into wind resistance."

The room turned to the Dhraka. Sarr stroked his

reptilian muzzle, teeth barely concealed. "We look forward to sharing the benefits of such an undertaking," he said slowly, fixing eyes with Osiris. "I anticipate hearing more about it from my soldiers as it progresses."

Osiris leant on the table with both arms. "If you attended more meetings, maybe you would not need to rely on espionage to discover our intent. This has not been a secret," he charged.

Sarr leant in. "Were I not more concerned with the greater world, I would have time to supervise your dangerous frivolity. Does this council even wander outside of these halls anymore? Have you forgotten your lands and the struggles outside them?" He pushed the table away as he stood. "But of course, that would be too much to expect from Arete, the champion of arrogant disregard. For all of your posturing about creating a free and open world, creatures still starve, and dissent still rages."

Virvel cast an accusing claw at him. "We've already done what we can to keep this city sustainable – everything we've achieved can already apply elsewhere. Or is it just that we haven't heaped our findings on you while you hide in your forges? You complain about the rest of the world being beggars but you've contributed nothing since this city's inception."

Sarr slammed his fist on the table. "We give you security! You think anyone would dare approach a city knowing *we* are stationed inside it? We deter scavengers and usurpers who would tear this place from under you within minutes."

Osiris rolled his eyes. "As if Arete would be any less of a deterrent," he growled.

Fulkore's eyes flared. "Perhaps you would care to test that theory."

"It would be no challenge, if you can bear the loss of your dependence on our knowledge."

Sarr's lip gnarled, his sharpened, jagged teeth glistening. "This charade is boring and pathetic." He glared at Aidan. "You established this farcical system; this was prejudiced from the very beginning."

Aidan glowered at him. "I'm not in control of how you negotiate agreements. If there's something you need then by all means ask, but you haven't, even once. For us to even know what you *may* need we should know what you're doing, but all we have on record is metallurgy and forging improvements, and your results get shipped out of the city. That's nothing to go on."

Aidan growled, rubbing his forehead. "I suggest we adjourn," he said loudly. "We'll continue tomorrow, after some time to cool down."

Teratai needed no prompting. In one swift motion she gathered her papers and swirled out of the door. Osiris swept round behind her, and Virvel and Nidjimes quickly strode out too, with Dhalen and Oakhe close behind. Aidan gave a quick, perfunctory bow to the Dhrakan pair and backed towards the doorway, only turning when Elysser joined him.

"I'll remind you once;" Sarr called to his back, "our scales were made for fire, your hide was not. We will endure, always."

Aidan turned his head, though not enough to face him. "And I'll remind you once: you do not know what I am capable of. Don't push me."

He swept out.

Chapter Thirteen

"Was that... was that the tipping point?"

"One of many escalations. I couldn't even say if it was the first."

"So... what happened next?"

"Exact details of the in-between are rather vague; some of it I had to piece together from Dhalen."

"Why Dhalen?"

Raikali turned to the dragons with a scornful grimace. "Do you see? Their hypocrisy has no boundary."

Sarr gave a baleful growl. "What they do will be of no concern as long as our achievements outpace theirs. Our power sources are far superior."

Fulkore turned his head to the window to look over the city, far below him. "I'm sure we can gain something from their techniques. They are far from useless, even if our end goal will render them ultimately inconsequential."

"Take whatever you can get," Sarr said. "Steal if you

must, but do not feign deference. We must always be strong."

Raikali scoffed. "I would have attempted a negotiation for materials if you hadn't disbanded the meeting with your pompous ire."

The grizzled dragon turned sharply. "I doubt that," he snapped. "What progress have you made with your paltry abilities? You are barely even considered a master of your lands anymore."

She recoiled. "What do you mean?"

"You are so engrossed in prowling this vain city and mewling at the adepts for recognition that your nation feels abandoned and seeks to dethrone you. You left inexperienced soldiers in a land of artists and farmers, weak and unprotected from enemies who have longed to erase your stain on the map. Your troops here beg for a reminder of the blood spilled in your name that brought them to supremacy, and you have delivered nothing but absence and petty spite. We entrusted a great many resources to you already, along with our allegiance, and you appear to be wasting them both."

Raikali's eyes flashed blue. She crashed her fist through the wooden chair next to her, blue streaks coursing from the tips of her claws. "How dare they! How dare *you*! I would have everything in my grasp had these simpering idiots not intervened!" she yelled, pointing furiously at the entranceway, indicating the recently-departed council. She rounded on Sarr, face to face with him, a claw angled at his nose. "I gave you soldiers for your machines! I hammered the metal for your drills and canisters in the forges myself! Where was *your* fire when Arete arrived? All you did was stand there sucking your tail, capitulating to the demands of a weak-minded missionary!"

Sarr lunged forwards, fist raised. Fulkore grabbed it, locking his father's swing in mid-air. Raikali had been poised to repel it, claws bared. Sarr craned his neck round to Fulkore with a venomous gaze.

"Don't," Fulkore rumbled. "We both share an enemy. Our differences are meaningless till we see them under our claws."

Raikali flashed her teeth at them. "I will tear this place to the ground to reclaim my right. I have every ounce of power that waif of a fox has, and more besides! I am stifled by the paltry rationing we receive of this material. I will not be trodden into the dust like a sickly calf!"

"Then what will you do?" Fulkore moved past his father, stalking up to her, looming, casting her in shadow. "I know your conviction, and your prowess against normal creatures, but anything further is nothing but a desperate roar."

She straightened. "My strength is limitless. There is nothing I cannot achieve when these crystals are in my grasp. I will keep my tribe and take my rightful share of this city. Just keep on with our agreement, you'll very soon witness my true power."

Sarr flicked his claws. "We had better."

She stormed out, her furious warpath through the corridors warning everyone out of her way.

Except one.

As she coursed across the resonant stone, walking breezily in the opposite direction was Oakhe. The chains on his ears swung with his swift step, and his armour shifted with a soft rattle. The purple markings in his fur gleamed even in the Tor's muted light.

She didn't see him rounding the corner.

The two collided; instinctively she rammed her claw out, but her body locked up before it reached Oakhe's body. He deftly swung out of the way, his eyes glowing a soft purple.

"Forgive me, Raikali, I had not anticipated such an event."

She shuddered, trying to pull free. "Release me, or I will tear out your throat."

He shrugged. "That sounds like a bad deal for me either way. May I take the chance to appeal to your sense of de-escalation instead?"

A growl rumbled in her gullet. "De-escalation; might as well remove my teeth while you're at it. You are all revolting, patronising, sanctimonious garbage."

"I never harboured any ill will towards you," he said, frowning. "Your reputation was very well-regarded as a warrior, and tales of your conquests reached our lands well before we knew your name. I often wondered how we could survive against you."

Her stern breaths subsided slightly. "This is your power, to subdue an opponent with flattery? We would have eviscerated you."

"I'm sure," he replied.

He released his grip on her and she fell free, shaking the stiffness from the arm that had been raised towards him. She looked him up and down for a second, then straightened, curious regard overtaking her anger.

"What can you control with your powers? Have you discovered any limits?"

Oakhe smiled softly. "It depends on many factors. It takes a remarkable amount of concentration, proximity, and quality of crystal."

"So I gather." She recalled the brief interaction she'd had with them in the crater. "A wolf would not ordinarily overpower a lioness of war. You alter your own bodies and can control others' as well."

He nodded. "That is part of our discipline. Our strength comes both through training and our affinity to the crystals. Each enhances the other, in balance."

After a second of thoughtful stillness, she took in a controlled breath and offered a determined half-smile. "I extend an offer to you. A joint research project, one that should help us both."

He blinked. "I… had not expected that. What kind of project?"

She cracked her neck, looking about them. "Despite my eminence, I require assistance, and have few to ask. I wish to experiment on the potential enhancement of resonance abilities using our powers combined."

He furrowed his brow; his tail flicked with curiosity. "What did you have in mind?"

She stepped forwards, taller than him by about the height of her ears. "This is where my experience is lacking," she intoned. "Your discipline is different. Teach it to me. Find a means of imbuing me with more energy so I can use it." She stood over him, dark and staunch in her conviction. "Make me stronger."

He leant back slightly, with a dubious squint. "That is an incredible task coming from someone with such a brutal reputation."

She held out her paw to him. "We have been at each other's throats for some time, but I am at an impasse. What you can do for me, Gauros will repay tenfold. We may be conquerors, but we recognise those who help bring us to glory."

Oakhe glanced behind him. "I… am willing to try, if it may bring us to new triumphs of self-improvement. It's somewhat of an imposition, however," he said quietly. "There are many who consider Gauros insurgent. I don't believe I could effectively dedicate many resources to your aid without protest." He leaned forwards. "Or supervision, as I assume this is something you wish to keep discreet," he murmured.

She scowled. "Would you contribute to a city that harboured perpetual mistrust and aggression towards you?" She paused for a second, then lowered her voice. "We are here to make use of each other, whether we like it or not. In truth I loathe it, but I find myself in need of a more open exchange. If not in public, then secretly. And if not with allocated resources, then with personal ones. You may be the only one willing to listen with courtesy to our plight and disadvantages."

She spoke bitterly, in a rising growl. "Grovelling is pitiful. You know as well as I do that we are not considered equals here. I was unmatched, unchallenged, the unequivocal ruler of my tribe. I had power to give, and here I have none, stolen away and given to those who barely recognise it."

He scratched his muzzle, regarding her carefully. "We're not as aimless as many believe." He produced a small purple crystal from the pouch on his belt, laid it on his open palm and held it to her. "Place your hand over the crystal."

She paused for a second, ears alert. Eventually she laid her paw stiffly on it, wary about touching him too closely. He gripped it and her firmly; she jerked to pull away, but stopped as the purple gem beneath her palm began to glow.

"Now, close your eyes."

"I will not. You will show me here."

"This won't work if your eyes are open. I won't betray you, I swear."

With a low, indignant hiss, she did.

"Now, feel the energy move through you. What do you see?"

"Nothing."

"Let it flow further."

She waited for a few seconds, darkness before her, when light and shapes blossomed into view. A figure, a lioness standing very close to her, hand outstretched onto hers.

She was looking at herself.

Her eyes sprang open and she reeled back; the illusion shattered. Oakhe placed the crystal back into its pouch.

"Do you understand? Our energy is shared, and our potential more than we believe. It is a matter of focus, turning the crystals within you instead of directing their energy outward. You *must* have an awareness of your body. To merely overpower your weaknesses with muscle is to ignore the channels that lie within and allow you to move, to breathe, to feel. To know this is to harness your energy, and that of others."

She stepped forwards again, eyes alight with determination. "This is it. This is it exactly."

He held up his paws in caution. "I can't promise to accomplish more than advice, but if this helps restore energies in Nazreal to something approaching unison, I'll be the bridge."

A decisive smile split Raikali's face; she took his paw in her muscular, tight grasp, then strode away.

Oakhe began to walk the way he had been heading, then stalled, ears swivelling behind. He turned, and Dhalen was in the corridor, arms folded, claws rippling impatiently on his biceps.

"Do you think that's wise?" he cautioned.

Oakhe opened his arms. "Where would we be if we had not taken the opportunity for communication, and growth? Still tearing each other's throats out on a mountainside."

"That was different." Dhalen did not move. "The scale of our conflicts here are far greater and reach further than a dispute between two clan leaders."

"Is that not what we are, though?" Oakhe responded, flicking dirt from under his claws. "Who ends a conflict, if not the first to suggest a truce?"

Dhalen rubbed his muzzle. "There are many reasons I appreciate you, Oakhe, and your compassion is one of them. But don't let what you hope for endanger what is the most likely outcome."

Oakhe stepped forwards and adjusted the collar on Dhalen's jacket, with a soft smile. "Compassion and mistrust are the two sides of us that may never completely entwine," he sighed brightly. "But that is why we work together."

Dhalen took his paw, stopping him from playing further with his attire. "You work alone if you choose this. There are some bridges too dangerous to cross. Raikali is not weak, nor will she ever be." The wolf huffed impatiently. "Your heart is sound, but you're looking in the wrong direction."

Oakhe stepped backwards, closing his eyes briefly. "Allow me this chance, Dhalen. We have this argument every time we encounter a stray, and many have been assets to us one way or another. You yourself have a strong rapport with Aidan."

"Aidan was never a destructive presence."

Oakhe shook his head. "You know we *all* are, at one time or another. And we all have the opportunity to alter that."

The lynx turned back round to the council chamber. "I'll see you tonight."

"I hope so," Dhalen said quietly, as Oakhe's departing footsteps faded across the stone.

Chapter Fourteen

"What would you have done, Osiris?"

"I was there, and made my choice; I cannot say whether it was correct. There was so much that none of us saw until it was over, and none of us alone may have changed enough individually to stop it. Together, we could have, but we were often too disparate. That is why it is vital you remain who you are. You are the difference this world needs."

Oakhe journeyed through the Gauros complex that evening, to the buildings Raikali had dedicated to her training and research. Her site was more of an arena than anything else; a paved stone circle with crystals placed at intermittent radii, connected by crystal-imbued chains and rivers of blue running through the slabs on the floor.

She was ready for him, no longer wearing her immense leather overcoat, and now in the form-fitting armour she wore to battle. Even without the bulk of the additional layer, her physical strength was easily visible and the custom armour harness and plating accentuated her covered musculature. Oakhe addressed her with a bow, which she returned.

"Are you ready?" he asked.

She punched a fist into her open palm. "Always."

"Good. First, a test."

He ran for her. She reacted quickly – as his punch aimed for her face, she caught it in her claw. He was strong, but she was stronger. Her arm shook briefly with the initial impact of his attack, but she quickly forced his fist away and threw him backwards, then twisted back round to strike at him with her left claw. He ducked easily under, but took her left foot to the crook of his neck. He rolled back to absorb the impact, and by the time he was upright she was on him again. He leapt backwards, then circled around her. She pivoted, right arm chambered, left arm outstretched.

He ducked down and charged forwards. She arched back but he caught her in a shoulder charge. She let out a deep cry but brought her right elbow crashing onto his shoulder before locking her left arm under his right, attempting a choke hold. He grunted as they both tumbled backwards; she still held him. He twisted and kicked his legs up, swivelling over her to break her hold and land his shoulder on top of her. She rolled and jumped back to her feet. Her nose bled. She prepared to strike again, but he had vanished. Her claws flexed.

A rush of air came from behind her. She whirled her elbow round just in time for it to be blocked by Oakhe, whose eyes were glowing virulent purple. With one push she cast him off and spun round to kick him, but he'd vanished again. Instants later he appeared at her side, landing a kick to her left leg. She flinched, but stayed standing, and reached out to him, grabbing him by his chestplate in her left claw and pulling him forwards. He raised his forearm to block her next blow, and the purple faded from his eyes. Their forearms met, and the impact echoed into silence in the dim arena.

He smiled. "Your reputation is well-deserved," he said through heavy breaths.

She licked the blood from her face. She had barely broken a sweat. "And your crystal empowers you just as I anticipated," she replied. "Do you think it feasible for me?"

He opened his paws. "You appear strong enough to handle anything I can anticipate, but focus comes with patience and discipline, not explosive rage. So how this power affects you will ultimately be down to you. Now," he began, as he once again retrieved the purple crystal from his belt pouch, "hold this, and remain still."

Focus was not alien to Raikali, as she often spent time absorbing crystal energies when she was depleted, or preparing, but this energy was alien; familiar, yet distinct, and sometimes unruly. Yet over time, when her ability to listen to the rhythms of its pulsing improved, she began to draw more energy from her own crystals, and channel it into diverse and nuanced applications instead of the brute force she had relied on so heavily. She was still attuned to draining energies around her, but soon enough she was able to concentrate on using a single crystal source instead of multiple, and the stockpile of resources she had been given was reducing at a much more amenable rate.

She could reshape crystals by herself now, where Gauros had physically chiselled them to purpose before. Their carving had been masterful in its detail, but still suffered from any faults within the crystals themselves. Her newfound ability changed their fundamental strategy, and Raikali was gleeful.

Her satisfaction swelled every time Oakhe rejoined her. The further she pushed, the more he responded in kind and found new challenges for her to ascend to. He demonstrated how to alter his own body using his crystals and how she could do the same. The changes she made were small at first, such as increasing her heart rate or muscle recovery speed, to begin combat at even faster movements than she had been able to reach before. At higher levels, he would show how his body, or those of others, could be distorted in the same way. She even began experimenting with her own resonance crystals, to see if they could similarly alter people. She could soon induce environmental changes, as in generating warm or cold air, or an atmosphere charged with disorientating low noise or high energy, but not bodily affectations yet. Their joint experimentation lasted for several months as her training increased. She became emboldened in the council meetings, demanding more, even being tactically amenable to council members like Virvel if it meant securing medical supplies that aided her healing and quickened her training. Dhalen and Aidan were still wary, but grudgingly trusted Oakhe's attempts to moderate, though Elysser and Osiris refused all but perfunctory conversation with her. They were busy and exhausted with their efforts elsewhere anyway, as the Coriolis was undergoing the heat of intense construction.

Eventually, she took her findings back to Dhraka.

She stood in the dragons' dark arena, lit in deep red columns of light, while around her in the darkness rang the movements of armour and chain, and the rattle of blades. She did not know how many awaited their command.

Fulkore raised his arm.

"Go."

Blurs of red and black streaked from the shadows, whirling metal, sharp edges glinting in the narrow shafts of light.

A dragon approached her from behind and to the right. She ducked, the impact of her body cracking the floor beneath her feet. Her eyes shone, and with a swift kick she laid the dragon on their back. They whipped their chain to bind her legs; she caught it in her claws and with another flash of blue tore it to pieces, scattering the remnants in the dragon's face.

Another swooped towards her from high, club drawn and poised. Raikali leapt onto the Dhrakan's back, and with one solid punch split the steel backplate. The force of her fist was so great the dragon plummeted to the ground; she leapt free before his prone form slid into a black pillar. As the third dragon rounded on her, she punched her claws into the stone column and dragged it across her body. The stone warped, forming a barrier directly over her chest. When it stopped the attacker's advance, she lunged forwards, palms against the stone, and it exploded outwards, pebbledashing the dragon with the debris. A powerful punch to his gut sent him sprawling across the circle.

Two more dragons advanced from either side. Raikali knelt, claws to the stone floor, eyes aflame with wild blue light. With a twist of her claws the floor formed into whip-like tendrils of rock; she thrashed and they stretched to lash out at the dragons. One caught a whip to the face and careened backwards, while the other was tripped at the leg, unable to escape incapacitation by a final flick of Raikali's rocky vine, slamming onto their chest with a punishing thud.

As the impacts reverberated around the arena, Sarr's tongue flicked hungrily.

"Now you have given us something worth our time," he salivated. "This changes our investment, and we will gladly lend you something to… further accelerate results."

He threw a scroll her way, which she caught in one outstretched paw. Her eyes narrowed as she unfurled it.

"Will this work?"

"It has not yet succeeded," Sarr said, deliberately. "But your ally may engage with it in ways we were not able to."

Fulkore's wings shook in the darkness. "This must not be seen by Arete," he thundered. "If this is discovered, we will be forced into defensive measures."

She nodded. "They will not be party to this. I have already forsaken any communication with their arrogant leadership."

A sharp-toothed grin split Sarr's battle-scarred face. "Good. I await your report with great anticipation."

The equipment hummed in the centre of Gauros' arena. Plugs and pipes thrummed with red energy flowing from the dark generators positioned around the periphery. Even in the arena's wide space, the heat coming from them was considerable. Raikali finished her preparations and stood back, glancing from the connections to the parchment she'd been given. The pipes led to a sloped wooden platform, lined with vials and needles mounted in sliding apparatus along the edges. A sturdy black barrel with a small pump handle, and a long glass tube with leather sections for articulation nestled behind it.

"It appears complete," came Fulkore's low voice.

Her ears flicked testily. "You could assist," she snipped.

He stalked around the edge of the room. "I intend to leave as little evidence of my presence here as necessary. My soldiers are ready to reclaim this as soon as you are finished but otherwise our presence is merely cursory. We have other devices we must attend to if we are to take full advantage of this city."

"How bold," she said flatly, sliding the end of the tube into one set of vials. An undulating blue liquid swirled through the clear container, shimmering as it passed through her grip. As it settled, she saw shades of purple glinting through. "Repudiation doesn't fit you," she continued. "I thought your race was too proud for that."

Fulkore let out a rare, mocking laugh. "You assume I am not proud. Subterfuge works best when influencing factors are reduced to a minimum. Your loss is mitigated and it becomes easier to reform if things fail."

She nodded. "So that's how you came out on top of the other Dhrakan creeds." She turned to him with a devious scowl. "How many killed each other through your machinations?"

"Most," he rumbled. "The remainder were easy to subjugate, or kill, depending on their level of resistance."

A faint noise echoed from the back of the arena. The

lioness' jowls flicked in derision. "Go. He will smell you and your soldiers on this equipment anyway, best not to confirm his suspicions."

She heard Fulkore's bulk shift away, and disappear into one of the antechambers. A few moments later the large set of doors at the end creaked open and Oakhe strode in. His pace slowed as he reached the dimly-lit centre. He took in the equipment very quickly, observing it with increasing dubiety.

"This is... new."

She clasped her claws together. "Our next phase. You have shown me the equilibrium of body and elemental crystal control, but I wish to test something with you – your ability to handle the energy of the crystals directly."

He gave her an uncertain stare. "Is my work not satisfactory already? You have already made great strides in the Council."

Her eyes flashed briefly with a look of anger, but it vanished, replaced with stern focus. "This is not a matter of satisfaction, it is ambition. You have greater control over your senses and abilities than I, and since you have been kind enough to show my affinity for different energies, I wished to return the favour and provide you with a boost that could see your lifeline and powers increase a thousand fold." She placed a claw on his thick wooden chestplate. "If you harness your control of this as well as you do your own resonance, you may become the most powerful of any on Vu-ori."

He frowned. "I'm not sure... if that's my destiny."

She raised an eyebrow. "How will you know if you don't reach for it?"

Oakhe studied the equipment as he circled it, tapping the glass vial and taking note of the long, thick needle screwed into it.

"I think I understand what your plan is."

She placed her claws on the plinth. "Do you accept? If this works, it could open a new world for all of us." She leant towards him, eyes wide. "We could change this world with our bare paws."

He looked at the platform for some time, running his claws over the worn wooden surface. "For the sake of discovery, and the promise of a future, I will try. But as a guide, not as a commander."

Raikali bowed her head to him, eyes brimming with victory. "A new step promises untold futures," she sang, gesturing for him to sit. He shifted himself onto the wooden surface, removing his armoured jacket and letting it fall to the floor. Purple tattoos cascaded down his chest, abdomen and back, in a swirling map of the energy paths he had instructed her about. She took his left arm and readied the needle at the crook.

With a deep breath, she pressed it into him. The blue liquid swirled and flashed as it passed through the base of the vial and into Oakhe's arm. He grimaced. A soft blue glow emanated from his fur where it spread within him. Slowly, more coursed into his body. His whole upper arm and shoulder were aglow. He gripped the table with his claws, his eyes tight shut.

"Are you with me?" she asked, clutching the handle that pushed further into him.

"S... stop," he said quietly. "I– I think it's enough. It's... I feel it."

She pulled on the vial. It caught.

She grimaced, straining harder. Oakhe let out a groan.

She pulled again. The needle refused to separate, as if fused to his skin. She tried to detach the tube, but the resonance liquid within flashed, blinding her briefly.

His body shook. The glow began to pulse and shift, sucking more liquid from the vial, illuminating his body in blues and purple.

He screamed. Straining through her disorientation she tore at the needle; it heaved away, but his skin and fur stretched away with it, like it was made of glue. He thrashed around on the platform, letting out a shrill, agonizing cry. He grabbed the deformed forearm skin and tore it free with his teeth. Glowing blue and splashes of red flecked the air as he arched back on the plinth, writhing and contorting.

A door slammed open behind them. Fulkore pounded inside, followed by several Dhrakan guards.

"What is this?" he hissed, as Oakhe rolled forwards, the muscles on his back expanding, distending, then shrinking at an alarming rate. Raikali shook her head.

"I don't know. Can it be stopped?"

Fulkore whipped the axe from his belt. "Definitely."

He bolted forwards. Axe aloft, he swung it at Oakhe's head. The lynx flung out an arm; at twice the distance his limb would normally reach his hand grabbed Fulkore's claw, muscles bulging and bubbling. He let out a terrified, pained screech, then lunged straight towards the dragon commander. He slammed into Fulkore's chest with his whole body, with such impact that his figure deformed and part-slid around him to reconstitute on the other side. He let out a spluttering roar of confused, terrified pain, and glanced down at his claws as they pulsed and twitched. His eyes shimmered purple, and darkened, irises flickering at unnatural speed.

Raikali froze. Without a word his head snapped to see her. His mouth opened, yet no sound came out but a hoarse, rising whisper of breath.

One of the Dhrakans stepped forwards. In a second Oakhe's attention whipped back their way, and he lurched forwards. A forest of claws erupted from his extended paws. He shredded the soldiers in a shower of blood one after another, throwing their bodies clear across the arena. The last two dragons tried to flee, but in two enormous, uneven bounds he was upon them, tearing into the neck of one with his teeth and piercing the abdomen of the other.

As the final Dhrakan fell with a rattle of blood-drowned breath, he froze, giving a desperate, hungry look to Raikali. For the tiniest of moments she saw his true face again, but within a blink it was overtaken by the dark, twisted visage he'd been turned into. He crashed into the half-open door, tearing it from its hinges, letting out a deafening screech into the blue night.

Chapter Fifteen

"*So the purple tattoos, that means... resonators like Vionaika?*"
   "*Correct.*"
   "*But then... does Kyru know?*"
   "*That would be up to you to discuss. He may not enjoy the idea of having such a historic connection to her.*"
   "*But... how did she come to be from that?*"

Alarms rang throughout the city. Horns, bells, and warning cries were a chorus of fear and danger. Guards leapt to their stations. Torches and beacons burst into light. Aidan, Osiris and Elysser all ran from their adjacent rooms to the roof of the Arete guardhouse. They heard the rumbling march of soldiers and the cries of officers, all heading towards the Gauros compound. Osiris took to the sky; Elysser and Aidan grabbed each other's paws and formed a platform that took them to the street, then skated swiftly to the centre of activity.

They arrived to see Dhrakan soldiers attending their

dead, carting them onto gurneys and carts, and Fulkore standing soberly by the arena's gates. Raikali, brandishing a dual-handed sword, asserted in roars her guards' directions and number. She saw the delegation arrive and immediately her eyes flashed in rage.

"This alarm is not for you! Leave now, we have this."

Aidan swallowed hard at the extent of the injuries, some of the dragons barely in one piece. "What happened?"

She snarled, claws bared. "This is nothing of your concern!"

"You're a liar," came a booming voice from behind them. Dhalen stepped forward, his severe focus directed solely at her. "Where is Oakhe?"

She shrank slightly. "How would I know?"

He lunged forward, taking her by her armoured collar. "You think I don't know my partner's own movements? What did you do with him?"

"I will contain him," she rasped. "My warriors are already in pursuit; it is only a matter of time. Spare your efforts for his rehabilitation."

Before she could speak further, he pushed her aside and ran into the arena. Aidan, Osiris, and Elysser quickly followed. With a vengeful scoff, she sprinted away, a company of lions at her heel. Fulkore, blood dripping from his breastplate and his right wing hanging at a crooked angle, began a lumbering march to the Tor.

Inside, Dhalen stood by the platform which now listed unevenly, bloodied and broken in the timid blue and red light. "Oakhe… something terrible happened here."

Elysser immediately went to the barrel, righting it and running her hand over its surface.

"This is resonance crystal, but… liquified. And… compounded with something else."

The gryphon's head snapped her way. He bounded over, then darted to the other materials strewn about the floor. He tossed the needle to Aidan, the blackened mass of Oakhe still dangling from its end.

"This is what they did to resonators past," he cursed. "This is Dhrakan technology at its most cruel."

Aidan stood opposite Dhalen, who stared towards the platform, although he could tell his focus was far beyond it. "Dhalen? What can we do? Can you find him?"

The wolf began to shake his head, then looked at the twisted doorway. "We have to. Everyone is in danger. This… this is monstrous."

Osiris rounded towards the exit. "I will warn the council to order a civilian curfew. It seems some patrols are already extant, but we will deploy more."

"It may do no good," Dhalen called. "Oakhe is subtle, he'll likely hide well. Let me search – put nobody else at risk, get them all away." He gestured at the shadows of blood still spreading across the brick. "We saw what he'll do to those ill-prepared. No normal soldier will be able to match him."

"We're with you," Elysser volunteered, as she and Aidan looked to one another.

Dhalen's jaw tightened. "Even we may not be enough."

Lhian trudged back to her quarters in Kitaia's region, rubbing her eye.

In the distance, the first alarm bells rang. She glanced

round. No smoke. The lynx turned back to face her path and quickened her pace. She heard doors opening, then some slamming shut again, as she rounded a corner.

She got to her doorway and turned the latch so quickly she didn't notice it was already open. She whirled inside and pushed it shut.

The fireplace shimmered faintly, bathing the room in dark, flickering shadows. As she reached for new wood, something shifted behind her. It sounded heavy, wet.

Breathing.

She whirled as something wrapped around her leg and immediately snapped tight. With a yell she was pulled over. Her head hit the stone hearth; for a second her vision flashed and her head swam in muted sound. The thing pulled her towards the darkness, and the tendril-like limb crept further up her body. A noise, not a gurgle, not a moan or a roar, but something between them all, overrode the noises of shadowy movement.

She let out a quiet, groggy groan; an attempt to scream. Another limb burst from the shadow and clamped around her jaw. As she tried to open her mouth again she felt the muscles of her face and jaw knit, bind together. She reached up with her claws to pry her mouth open.

Only matted, lumpy fur and bulbous tissue covered where her mouth had been.

The two limbs constricted further, pulling her out of the fire's glow.

In the distance, more alarms pealed.

Osiris's lockdown went into effect immediately, with civilians ushered into guarded quarters and locked buildings. There was no choice but to comply, and the lack of explanation threw many into anxiety over the safety of Nazreal itself, and demanded to leave. Guards from all nations stood on alert outside their respective buildings, with orders to raise alarms as soon as anything was sighted. Teratai flew to the Tor, where she stayed with Virvel and Nidjimes to eliminate search areas and collate reports.

An alarm rang to the south, in the Aretian quarter. By the time anyone arrived, the sighting had passed, and the gryphon admitted he was not entirely sure what he noticed, only that it wasn't a form he recognised, and it was darker than the night above them. No sign of Oakhe appeared, even with Dhalen and Raikali lending their efforts to track him. They returned to their squads, saying nothing directly to each other. The search went until daybreak with no luck, aside from trails of blood that seemed to appear from nowhere and stop just as suddenly in the middle of an open space, with no clue as to their onward direction. With great care, researchers were allowed back to their rooms under heavy supervision and in strict rotation. No-one was to be left alone.

Fulkore was in the Tor's command centre, mainly to be attended to by Kitaian physicians. His breathing was laboured from a series of broken ribs, and his dorsal ridge bore several split and shattered spines. His right wing was unable to fully extend, a signal of the stiffness in his body and back from Oakhe's terrible impact against his chest. He was a belligerent patient; between his attitude and news of Oakhe's disappearance, the Kitaians had eventually left him to medicate himself with aggression and militant, distracted pacing. With intense suspicion and silent disdain he watched Nidjimes, Virvel, and Teratai plan where to assign troops or searches next. Occasionally he made low comments about strategy, and although all were delivered with a snide and dismissive tone, some were useful. When it came to the second night, he and Teratai were even openly discussing methods for covering more ground and how to bolster their strength.

More Dhraka appeared, summoned on Fulkore's orders, and although Osiris protested initially that they weren't necessary, he relented soon after he saw how much it aided the search. More patrols meant more streets were covered at once, and nobody could argue with the Dhrakan strength, even if Oakhe, or whatever he was now, could still overpower them.

Dhalen was with Aidan and Elysser again, this time scouting through Kitaia's buildings. Ahead of them were two sets of guards, knocking on doors to ascertain who was inside. The two foxes had their resonance devices ready; the blue elements pulsed softly. Dhalen's eyes radiated their deep purple as he scanned alleys near and far. His tail swung behind him in a rigid arc, and his footfalls fell with great weight, power-charged and ready.

One of the guards rapped on the door ahead for a second time. No answer. He looked back to Dhalen and the others, who positioned themselves around the door. The guard twisted open the latch and aimed his sword at the gap.

The smell of smoke and blood hit their nostrils. Dhalen

pushed inside.

"Lhian? Oh hell…"

The fallen lynx had been slung against the wall, below the torn window shutters. Her body was a ragged mess of scratches and lesions, and one of her legs looked completely crushed. As her mouth had been sealed shut by her own boiling tissues, she was breathing through her nose, but barely, as it seeped with blood.

"She's alive," Dhalen snapped. "Get her away immediately."

One of the guards leaned outside and blew a whistle; within seconds others responded, running from their posts to aid them. Dhalen watched them gather the lynx up, while purple glows emanated from their paws as they performed enough rudimentary healing to keep Lhian alive as they moved her.

Elysser shivered, grip tightening on their hand axe. "How… how could he come to this?"

"Osiris told me…" Aidan began quietly, unable to tear his eyes from the injuries on Lhian's mouth, "…that when resonators were forced into power, as the Dhrakans once did, often the bodies would try to reject it. Even slow exposure to resonance energy wasn't always successful. If Raikali tried to infuse him with this much at once…"

"It may have conflicted with his own resonance if he tried to reject it when it became overwhelming. The mixing of energies spawned something far more disastrous," Dhalen finished, inspecting the gouges on the door and the strange trails of red that looked more like the smear of dragging carcass than the movement of something legged.

He dabbed at the blood. "This is not all hers," he said

quietly. "Some of this... feels like Oakhe's. His body may be tearing itself apart."

"Do you think it will just be a matter of time before he falls?" Elysser asked, looking through the window for further signs of a trail.

Dhalen shook his head. "I don't know. I wouldn't risk it. I hope something may be able to stabilise him first."

Elysser laid their hand on his shoulder. "We will try."

He stood up. "Oakhe was always pragmatic. If he has any awareness of what he's doing, he would want to be taken out before more lives were destroyed."

That night there were two more attacks, and several sightings. A pair of Gauros guards were targeted: one killed, and the other had his arms snapped almost completely off. A mangled body was found in the aqueduct, missing eyes and teeth. Dhalen and his soldiers found another ghastly scene the next morning. Someone had been sliced into ribbons with precision unlike any natural claws could accomplish: strikes and cuts as fine as any butcher's knife.

The name 'Daemon Stalker' spread in hurried, frightful whispers around Nazreal. All work had more or less stopped, and many had already requested to leave the city. Teratai and Virvel placed dozens of guards around routes to guide those who wanted to leave; once the midday sun struck the sky, several carts an hour began a frantic pace to escape. Archers from all nations patrolled the walls and rooftops, and exhaustive searches of warehouses and grain storage still turned up nothing, despite continued random instances of blood littering the streets.

The following night, with fewer citizens to guard, patrols increased. An organized sweep of the city began from the west, moving outwards. As they passed a well, some of the soldiers noticed a dark liquid dripping from one of the aquifer pumps, and a mad scramble began to access the underground pipes. Dhalen, Aidan, Raikali and Elysser all ventured forth with the patrol into the caves, and although a thick, acrid smell clung to some areas, they could see nothing, and the water remained clear.

While the group patrolled the underground tunnels, in another part of the city a young jackal had tried to investigate a sound inside a house. When he received no response, he turned back for support, and saw the bodies of his companions. All fifteen of his company had been eviscerated in complete silence. As he opened his mouth to cry for help, he felt a tiny, yet forceful, scratch crawl across his neck. His paws instinctively moved to his head in fear, yet nothing more happened.

When Osiris' patrol found him half an hour later, he was standing in petrified silence, clutching his head to his neck. Soldiers tried to comfort him but he refused to move. A physician who had tried to attend to the massacred fallen assessed him and immediately sought help; the jackal's head had been all but completely severed. Something in the way Oakhe had cut him kept him alive as some test of grim endurance. The soldier was now recovering in the Tor, but his terror was immense, and the loss of soldiers felt by all who remained.

Many deserted that night.

In the early morning, as the sun crept solemnly over the mountains, Aidan leant on his paws in the council room, sitting on his tail, poring over the city maps in a daze. The attacks seemed to have no connection, no pattern, and no trace left to point to any hiding space. Dhalen had kept the scraps of his friend's torn fur in the hope it would be useful for tracking, but its burnt, decaying smell never lingered at any site, where all that filled the air was the stench of the fresh kill. The wolf stood opposite Aidan, arms folded, claws clamped around his armour. None of them had slept since Oakhe disappeared.

"We need a way to bring him to us," Dhalen muttered.

"If we gathered everyone in the Tor, would that have any effect?" Elysser chanced.

The wolf shrugged. "We don't even know he's looking for food."

"Minimizing the area for him to attack makes our job easier regardless," Teratai said, flipping over a map of the Aretian block.

"Or provide the perfect scenario for a complete massacre," Fulkore rumbled, leaning against the wall, watching the caravans course into the desert pathways.

Osiris glanced up with a murderous stare. "As if your judgement gave us anything more than disaster in the first place."

Fulkore's wings flexed. "Our soldiers were the first killed by this mistake. We were assured it would be under control. The fault was not with our equipment but the greedy miscalculations of the operator. Which may not have happened had you not forced us both into the shadows with derision and–"

"Stow it!" Osiris roared. "Your ruinous aspirations have long been your responsibility, but your pride refuses to keep them in check. Had your soldiers not been among the dead, you would be laughing at us from your mountain."

"And rightly so," Fulkore replied, turning to leave. "Better to prove your self-obsessed folly now than later. My soldiers will be here to pick up the pieces regardless of your accusations."

He sailed out of the chamber, his wings beating a gust over them all as he went, lifting papers and rocking tapestries. Elysser brushed a paw over their ears. "Is that our best plan, consolidate the remaining civilians and hope we can corner him?"

"It may well be," Dhalen said, his clenched fist resting at the end of his muzzle. "If nothing else, we may guarantee a quiet night for the rest of the city."

The cordon and movement of the citizens went quickly, but not without further fear being cast among the populace. The Tor, although defensible, was not best made for a thousand or so refugees. Some were camped uncomfortably on the stairs leading to the resonance chamber, while others crowded into the lower chambers and libraries. If the city had been any larger the rooms may have been more populated with shelves and scrolls, but for now the rooms were just about barren enough to make room. At each potential opening stood a set of guards, but most were outside, stationed around windows and the tower's base, while other soldiers stood on rooftops above the flame-lit streets, completely emptied of activity. Between the dim glint of the resonance gutters and the torches, there should not have been a place for Oakhe to hide.

Returned to the council chamber was Fulkore, with Raikali, who mostly skirted the edges of the room in churlish silence, making sure not to cross behind Dhalen, who kept watch outside one of the windows. Virvel, Nidjimes, Teratai, Aidan, Elysser, and Osiris stood around the table, waiting for any sight of Oakhe.

Hours passed. Soldiers came and left with reports, sentries switched, but overall a thick quiet hung in the air. Suspense layered like a blanket over the city, one that could be torn off at any moment.

Virvel had been piecing something together on the table, a device similar to a crossbow, with a much deeper flight groove. She muttered and cursed under her breath as the tension in the string kept refusing her commands to yield. Nidjimes moved from window to window, in opposition to Raikali, checking on sentries, clutching a clay ball on a spiked shaft, winding his claw around a rope that protruded from the top. He jumped upon noticing Raikali had broken her rhythm to walk towards him, so he quickly changed direction and walked back. At the last window he'd checked, something seemed different.

"Wasn't there a soldier–"

With a growl, something catapulted through the window, knocking him under the table. Everyone in the room turned.

Skidding to a halt, heaving, sweating blood, was the distorted, hulking form of Oakhe. His armour and clothing, where not torn by his distended muscles, had sunken into his fur. His tail, once a short lynx bob, seemed to have partly melted, and hung limply from the remnants of his jacket.

Blackened eyes with empty purple irises darted erratically. His ears hung lopsided, but twitched and swivelled. His teeth, now needle-like, oozed with red-tinted saliva.

Osiris moved first.

The gryphon whipped a chain from his side and cast it across the room; Teratai caught it and slung it back round; with both ends Osiris now heaved back, trying to hook Oakhe's head. The once-lynx rolled his head sideways and under the chain, then cannoned into Osiris, denting his breastplate. His teeth loomed at the gryphon's neck.

"Arrogant," came an unearthly, guttural tremor.

A slab of stone twisted from the ground, aiming for Oakhe's side. It slammed into him but he twisted and rolled away before it could close into a ring. Aidan withdrew his stave, brandishing it. Just as Oakhe readied his legs to leap again, another rock descended from the ceiling. He half-slithered half-rolled out of its path, rounding towards Elysser at devastating speed. Teratai pushed them aside, as Oakhe's arms thrust forwards and slammed into her abdomen, twisting together to form a ball of flesh, constricting and gnarling into her.

"No future."

Bone snapped. The vine-like limbs crushed further and further.

She let out a breathless gasp, trying to pull herself out, her legs hanging limp. Dhalen leapt forwards, bringing his clubbed fists down on Oakhe's forearms. He landed with such force the creature fell forwards, rolling, still with Teratai in his grasp. Oakhe's legs whipped around and landed over Dhalen's shoulder, pinning him to the ground. His head sagged before Dhalen.

"Y... You... love... abandoned..."

Dhalen grabbed Oakhe with his free paw; purple sparks flashed between them. Oakhe let out a pained roar but did not relent. The claw pinning Dhalen shook and constricted.

"HURTS!" Oakhe shrieked. He writhed and pulsed. The muscles on his back whipped, rippled. Another pained howl pierced the room, then he tore himself away from Dhalen, landing heavily on the table. Oakhe kicked out, limbs extending in random directions, and when he righted himself he looked straight at Raikali.

His eyes widened. *"YOU."*

He lunged.

She ducked and threw him over her head, sending him into a set of shelves, which disintegrated under his weight. He slithered around to fly at her again; Aidan and Elysser both used their resonance to shoot beams of stone into his path. He leapt over them all, and with an unhinged jaw sunk his teeth into her left shoulder and rolled over the top of her, arching her back and tossing her onto the stone table, which split under the force of her body. Virvel pulled Nidjimes quickly away from underneath the other side of the table, and he clambered desperately for the spiked projectile he'd been holding as it rolled across the floor.

Oakhe's breath roared from him as he shook his head and his needle teeth tore at Raikali's body; the lioness roared in response and pierced his flesh with her claws.

"You will *not* overpower me," she growled, rising to her hind paws under his weight. She drew her right claw back and plunged it into his eye. He shrieked and fell backwards and she toppled on top of him. Red-black liquid spewed from the wound. Aidan and Elysser kept aiming their crystal tools for a shot, but their movements were too erratic – Raikali would be injured or killed first if they tried.

Oakhe roared and withdrew his teeth, but his other arm slammed into her neck. Once again his tendril-like claws undulated and morphed into a ball-like growth, but this time leech-like appendages burst from his fur and burrowed deep into her skin. She froze, wide-eyed, and her body shook.

"Deserve," he rumbled. *"No more."*

Tendrils wriggled under her fur, digging, tearing. Blue light flickered at the ends of her claws.

"S…stop…" she faltered.

"WHAT OF ME?" Oakhe roared. *"Pain. Nothing. Pain."*

Raikali's eyes rolled back. Her paw dropped.

Fulkore raised his axe and swung it at Oakhe's head. The lynx shifted away, but the serrated blade struck deep into his shoulder. Blue-green liquid, mixed with his darkened blood, sprayed out. As Oakhe swiped at him with his other claw, Fulkore reared his head back, an acrid yellow glow rising in his throat. Yellow-green flame erupted forth, coating Oakhe's face. He let out a piercing shriek and snaked his arm out of and away from Raikali, who crumpled to the floor, convulsing.

Virvel snatched the parts Nidjimes had been piecing together and snapped them home – a catapult, loaded with a bolt-mounted grenade. She punched the lit bomb into its nest and took aim, while Elysser swiped their red-hot crystal blade over the match, lighting it instantly. Virvel pulled the string back and launched it directly at Oakhe. The bomb impaled his chest, but the long match was still seconds away from rupturing. Seeing their chance, Elysser glanced their axe along the ground and a whip of rock encircled Oakhe and the bomb, trapping them together. Aidan cast the end of his staff towards the floor, which rippled up and backwards, toppling Oakhe's burning, screaming, flailing mass out of the window. Two seconds later there was a thunderous boom and a flash from below. Those who could reach the window saw the flames cascading downwards and specks of blue crystal disappearing into the streets below. The guards on the streets scattered.

Aidan looked back at the room. Osiris was cradling Teratai, unconscious, her midriff completely collapsed and contorted. Nidjimes fell to his knees, and Raikali was limp on the ground. Dhalen sat with his head in his paws.

"It's done," he croaked.

Osiris' eyes flared with anger, directly at Fulkore.

"We are far from done."

Chapter Sixteen

"I can't... I can't ever imagine the horror of that. Was that the start of the end?"

"In a manner of speaking. The spiral encircled slowly, then all at once. But... I played my own part in furthering the collapse."

The Kitaia, led by Dhalen, held a funeral for Oakhe in a circular garden behind their living quarters. They built an altar for him under a tree with wide, flat branches, carving his name and the shapes of his tattoos into its pointed headstone. It was markedly sober, not least of all for him having been such a calming and well-respected presence, but because there had been so little left to pay respects to. Many were anguished at the sudden and shocking nature of it. The fear that gripped the city still hung in their minds; knowing such a companion was at the heart of it meant they felt the loss doubled with disbelief.

They built a small pyre at the base of the headstone, and his remains were cremated there. Dyes infused in the leaves used for kindling sparked flames of rich purple and dark red. The smoke swirled and bloomed up, through the leaves, disappearing into the air.

Dhalen gripped Oakhe's metal headband tightly as he prepared his solemn address.

"What darkness we suffer, may it be repaid in light and love in our souls hereafter. What life we fail to live, may it be repaid in time after time. What words we do not say, may they be known eternally in the voices of our loved ones and spoken in our stead." He paused, his jaw tight. The paw gripping the headband trembled. "What love we cannot give, may it be known in the hearts of those we leave behind and kept as a shroud of safety for all eternity. So we bestow these blessings on Oakhe, our friend, our mentor... our family."

He took a small handful of ashes and rubbed it into the carvings. The Kitaia bowed their heads. Standing near were the council members, aside from Raikali and Fulkore. Aidan held Elysser's paw tightly, while Osiris stood with his claws behind his back in solemn forbearance. They stood in silence for a few minutes while each Kitaia member paid silent respects to Oakhe, then left at their own need. Dhalen was the last to remain, with Elysser, Osiris, and Aidan gathering behind him.

"I could stand here forever, and there will never be enough to say." His voice held an emptiness; a quality both on the edge of sadness and far beyond it. He pulled the headband up to his own and held it there for a few seconds, closing his eyes.

"Thank you for being in my life. I will ever be in your debt for showing me who I could be. I'm sorry that... I could not show the same compassion you did. Maybe things would be different. I hope, even though I tread this future without you, I can yet make you proud."

He took Oakhe's headband and tied it around his neck, then let out a long, wavering sigh before turning to the others. Aidan hung his head, rubbing his thumbs over the haft of his stave, as if somehow it would conjure to him words of comfort or a means of making things right again. But no power could bring someone back like that.

"What now?" Dhalen asked, mainly to Osiris, as the sadness both Elysser and Aidan displayed mirrored his own too closely to bear.

Osiris gave a low, spurious look sideways. "We must decide what happens to Dhraka and Gauros."

"I hope my position is clear," he stated, with marked bitterness.

Aidan nodded sadly. "I don't blame you. This... this should never have happened. I'm sorry."

"If you're about to blame yourself, don't," Dhalen said. "You are not accountable for the destructive judgement of others, even those we love."

Flashes of Oakhe's grim, bloodthirsty visage hit Aidan's mind. He'd been close enough to see him in light; he couldn't tell if the darkness would make him more terrifying or spare someone the full horror. He shivered.

"More soldiers from Arete will be arriving soon," Osiris said, turning towards the Tor. "I have notified them of all that happened, and they wish to bolster our defences ahead of our next council meeting."

"That's a little more time for Raikali to heal," Elysser murmured.

For a second the gryphon's gaze was of fury and fire; he calmed quickly, though. "I give Raikali the same consideration she afforded us when she conceived this plan – none. Her injury is of her own creation, cast with the Dhrakan machines."

Elysser held up their paws. "I'm aware. I mean that she should be present for what will essentially become her disciplinary."

He stared ahead.

"You phrase it too kindly," he rumbled. "I will see to their complete expulsion from Nazreal. Were it completely down to me, their futures would be nothing but the most abject of darkness."

Aidan frowned. "I can't blame you. I just… hope we're not already on that path."

The hospital near the Tor, in an area adjacent to Kitaia, Arete, and Skyria was the most neutral of any area in Nazreal, as all were welcomed in sickness or injury and helped to health, where possible. Oakhe's victims had been the first deaths the city had seen, and while it was an inevitability to many, and an experience some had witnessed in battles prior, a grim atmosphere hung in the air as the gravity of a power's misappropriation hit the city. While not a big facility, the wards and rooms were staffed by many from Skyria and Kitaia, and some of the medicinal specialists from Gauros, so conversations were sparse, and energy high but guarded.

The four walked solemnly through the corridors till they reached a side room bathed in brilliant, warm white light. As they entered they saw Teratai, sitting up in her bed, with a gilded drawing board leaning up in front of her. She was deep into her sketching, although she did acknowledge them with a brief glance.

"Just a second."

After a few moments and some more broad stretches of her pencil, she laid it on the small shelf at the bottom of the board and looked to them expectantly.

"A pleasant surprise; I had expected you to be busy."

"We were," Aidan blundered. "I mean," he suddenly panicked, looking at Dhalen. "Have been. Sort of. Uh…"

Dhalen shook his head and patted Aidan's shoulder, in that inscrutably sympathetic condescension that's only comforting when friends do it. Aidan was glad for the patience.

Dhalen gave a bleak frown. "A ceremony is performative when you spend a lifetime saying goodbye in your heart. But for what it was… I hope it will bring some peace to those who loved him."

She nodded. "I am heartbroken for you, Dhalen. Please tell me if there is anything you need, even just for want of conversation. Do not find yourself alone unnecessarily."

He bowed kindly, as Elysser approached the gryphon's bed.

"How are you feeling?" they asked quietly.

Teratai gave a gruff sigh. "I will not walk again. There is no knowing how my lack of mobility will affect flying, so for the time being I am grounded. The damage is still being assessed, but it seems I am out of immediate danger."

Aidan gave a quick look to Osiris, who appeared to be deliberately not saying something. He gained this distant yet piercing look in his eye, as if gazing into the infinite at something very, very specific.

"So, with that in mind," Teratai continued, "I am designing something."

She rotated the paper and swivelled the drawing board over. Her diagram depicted a set of mechanical legs, looking like a close-fitting set of armour, with wires and cables imitating musculature underneath.

Elysser's eyes gleamed. "This is beautiful," they whispered.

"Nonsense, this is only a rough concept. I am still discerning the nature in which they should move and balance, if they should augment my legs or completely replace them, but I would dearly love your assessment as to the materials."

The fennec nodded, stroking a claw over the sweeping, sharp lines. "Absolutely, your work is always impeccable."

Aidan cast his eyes towards the doorway. The room opposite them was much more darkly lit, with candles flickering dimly and pronounced shadows, even in relative daylight. Osiris caught his attentiveness towards the doorway and looked back to the others.

"We'll be out here for a moment."

Elysser and Teratai waved briefly as they talked over engineering and metal formation, while Dhalen followed the others back into the corridor.

Aidan clasped his paws together between the rooms, looking sideways at the darkened threshold on their left.

"I know that look," Osiris said sternly. "Pity will undo you when misplaced."

Aidan returned him with a sullen look. "I'm not... I'm

not endorsing what they did. But she was hurt, and is still a council member for now."

Osiris' expression hardened. "Be careful, Aidan. Creatures are often at their most dangerous when wounded."

"While you do that, I'll check on Lhian," Dhalen said, with a hint of bitterness.

Aidan's ears flattened sadly, remembering the grisly state they'd found the lynx in during the search for Oakhe. "Is she stable?"

"Somehow, although her injuries are still severe and we will not know the full extent of her condition for some time. She had not yet woken from the attack when I saw her last. I hope for her sake she does not remember much."

He strode up the hallway, while Aidan confronted the ominous quiet of Raikali's room.

He stepped through. In the dim, bare room a high table and a desk covered in medical supplies stood beside a single bed. On the edge of her bed, facing the window, was Raikali. She was staring through the slit of light between the sheets of fabric at the city beyond. Her body, stripped of armour aside from her thick leather trousers, was covered in scars even before Oakhe's attack. Her chest was bound, as were parts of her arms. She kept her grim countenance focused on the part of Nazreal she could see, and didn't turn to face him as he entered.

"Come to admonish me, have you?"

"No," Aidan said quietly. "I came to check on you."

She gave a quiet scoff. "How gracious. So this is a diplomatic visit."

Aidan sighed. "I can't make you trust me. And after

what you did to Oakhe I can't say I trust you either. But I came here with no ill intent."

There was a grim silence. She glanced down briefly. "It was an accident," she growled.

"I don't doubt it," he replied, bitterly. "You already know the cost. Any lecture I give will be pointless. But we're still going to have a formal vote on how to move next, with the council."

"Spare me," she growled. "You'll throw me out anyway."

He shook his head. "Like I said, I can't make you believe anything I say. But I can still act the way I always intended. That's the beauty of individuality."

He took a small crystal from the pocket on the inside of his belt and threw it into the bedsheets beside her. She glanced at it for a moment, then rested on her claws again to stare outside.

"I didn't stop believing you could be an asset to this city. It's up to you whether you want to change that. See you soon, Raikali," he said quietly, before disappearing back into the other room.

Osiris and Dhalen were waiting in the corridor, talking quietly. They looked to Aidan expectantly; he could only give them a defeated shrug in return.

"I said what I could. I have no other sympathy, and I won't force you to show any grace. She should have known."

Dhalen dusted off his forearms. "Well, she soon will regardless. Those who forfeit the lives of others should themselves learn what it means to be forfeited."

"I know," Aidan replied.

He heard a soft sigh from Osiris. "Hard to save the world when many are intent on destroying the things that make it unique, is it not?"

They began moving into the other room. As Dhalen went on ahead, Aidan took Osiris' arm briefly to pause.

"You know I don't want her here either, right? I just… this is my responsibility as much as anyone else's. If this is to last, I want to do it right."

Osiris nodded. "Your respect credits us all, but you could stand to be more severe. The more tolerance given to greed, the more it will take from you. Subtlety is a privilege afforded only to those with time and position. In our first steps we must establish rules quickly and emphatically, or they will forever be incrementally pushed into irrelevance."

Aidan nodded. "I'll… I'll do that. Thank you." He shuffled awkwardly, peering round the doorway at Teratai.

"How is she doing, honestly?"

"She is remarkably strong. But…" he paused, and the sting in his eyes faded a little. "Even for her strength, she is finding it hard to bear what she lost."

"Isn't she working on her flight when she heals up more?"

"Not flight," Osiris said. "She was pregnant."

Aidan's eyes widened. His paws raised to his muzzle in shock. "Oh… oh no…"

"We had not told anyone yet, because a hold can be tenuous." The gryphon continued, solemnly. "Now… there is nothing. You see why our response is so measured, why Arete is sending legions over to secure the city. Acts of subterfuge do not merely affect those who fail to undertake them. There is always a cost, and a life has infinite scope. A whole world was lost before it even saw the light of day."

"You…" Aidan began, before choking down the lump in his throat. "You'll always have me. I mean… I'll be here. And I promise to do what I can to keep this world going. For you, and Teratai, and for those who should still be here."

He gently laid his paw on the gryphon's arm. Osiris put his own claw on top of Aidan's, gripping it tightly. The gryphon stared at the window past the doorway, at the quieted landscape, the sadness brimming in his eyes steeled with determination.

"Thank you, my friend."

Left in her darkness, Raikali released her claws from each other. She pulsed them in and out, trying to quell the constant quaking. Only in the shaft of light could she see the bruising through her fur, which ran all the way down her arms. Her face and neck throbbed with the tears under her skin, the swelling of bloody lesions. She grimaced with each stiff, erratic movement and her breathing became more ragged and angered each time the pain jerked up her arm, causing it to seize. She glared at the lump of crystal at her side, pushing through her discomfort with slow determination. She grasped it, but as she turned her paw over she saw it changing at her touch. She gasped, horrified, as the smooth surface crystallised like frost, creeping across its many facets, then crumbled to brilliant blue dust that slipped through her claws.

With a growl of frustration she punched her paw closed. The remaining dust in her palm burst out in violent blue flame from between her fingers. She held her fist closed for a few seconds, shaking, as the light vanished, sparking through the floating dust like smoke. A gruff, furious growl swelled in her chest.

"You dare mock me," she whispered. Slowly, she opened her palm again, and in its centre lay a tiny crystal shard.

The blue dust glimmered on the blanket and floor. She looked between it and her palm for a few seconds, then a low, quiet laugh escaped her lips.

Two days later, a flight of Aretian soldiers arrived at Nazreal's gates and marched directly for the Tor. They surrounded it, stood at every outer gateway, and at the entrance to the council chamber. Osiris was already inside, arms folded, staring at the entranceway through which the other members would soon enter. Aidan was already by him, nervously rubbing his stave handle.

"You'll wear through it if you keep doing that," Osiris murmured.

Aidan laughed nervously. "Sorry. I'm not looking forward to this."

Osiris remained firm. "I have been anticipating this since Nazreal's birth. That does not mean I enjoy its prospect."

The other delegates arrived in turn; Elysser first, followed by Dhalen, and the Skyrian pair, and other representatives from the collected regions. Fulkore and Raikali were summoned when the rest had arrived, and the two strode in past the gryphon guards, who pulled the large doors shut behind them.

Osiris let the boom of their closure echo into silence before speaking.

"You understand the nature of this meeting."

It was not a question. His eyes were piercing, with increasing vehemence directed at the crimson dragon, whose own yellow eyes flared with indignation.

"I understand this is the rout you always desired," he gnarred.

Osiris slammed his fist onto the table. "Your recklessness created a monster. You are responsible for the deaths of many Nazreal citizens and the torturous murder of a respected council member. You furnished yourselves with dangerous and illegal equipment and put every single creature in this city at risk." He glowered at Raikali. "Your impatience terrified many, drove researchers from our walls, and destroyed progress that had taken years to accomplish. Nothing in your excuses has justified the cost of such a ridiculous endeavour."

Aidan's eyes narrowed. Raikali stood tall. Even though he could see the flicker of her spasming muscles every so often, she held a determination that unnerved him, much a return to the focus and drive she held when he met her on the battlefield. This was not the manner of someone about to lose control of resources they had almost fought a war over.

"Is there anything you wish to present to the council before we pass a judgement?" Osiris boomed. Aidan glanced between him and Raikali.

The lioness stepped forward.

"You do not belong in this world. You know nothing of the ravages of famine, the fight to survive, when you've had the privilege to ignore whatever you please and live above us all. There is no progress without sacrifice, no victory without struggle." She shot a glare to Dhalen, whose venomous scowl threatened a world of pain in the teeth behind it. "Your friend was noble, and his loss unfortunate, but the choice was his. He was as much to blame in this as either of us." She cast her venomous gaze back to Osiris. "But look how you play favourites, blame our entire sovereigns yet vindicate Kitaia as if they had no hand in it. What does that say about the privilege of your choice? This is a demonstration of your elitist eugenicism. You wish to choose who survives and curtail the freedoms of those who disagree with your principles."

"Oakhe wanted to help you reach an understanding with us, independently," Dhalen bit back, "and you desecrated his legacy by turning him into a dying creature tormented by darkness and pain. If this is your means, the only end it will lead to is yours, or all of us together."

Aidan looked between them all, and finally broke the encroaching, embittered silence: "I think we have said all that can be under decent circumstances," he cautioned, casting a warning glance at Osiris, Fulkore, and Raikali. "We decided to put this to a vote between the council as to whether you should be allowed to continue experimentation within Nazreal's walls. This does not mean you will not benefit from our work. If you remain open, we may convene in the future to address your re-entry when enough time has passed."

Raikali scoffed again. "Spare us your theatrics. This was

written from the beginning. We will leave, and you may keep your diplomatic facade."

She and Fulkore turned. As they reached the threshold, Fulkore gave a spurious look over his shoulder to Osiris. "Do you believe in your prospects so much to hold up two cities on your shoulders?"

Osiris leant on the table. "Two to begin, then a thousand more. All without you, or even against you, if you so choose."

A grin split Fulkore's face again. "I'll leave that choice to your children."

Osiris' claws ripped gouges in the table as he made to leap ahead; Aidan, Dhalen, and Virvel all leapt in to hold him back, and barely succeeded, as Fulkore's deep, callous laugh echoed in the hall.

Chapter Seventeen

"*Osiris, I'm... I'm sorry.*"
"*It is long passed. But... thank you.*"

Osiris and Aidan watched from a rooftop as the Gauros and Dhraka marched along designated routes marked by companies of Aretian and Kitaian soldiers. They were allowed to take with them any resources they'd brought, and an amount of Nazreal's stockpile as a token of goodwill, but otherwise they were under strict instruction to leave quickly. Something about the scene troubled Aidan; his brow furrowed as he watched the troops march through the gate.

"Is it me, or... are there fewer leaving than you expected?"

Osiris scanned the exodus trail. "Did some not leave during the lockdown?"

Aidan shook his head slowly. "I don't remember. But we were all preoccupied then, I could have missed it. But... something feels strange."

The gryphon folded his arms. "Nothing has ever settled me with those two sovereigns," he muttered. "We will keep vigilant. Arete's guard will stay stationed here to bolster our numbers until more nations come to join us."

Aidan frowned, looking down. "Do you really believe they will, after all this? I'd... I'd be lying if I hadn't thought about returning to Mahrae. It'll be slow and quiet here for a time, I suppose."

Osiris nodded. "Sometimes there is great value in that. Patience is sometimes a product of necessity, and not discipline."

Osiris' words proved prophetic. He, Aidan, and Elysser worked tirelessly working to bring the Coriolis to completion, in an effort to focus on moving forward. They envisioned the ship as a persuasive emissary of Nazreal's prospects to counter the stories of terror told by those who fled the rampage of the 'Daemon Stalker'.

Elysser's extensive knowledge of metal properties accelerated construction a great deal – before Teratai's injury they had made great pace, but the gryphon was still relegated to her hospital bed, so had to pore over scrawled diagrams and furious notes from there, while Osiris frequently swooped back and forth conveying messages between her and the group at the dock over the best methods of creating the intricacies of the ship. Teratai already knew of hydrofoils and aerofoils, having helped create efficient windmills for crushing grain and a water turbine to increase the power of Arete's forges.

But even to advertise the illustrious work still going on

within Nazreal's walls was not enough to stem the flow of opinion away from the city. The horrors of the Daemon Stalker's massacre had become a violently-spread warning fable outside the walls, something that Osiris kept sensing a Dhrakan tongue in. Amongst all this, conflicted by the portrayal of his dearest partner as nothing but a grotesque monster, Dhalen had been listless, wandering the city by himself and venturing on solo patrols far into the mountain ranges. He always returned, but looked continually sullen, and spoke little unless pressed.

Elysser and Aidan reached out as much as they could, but were wary of chasing him permanently into the space he sought. Eventually he began spending time on the ship to move objects, heal minor injuries, or deliver food from marketplaces and kitchens. Aidan hoped keeping Dhalen busy and in open company would go some way towards healing his spirit. Currently the wolf was investigating a sudden drop in the Skyrian waterway's flow. Although serious, the issue was not immediately life-threatening thanks to the reservoir and the still-functioning aquifers, but it left everyone on edge all the same.

Since Dhraka and Gauros left, a restlessness grew in Aidan, an adirectional struggle against something intangible that could only be quelled by spending time with Elysser. But despite how many evenings they shared or projects they worked on, the building tension kept disarming him of true security. He would have dismissed it as sheer anxiety, were it not for the subtle fluctuations in the energies coming from the Tor that rippled on an increasing basis. The beacon seemed to surge with incredible intensity some days, such that he wondered if his control system had become damaged at some point. Every check he made found nothing awry, even if he spent hours in the resonance chamber doing nothing but meditating on it and searching for anomalies. The sensation felt like approaching footsteps; thunderous, from no discernible location but everywhere at once, or within. Every now and again he staggered unsteadily as if the ground suffered an upheaval, but the stone on which he stood remained completely level. Neither Dhalen nor Elysser could find anything amiss in his body, but he felt ever on edge, constantly and increasingly as if he were about to jump over a precipice.

He was not the only one suffering from restlessness. After several weeks, Teratai had designed and commissioned Elysser for a gilded wheelchair, to be used until she had the workshop space to build her mechanical legs. She said very specifically in her brief that it needed to be self-propelled, be easy to use both indoors and out, and look eminent enough to sit in at council meetings.

With great enthusiasm, and a welcome break in attention from the Coriolis, Elysser had completed the task within days and delivered it personally to Teratai's bedside.

"Perfect!" the gryphon whistled, pulling her breastplate on and securing it in place with its staunch straps. Elysser handed her the ornate vambraces that completed her armour set and helped her buckle them. Teratai's greaves, with their golden embossed fish-dragons and fine wave detailing, had been incorporated into the chair's lower section, a swivelling platform she could rest her legs on to stay level.

Elysser pulled the chair right up against the bed, and in a few strong movements Teratai had lifted herself into it, shedding herself of the confining bedsheets. She swung the leg armour into place and beamed.

"Yes, this is much more suitable." She looked up brightly at Elysser. "Shall we?"

The fennec gestured to the corridor as a maître d' would to an esteemed guest, and Teratai rolled herself free with the staunch rings mounted over the wheels. Elysser followed gleefully, admiring their work with pride.

The two of them shot past physicians who could only watch wide-eyed as their patient made her escape.

"This place will kill me as fast as my injuries do," she'd growled at an attendant who tried to grab the handle at the back of her seat. Reaching the stairs, one swift movement of Elysser's axe transformed them into a sweeping, even slope. The gryphon launched herself over its summit and careened straight outside, where she breathed, with a great sigh, the scent of the outdoors straight from its source.

Elysser strode alongside her, tucking their axe into the ring on their belt. "Do you need help?"

"No, I have this," Teratai said, with cheerful determination. The high-backed chair had padded cradles above her shoulders to prop her wings on. To counter the potential balance issues, Elysser had added weight below the axle and in the platform on which Teratai rested her legs. Overall its sleek, sweeping design had an aesthetic similar to waves in motion. The fennec watched their work as the two of them moved at brisk pace towards the dock.

"How does it feel?"

"Excellent!" Teratai beamed, pushing forward with another powerful stroke of her arms. "I had no doubts you could pull this off."

Elysser smiled quietly to themself. "Thank you for

trusting me. With this and the ship. It's an honour to work with you."

Teratai laughed. "The honour is mine, believe me. I was held back by what I could do in Arete; you blew my ambitions out of the water. Aidan too, but mainly you."

Elysser's tail flicked proudly as they walked, breaking onto the long, wide dock that the nearly-complete Coriolis was moored in.

"And actually," Teratai continued, "I am glad to have met you here. If you had been scouted by Venedreus' outreach opportunists, you would have been relegated to study like Aidan. While I am not in denial of his skill, you face your tests with a boldness that he lacks. That may be a timidity inherent in himself, but I am thankful for your forthright pursuit of what you create."

The fennec pulled at their ears in thought; the thin patch of fur under the thumb indicated this was, or had been once, a regular habit. "He's still very good, though. And brave to have done all he has already."

"Oh, without question. Ability and boldness are two different things. And one can be brave in different ways. I see you two as complimentary, yet distinct. As we should all be."

Ahead, the ship gleamed in its bright gold and silver metal. The Coriolis was long and wide, with a high sterncastle and two large masts: the main central mast, and a three-pronged mizzen-mast angled forwards at about seventy degrees. The specific construction had been devised between Teratai, Elysser, and Osiris to gain enough lift for flight and maintain balance in the air, and also provide drag to land again. The sails and wing arrays were still folded within, the hydrofoils sat just at the water's surface. The four resonance engines had been calculated to provide power enough for something almost twice as large, but as with any such construct, they all felt it better to be safe than sorry.

"I hope we get to test it soon," Teratai breathed.

A laddered tower led up to its deck, which, although not particularly high, was still forbidding enough to a wheelchair. Teratai frowned.

"That will need a swift address," she muttered. No sooner had she said it than the stone her chair rested on rose up and dipped over the railing, placing her neatly on the gangway. She nodded appreciatively to Elysser, who was already inspecting the railing for a place to put a proper gangway.

Teratai wheeled herself to the sterncastle door, thankfully already wide enough to accommodate the chair as it had been made for gryphons and their wings to walk through with ease. Inside was almost complete, with ornate plating adorning the walls. A vine-like nest of cables wound its way around the edge of the room towards the helm above them, awaiting proper fixture to the casing. There were many tools, piles of materials, and plenty of papers and parchments strewn around, but no furniture, save for the bed she could see through the doorway to the Captain's quarters. She half-smiled, wondering if she and Osiris would take turns claiming it as theirs, or whether their companionship would still be viable enough for them to share again. Before she could dwell too deeply on those thoughts, she felt a tap on the back of the chair, and Elysser appeared by her shoulder.

"Is it looking all right?" they asked.

"Seems to be," Teratai responded, glancing around the room. "Why?"

Elysser shrugged, with a nervous smile. "We tried to finish it as a surprise, but you escaped early. Honestly I'd have you here anytime over a perfectly-formed surprise."

Teratai smiled appreciatively. "Well, it is kind of you. I think... this will be my home for now; something unique that grew from our spirit and creativity, not the history of our nations."

Elysser could hear the dull echo of voices and movement below. Just as they started to move towards the lower deck, a cheerful voice rang out.

"Oh, you're here!" Aidan called. Elysser looked about, but couldn't see him immediately. Then, a shape in the corner of the room caught their eye.

Aidan's head was poking through a hole in the floor. A surprisingly strong light source beamed underneath him, casting his face in shadow as if he were a very diminutive messenger of some fiery deity. Elysser's eyes almost bulged from their head.

"What are you *doing*?" they hissed. "Stop making holes in the ship!"

He pouted. "I wanted to see you, and this was the fastest way to do it. Besides, I can fix it really quickly."

Teratai wheeled over to him; a shadow of fear crossed Aidan's playful expression.

"My legs may not work," she threatened, "but I will have no issue beating you over the head with them if you play games with my vessel."

He gave a nervous laugh. "I understand, that's, er, yes."

"Are you done?" came Osiris' voice from somewhere

below him.

Elysser peered over the edge of the hole to see Aidan standing atop the gryphon's back. They smeared their paws down their forehead and rubbed their eyes. "How long have you planned this trick?"

"Oh, a long time."

The fennec shook their head. "The most impressive part is you convincing Osiris to help."

"I was misled," came the irate gryphon's reply.

Elysser sighed. "I don't know what to do with you, I honestly don't."

Aidan grinned. "I have some ideas."

Immediately he disappeared. There was a crash, and some assorted grunts and yelling. Osiris' disparaging eye appeared at the hole.

"If you would do the honours, Elysser. I apologise for his behaviour."

The fennec ran their axe around the edge of the hole and it swept back into place, smooth as if it had never been unbroken. Together, after forming the stairs into a suitable ramp, they and Teratai journeyed to the deck below to meet Osiris and Aidan, who was rolling his shoulder, looking apologetic but also incredibly self-satisfied. Elysser shook their head at him again, but could not hide their smile.

The source of the light beneath Aidan was immediately clear. A sphere of brilliant white light, almost a foot in diameter, fizzled softly above a strange, propeller-like array with a spindle at its centre. A protective glass orb surrounded it.

"What is it?" Elysser asked, circling around it.

Teratai raised an eyebrow. "Is it not dangerous to have

lightning onboard?"

Osiris shrugged. "An experiment. I told stories to Aidan about the things we had seen in the skies, and our own ships, as we travelled, and ball lightning particularly intrigued him. Knowing of the dangers, it appears he has found a way to contain it. This may reduce our need for indoor crystal light sources, saving on weight."

The blue-feathered gryphon ran a thoughtful claw down her beak. "Is it tethered?"

"Yes," Aidan said firmly. "It won't fly off."

She gave him a sly look. "Can you change that?"

He looked a little unsure. "I can probably build a trigger release into it, but… why?"

She gestured around her. "If we are to make any realistic journey, we will need defence. If this can be made into viable protection, we won't even need cannons."

Aidan looked doubtful. "I mean, these take up a lot of energy. And even if they burn things, I don't know if it'd be enough to deter a dedicated attack."

She flicked her claw. "We shall look into it, anyway."

With a twist of a dial, Aidan turned off the generator and the brilliance in the room faded to be lit only by the crystals around the room's upper edges. It was still more pleasant than many other ships, given their usual cramped and imposing darkness, but the room's bare, unfurnished nature made it look very stark all the same.

Osiris stood and gestured to Teratai. "Would you like to check the engines, as you're here?"

She gave an affirmative nod. "I want us to be ready to test as soon as possible. Especially if we need to make a swift impression with other nations. I am eager to separate ourselves from the disaster we left behind."

They moved to the stern, and descended to the level below.

Aidan sat quietly in front of the ball lightning generator. Elysser thumbed through some parchment lists to the side, but kept glancing up at him.

"You don't like weapons, do you?" they said.

He shrugged defeatedly. "I see their value in defence, but… it's still a strange feeling to see something you created in earnest immediately have its purpose reassigned. I'm… I can't say I'm not naive, but is it wrong to strive for something peaceful, even under threat of violence?"

Elysser pouted. "Once a sword is drawn, there aren't many questions as to its wielder's intent. At best it's intimidation, at worst, death. Time's already against you at that point. For some, their only language is violence, and you have to be stronger to protect what needs to be protected."

He nodded. "There's… so much I didn't anticipate," he said quietly.

"Would you think differently of me if I said I had designed weapons?" the fennec asked, shifting to sit next to him.

"I saw your axe the day we met."

"Right," they said softly. "And trust me, I know how to use it as a blade as well as I do as a resonance tool. But I made plans for many others too, including siege weapons." They leafed through a pile of parchments until they uncovered their journal, from next to Aidan's, and flicked it open to a page detailing a large mounted projectile system. "This is a railgun. It launches a large metal bar at incredible speed at something you never want to see again. I think it's fascinating." They looked at him closely. "Do you see me as unstable or dangerous, even for my part in this?"

"No. Never."

"There you are." They set the paper down and played their paw over their axe. "I'm not saying you *shouldn't* be wary of someone's weaponry fixation, but knowing how to protect people, or yourself, isn't the same as preparing to assault others." She gestured to his own tool, resting on the floor. "You made your staff with blades. Have you ever practiced combat with it?"

"Well... barely. Only the movements I use to summon resonance itself." He turned the stave over. Admittedly, he'd fashioned the blades for practical reasons, and ironically, because many of the heroes he'd read about in legends used great weapons. It seemed fitting to have a bladed edge just for the image, if nothing else. All too quickly he found Elysser's point proven, even just partly: he knew, even subconsciously, that he needed to present an image of strength, and the first means of doing that was to give himself something that looked like a weapon. Every time someone asked, he insisted it was a tool, but the fact he had to deny it often enough meant it already gave the impression of violence. And it *could* well be used for violence, if he so chose.

"I know a place of safety should never tolerate ideas of brazen, oppressive violence," he murmured, staring into the ball lightning array. "But I've been uneasy since Dhraka left. I don't know whether I felt safer having them here, knowing I could see what they were doing, and maybe prevent it. I'm worried about what they can do in a world where they don't even have to hide what they're attempting. Does that mean we should come to them, and stop them pre-emptively, or wait till they're at our door to strike back?"

Elysser shook their head. "If we believe in righting the world we have to start where we are. As for after that... we should keep an eye on what's happening outside, and if necessary, protect those who need it, and especially those who come to us for help." They rested a hand on his knee. "I've felt uneasy too. We can always do more, to prepare and prevent. Now is the time to start, I think."

Aidan reached out to take their paw in his own, but as he did, his stomach lurched and his palm shot instead to his abdomen, trying to massage the sudden nausea away. Elysser gently laid a paw on his shoulder with a sympathetic smile.

Footsteps pealed across the deck above. Dhalen charged down the ramp, skidding to a halt right by them. The purple glow in his eyes subsided as he saw them, his body shrinking as the power withdrew from his muscles.

"I just came from the mountains," he said, his voice darkly ominous. "Something is coming."

The turning in Aidan's stomach tightened. "What is it?"

"A black pyramid."

Chapter Eighteen

"*The Gargantua?*"

"*No, another. There were three; Leviathan, Gargantua, and Colossus.*"

"*So... the other two...*"

"*They... this was the end. Of everything.*"

"How far is it?" Elysser asked, as Aidan ran for Osiris.

Dhalen shook his head. "Stopped at the second mountain ring to the North. As we travelled along the aqueduct we discovered a huge section had been destroyed, then we sighted the machine past us, already on its way." His voice was a dangerous growl. "It's enormous. Huge enough to contain thousands of soldiers."

The two gryphons returned at extreme pace, led by Aidan.

"How did it get through the first ring?" Elysser grabbed a nearby map and laid it before them. Dhalen pointed at its current position, then traced the trail back in the direction he saw.

"They broke through the aqueduct, then navigated around to a significant gap."

Osiris' countenance was already grim. "What is it?"

"An immense war machine made of black metal," Dhalen said.

The gryphons exchanged severe glances. "Dhraka," Teratai glowered.

Aidan looked to the others. "Do we prepare for an evacuation or a siege?"

"Likely both," Osiris replied. "They will aim to damage us enough to force a surrender, then evict, execute, or enslave anyone they deem useless. Everything we have will be deemed forfeit if they succeed in their approach."

Aidan stared at the map. "I could… try moving the city. I might be able to take us somewhere safe."

Osiris looked askance. "I would rather destroy it. You would not outrun the pace of their engines. All they would do is chase us into the sea."

"And the crystal we leave behind will still be theirs for the taking," Elysser said with bitter resignation. "We haven't got enough resources to combat them, aside from a handful of resonators. We may be able to sink the pyramid into the ground between the two of us."

Aidan grimaced. "A disturbance that big may disrupt the crystal, but it may be our best chance."

"If you can get close enough," Osiris growled.

Elysser bit one of their claws. "Could we send word to Arete?"

Teratai shook her head. "They would not arrive in time to help us with the initial battle, but… if we could hold here long enough, they may bring numbers enough to push Dhraka back. In the meantime, we may find a way of sabotaging their engine."

Aidan bit the fur on his knuckle. "Should we assume Gauros is with them?"

"I would," Dhalen said gravely. "I will prepare our soldiers for battle with them again. Fighting resonators will add an extra level of danger to this. Even if none are especially powerful, their numbers and physical strength are not to be dismissed."

Osiris nodded. "In the meantime, we will move all of Nazreal's vulnerable and essential to the Coriolis. When the time comes to seal the city, we will take flight. Teratai, will we be ready?"

She nodded. "We have no choice."

They set to their tasks; Elysser and Teratai worked on the Coriolis at desperate haste, while Dhalen, Osiris, and Aidan rounded up the injured, researchers, and families to bring them to the ship. A section of Arete soldiers left immediately to bring reinforcements, while another circled back and forth between Nazreal and the pyramid to provide updates. It sat for a long time, while rumbles and explosions rang out in the distance as they began to break down the mountains to pass through. Once it crossed the barrier, the time Nazreal had left diminished rapidly, with only one set of mountains remaining between them and the Dhrakan arrival.

On the second day, as the evening of broken cloud turned

the sky a deep, rich purple, a horn resounded through the city. The council members had been finishing the final preparations for the Coriolis' evacuation when the harrowing warning call split the air. Osiris immediately took flight towards the walls; Aidan leapt onto his back just in time, and together they swept to the northern gateway.

The sentries pointed wordlessly to the jagged, uneven peaks before them. Rumbles and crashes rang out, under which lay the grim, haunting note of grinding and crushing rock. But for all the noise, they didn't see it at first; they simply saw the mountain the guards pointed to.

Then dawned the horror that the mountain itself was the intruder, and neither Osiris nor Aidan had been prepared for the gravity of Dhalen's warning. A black pyramidal mass churned the rock before it, pulverising the ground, shredding the landscape under enormous treads. It thundered forwards at a menacing pace, deterred by nothing, its rumbling, shaking, and screeching of metal roaring into the twilight air.

More guards mobilised by them, and although their weapons were ready, they could do nothing but watch as the immense machine rolled ahead until it reached the edge of the grassland, close enough to loom over the city walls, and came to a halt with a piercing hiss.

From its nearest side, about midway up its structure, a hatch shuddered open, and from it billowed a torrent of steam. Three long cylinders spiralled upwards, then angled down towards Nazreal: an array of gigantic cannons shook the valley with its mechanical boom into position.

Above the pyramid's tracks, the ebony plating yawned open like a carapace. Two monumental platforms rattled out and down, slamming into the ground, sending soil and grass flying into the air. Standing aboard them, descending from the newly-extended stairway, were scores of lions and dragons. They sprinted out in relentless formation to encircle the front of the city, blades drawn, teeth gnashing, howling with derision at the wall they stood to conquer.

Osiris, with vision far more acute than Aidan's, picked out a figure standing at the heart of the shell's opening, arms and wings wide, twin metal clubs in his talons, their spikes glinting in the light from Nazreal's beacon.

"Sarr!" he spat. He spread his wings wide.

"Wait!" Aidan called. "Take me too."

"You need to defend the city," Osiris hissed. "If they open fire, you will be the only chance we have to seal over the walls and shield us."

Aidan gripped his staff. "I may still be able to sink the pyramid, if you can get me close enough. Try and stall him with some kind of parlay."

The gryphon let out a deep breath, analysing the field before them. The joint Dhraka-Gauros forces bayed and clashed their weapons against breastplates and shields, a louring choir of vengeful bloodlust.

The pair took to the sky once more and swooped to the front of the line, where they were met with merciless jeers by the soldiers. Some spat, some howled with mocking laughter, but all of them were ready within a moment's notice to completely tear them to oblivion. Osiris stood tall, drawing his rapiers, and Aidan readied his staff, as they faced up to the Dhrakan General.

Sarr reared his head back to laugh, and cast an arc of bright yellow flame above his head.

"Captain Tallon!" he sang, in a gesture that mocked hospitality, not only for the derision with which he spoke but also for the weight and dangerous glint of his clubs. Aidan could see they were coated in some kind of oil, likely flammable, to immolate and crush simultaneously. "We demand a reconsideration of our expulsion."

"One wingbeat closer from a single soldier and all of you will be made to pay," Osiris shouted. "Your machines failed once; nothing will guarantee your success this time."

Sarr gave a humming laugh. "Come, Tallon; I knew you were deluded but even you can see our might is unassailable. All the pride in Arete will not save you from my Leviathan, my beautiful and perfect war machine."

Aidan saw the advancing blades begin to train on him as he prepared to lower the stave. If he was quick enough, he could create a wave in the ground to separate them from the troops, and might be able to disrupt the pyramid, but he'd need to be quick, and an energy burst that intense could damage the Tor and set off a chain reaction beneath Nazreal.

He took a deep breath.

Before he could even move, the ground shook. He stumbled forwards. Osiris' wings opened to steady himself. Even the troops rocked and swayed, and a number toppled over. Only Sarr remained defiant and still, his chest heaving with laughter, bellowing over the catastrophic noise.

Aidan looked behind them. Dust rose from the city by the Tor, but not the dust of an explosion or cannon shot. Blue wisps spiralled up and around the tower like snakes of fog, wrapping around its walls, climbing up to the beacon. They flattened against the stone and began spreading in geometric veins.

"Fiends!" Osiris cursed. "They were coming from underground!"

"We have to get back," Aidan said, his fur on end.

Osiris turned to face the city. "Can you make us an opening?"

Aidan growled as the dragons began to approach them. "Get ready."

He slammed his stave into the ground and the grass whipped into a frenzy, twirling into a huge mesh that loomed over the nearest soldiers. Aidan spun on his paw and leapt onto Osiris, almost slipping off his pauldrons with the force of the gryphon's wingbeats. A lion swiped at Osiris's tail, missing it by an inch. Several dragons took to the skies in pursuit, but in the distance Aidan heard Sarr roar a command to belay.

"They have nowhere to run," he oozed.

Osiris circled as the blue veins continued their creep up the middle of the Tor, chasing its own patterns.

"Set me down," Aidan said firmly.

Osiris landed in front of the Tor, just short of the rune-like crystal shapes now burning into the stone like cast molten metal.

"What is it?" Osiris asked, swords still ready, as if the runes may come to life and attack them.

"Raikali must be underneath somewhere. I've felt something in the ground for weeks, but…" he clenched his fist, a gnarled and angry grimace crossing his muzzle. "I should have known. They made us see the Leviathan so they could break through the crystal without suspicion. Osiris…" he took a deep breath. "Get the Coriolis into the air. Get everyone out of the city, now."

"Aidan, I will not let you do this alone."

The fox turned to him, resolute. "You must. Nobody else can stop what she's trying to do. You can save the rest of us. I'll seal off the city if I can, but if things go wrong... there won't be anything left standing for miles."

Osiris gripped his swords tightly, then slipped them into their scabbards. He laid his talons on Aidan's shoulders.

"Do what you must. Once we are safe in Arete I will return for you. Please, be safe, Aidan."

Aidan nodded. "I'll keep them distracted till you're in the air. Listen... if I don't see you again..."

"I will not accept that," the gryphon barked. "I *will* find you."

Aidan took Osiris' talon firmly. "Go."

With a massive leap, Osiris burst into the sky. Aidan broke into a run, entering the glowing, humming Tor.

Chapter Nineteen

"*Leaving Aidan will forever be burned into my memory. It was... a painful choice.*"
"*But you saved so many, Osiris... right?*"
"*...Not enough.*"

The walls were vibrating. A low rumble shook the air and rattled the fixtures. Aidan darted over the stones to the staircase leading to the resonance chamber, then descended the wide, arching steps. The further he ran, the stronger the glow became. Rounding the walls he began to feel heat on his face from the energy coursing from ahead.

The resonance chamber thrummed with the roar of machinery, and the air was thick with fumes. At the centre of the dome's floor loomed a huge black column, at the top of which a circular drill pointed directly up, with torn brickwork all around it, a web of glowing blue cracks stretching in all directions. As he crossed the threshold, sections of the machine's protective casing collapsed to the floor like a discarded carapace, signalling its deployment. At the drill's heart lay some kind of engine, whirring vociferously, surrounded by a ring of imposing canisters similar to the ones found in Dhraka's arena, only much, much larger. At its base a circular metal platform spiralled outward, stabilising the strange and intrusive device. He took a timid few steps forward, stave close to his side, but pointed ahead. Before he had even crossed halfway to it, a familiar figure strode from behind it.

Raikali stood before him in full plate armour. Even though he had seen her at the Zenith in exactly this, a new aspect to her physical arsenal filled him with an electric fear.

"What have you done?"

Her claws and legs were encircled by spiralling crystal dust, so fine that it looked more like smoke. Even with the fumes beginning to cloud the room, Aidan could see its dangerous shine with perfect clarity.

She grinned under the shining metal of her helmet. "What you were always too afraid to do. I embraced the true nature of these crystals. What I thought a curse has turned into my greatest asset."

With barely a movement, the dust around her claws coalesced into a crystalline gauntlet, perfectly moulded to her shape, and infinitely sharp. With another movement it evaporated, and the crystal mist swarmed about her like a ghostly, patrolling serpent.

"None of this would have been possible without the sacrifice you so protested. Now do you see how my way of the world always triumphs? You are a child playing in the sand before me. My powers are infinite, and immediate."

Aidan's eyes were wide, furious.

"You don't know what you're playing with," he raged.

"On the contrary," she grinned. She circled her wrist and a cloud of crystal dust flew at Aidan. He blasted a cone of air from the end of his staff at it; briefly it dispersed, but just as quickly it regained shape and charged for him again. He swept the bladed edge across it and it solidified like a glass web, dropping to the floor. She scowled at him, and he glared defiantly back.

"You won't win on force alone, Raikali. There's still so much you refuse to learn."

A vortex of dust enshrouded her and she took flight, looming closer to him. Her voice buzzed and echoed from within the pulsating cloud, reverberating off the walls.

"Nothing but pathetic, desperate mewling. Remember what I told you? Strength or ability alone may make a warrior great, but together make them unstoppable. Now I have them both, fuelled by limitless energy. You will never match the power I wield."

The light in his staff sharpened with his focus, as did the points of his blade, which began to glow a brilliant blue-white. "We'll see."

He sliced it into the air in front of him. A razor-sharp wave of energy careened towards her. She raced away and the razor energy crashed into the wall. Raikali spiralled round, aiming straight for him. He twisted backwards, using his staff to pivot the ground underneath him to enhance his dodge. A nest of claws swiped past his right ear with a piercing whine, distorting the air itself. Whirling his staff around again he managed to solidify a section of crystal, but Raikali's smoke tendrils caught and dissolved it, assimilating it into her thunderous veil.

In the growing smoke he lost sight of her. A second later something slammed into his back and he was cast against the wall. Almost too late he softened the blow using the crystal in the wall to cave the brickwork in, but his head still shuddered against its hard, hot surface. Light shimmered before him. He rolled desperately forwards, missed, by inches, by two large crystal javelins that would have torn his body in half, instead piercing the wall just over his shoulder.

He ran forwards, spinning the stave, trails of blue-white light radiating from the blades, and with another thrust of his arm he threw two more slicing arcs of crystal towards her. She parried both, deflecting them into the domed ceiling.

Aidan caught sight of the crystal prism above them. It shook with a strengthening, pitching hum. The tip of the drill was rising. Its flutes gleamed with crystal, and as it rose, a column of crystal light began to form at its tip, synchronising with the crystal nest directly above it.

"What is that?" he bellowed.

"You won't live long enough to find out," Raikali gloated. She charged for him again; with a whirl of his staff the floor beneath him slid in a wide circle to the other side of the chamber.

"You have no idea the power contained here!" he shouted. "You'll blow up the city!"

"Not this city!" she laughed.

Suddenly Aidan realised what the runic crystal channels on the walls were: a means to control the beacon's energy – not just its intensity, but its direction. With so much raw power, it was now an enormous, possibly infinite, energy cannon. He gritted his teeth.

"You're too late to stop it!" Raikali roared, spreading her arms wide. "It's die and let die!"

His staff glowed. "Only for us."

A beam of resonance streamed from his stave, hitting Raikali's crystal shield. Her crystal swarm twisted about her, splitting it into streams that bounced harmlessly away, and she smirked.

"You are powerless."

His eyes shone. The beam strengthened; she raised her paw to obstruct it but a sphere of crystal clamped shut around her – Aidan had used the beam to connect with, and solidify, her protective cloud.

A second was all he needed. Before she could dissolve her floating prison, he sprinted to the drill and, winding back as far as he could, plunged the blade of his staff into the engine's heart, splitting it between the canisters.

The engine's pitch increased to almost noiselessness, and the drill stopped rising. The mechanical noise faded.

The rumbling continued.

He looked around, and *slam*.

He barely caught himself after the strike to his muzzle, as Raikali clawed her way free from the spherical cage.

"Reckless fool!" she shrieked. She charged for him.

He fell backwards and rolled as she lunged, claws passing just over his ears. He raised his staff, and gripped it tightly. A blast of energy exploded from its tip and punched into Raikali's chest. She flew up and backwards, crashing through the layers of rock, shooting clear out of the ground and into a building beyond.

Shaking his head, Aidan clambered upright. Raikali's gargantuan punch was making the floor list under him. Or, was it…

He wiped the blood from his muzzle and looked back up at the drill. The canisters had already leeched some crystal energy, which dripped and fizzed onto the chamber floor, running into the runes and channels. The drill was shaking, rattling, but not under its own power. The stabilising disc was beginning to warp.

"No…"

On the Coriolis' flight deck, Osiris twisted the golden communication funnel round to face him, watching in the distance as the Leviathan's rotation finished to face their direction, and the monstrous cannons took their aim. "Teratai, we need to leave!"

"One second more."

An orange glow and thick smoke oozed from the cannon mouths.

"Teratai!"

"NOW!"

Osiris punched the throttle forward. The golden ship's turbines thundered ablaze, and the ship hurtled across the water in its maiden flight. The walls shuddered, the evacuees below deck screamed in panic. Osiris hauled back the control wheel with a determined roar and the ship broke free of the reservoir, as the fiery projectiles punched through the water in their wake.

Raikali twisted herself free from the rubble with a furious growl and took to her feet. She pulled at her breastplate, smoking, and glowing at its edges with the ire of Aidan's energy blast, and tore it free, leaving her leather arming jack in its place. She began a march back to the Tor over the top of the ruins, claws poised, drawing in crystal dust and flickering light from the streets' torches.

An enormous *boom* rent the air. She looked about, hearing the screech of metal and the rumble of engines. She saw the smouldering trail of the cannon fire barely missing the Coriolis' stern, and the golden caravel riding on an ascending blue flame, streaking across the darkening sky. The Leviathan's cannons would never be able to track such a wide, fast arc.

But *she* could.

She raised an arm, and the dust coalescing at her claw tips formed into a massive blue javelin.

She took aim, and released.

At that instant something forced her forearm outwards, and her missile launched into the distant sky far between both the pyramid and the Coriolis. She snapped her head round at her assailant. Aidan stood at the mouth of the hole she had been ejected through, a rippling trail snaking between the two from which he'd summoned the stone to break her shot.

"Let them alone!" he roared. "We have to get away from here!"

She stalked towards him, cracking her shoulders.

"I told you, this place is my birthright. I will leave when all who challenge me are slain!"

More javelins rotated in front of her, widening into missiles that she cast towards him in rapid succession. He swept his staff across the ground and a wave of stone formed in front of him. The first missile shattered on impact, the second broke his barrier and he dived away before being crushed. Raikali pounced immediately, and her crystal devoured the rocks around her to generate more projectiles to mark him with. He retreated desperately, trying to reach the shelter of the Tor again, throwing more stone archways over himself to protect his body until he could get to his hind paws. Her barrage relentlessly pursued him at greater speeds, until one streamed right for his head.

An explosion of stone dust obscured him. Raikali floated forwards, siphoning more crystal dust from the debris, hungrily looking for his mangled corpse.

Nothing. Only stonework.

A strange ripple remained in the brick where his body had been, as if he'd slipped underwater. She scanned the rubble, stalking through debris, claws bared.

A rumble grew from close by; she readied herself to strike.

Nothing. Yet the rumbling grew louder.

Now, the Tor shook. From deep within the cavern she'd been blasted through, she heard the sound of metal striking the floor.

The lioness streaked towards the hole, punching it wider with crystal-imbued fists as she descended. She emerged directly into the chamber where Aidan was atop the drill engine. He cast his stave across the half-risen shaft and decapitated it. The massive drill blade crashed to the floor.

The quaking grew, ever steadier.

"It won't stop!" he cried.

Her scornful laugh rang out even over the heightening rumble. "Do you see the folly of your compassion? This is your testament – the world will always reject the weak."

He clutched his staff tightly, watching the resonance liquid spill further and glow brighter, and the runes' terrifying luminance creep closer to the crystal nest above.

He only had a few seconds before the cannon would ignite itself. He locked her in a defiant stare, then raised the staff and slammed the point into the drill's severed neck. Spirals of metal swirled about him as the machine unravelled in steel ribbons. The resonance canisters split and fell to the ground, and suddenly freed the resonance liquid whipped round in a blinding, cascading gyre. The whole room began to whine; the energy coursed and rippled over the walls, and parts of the floor began to vibrate into the air.

Aidan clenched his eyes shut, focusing all he could on drawing the energy back down from the Tor above him.

Raikali took to the air again, coming level with Aidan. "By my paw or your own, you will never outlast me." She barrelled forwards, crashing into him, sending him sprawling across the stone floor.

The whirling resonance exploded outwards with a powerful shockwave, imbuing the walls with intensely-glowing flux. Rocks and shards of crystal dislodged from the ceiling. The floor rippled, warped, and burst. The remnants of the drill listed to one side and its engine burst open, lodging debris into the walls.

The crystal above rocked and shifted from its mount, glowing erratically, and now, above the deep tremorous vibrations, a deafening whine rose above the noise.

Raikali hovered triumphantly over Aidan.

"Die with your old world," she spat.

She burst away, disappearing through the cave entrance to the surface.

Aidan pushed himself upright, wiping glowing blood that dripped into his eye from just below his ear. He stumbled, falling once again to his paws and knees, his staff clattering a few feet from him. The tips of his claws burned at the floor's touch. The fabric over his knees scorched and singed.

"It's… I can't… I have to stop this…"

He looked up at the crystal ceiling, a brilliant guillotine waiting its plunge. Below it, just in front of him, was the rift the drill had emerged from.

A section of ceiling collapsed opposite him. The room shook, and the heat began to burn his pawpads. An electric taste burned his mouth, his fur rippled with needle sensations, and his staff shook like a tuning fork. Fighting against a body that wanted to collapse, he crawled into the hole.

The walls were hot as an oven in the tighter space. He could barely breathe.

The drill had damaged the crystal so substantially that any chance of regulation it formerly served as a siphon atop the subterranean mass of the Zenith was impossible.

Between its attempt to harness the crystal, and its rupturing in the battle between Aidan and Raikali, the machine's battery had imbued the crystals with an unstoppable, catastrophically-recurring power. Jagged shards erupted from crystal fissures all around him like the closing jaw of a huge, electric dragon.

He stood atop the quaking crystal mass and, head pounding, forced his staff to its surface. Instantly he felt his body aflame, such incredible energies powering through his entire being. Every inch of him felt like burning blades scraping into his fur and flesh, searing his bone. His eyes flashed with a blinding blue-white light, streaming trails from their corners, cascading tears of glowing white down his face.

He screamed.

This would *not* be the end of the world. His world.

Outside, the Leviathan shifted unsteadily. Many soldiers had retreated to the Leviathan's interior. Raikali had landed on an outer platform, but clung to a railing to steady herself in the mounting tremors.

A violent shockwave rocked the machine, lurching it upwards. With no time to take to the air, Raikali tumbled to the ground.

She rolled upright to see the Tor listing, shuddering, and a monstrous glow erupting from its base. The beacon engorged erratically, and flashes of blue lightning sparked from the tips of nearby buildings as the light swelled even further.

Desperately she whirled her uninjured arm and crystal encased her like a blanket, folding the metal next to her over and over with it, compacting it into a shield. As the shockwaves kept coming, and the beacon grew to an even greater size, lightning began to strike the land around the pyramid, coursing over the plating. It danced over her encasement, drawing more metal into her shell like the flow of water into a drain. The pyramid began to twist and implode towards her, shrinking, breaking apart, until the white-blue glow engulfed the entire city, and the pyramid beyond vanished in its aura.

The Coriolis had circled back round, keeping what they believed was a safe distance from the city. Osiris scanned the landscape, keeping a close eye on the Leviathan, too slow to turn their cannons completely around the pyramid's axis. Teratai and Dhalen were on the flight deck with him, watching with grim realisation.

The ground bulged and billowed. Blue streaks of energy snapped across the ground for miles. A blinding light fissured from the Tor and ruptured out. The ship began shaking. A terrifying, deafening rumble and infinitely pitched whine shook the ship. Panels rattled and the Coriolis tilted, resisting Osiris' controls. Below decks, he heard screams from the confused, frightened Nazreal citizens. Lurching back on the control wheel, he pulled the golden ship into a steep, desperate climb. Further shockwaves threatened to buffet them out of the air, and a shower of debris cascaded into the sky from Nazreal's direction. Osiris tried to pull above it, but stones and crystal sparks rattled against the hull, some overtaking his field of view. The ship ascended further; he steered it to ride the shockwaves, using their force to bolster the engines' frantic drive and push them even faster, higher, ascending past the dispersing clouds.

Elysser hauled themself to the outer deck, wrapping their paw around a chain on the railing, using their axe to summon an energy shield to deflect the hail of debris. Their barrier fluctuated with the tearing, coursing energy beneath them, sparking and jittering even at this distance.

They gripped the chain so tightly it bit into their paw. The land was being swallowed by the resonance blast. Pillars of dust split from deep rifts that thundered along the land, snaking ahead of the energy's blue expanse. The desert sands shifted in movements like a tsunami. The Skyrian waterway crumbled and vanished into a rumbling abyss. In two directions, a deep rift began to form as the land shifted apart. The continent split, shifted, quaked.

"Aidan…"

Aidan felt the depth of the world opening up below and around him, the terrifying emptiness of its centre, and its fragile shell on the brink of shattering. He held his staff in a death-grip, thinking of nothing but keeping the world whole, in any way. He would disappear into the rift to keep it stable, if he had to. There were too many who deserved to live, who had given him life, ones who he desperately needed to protect.

They all had to live.

"Please… please…"

He envisioned walls to close off the city, seal off the energy. He tried to lift Nazreal to keep it from pushing everything aside. If the shockwaves only hit the air, maybe the land would be spared.

The energy fought him, resisted, tried to pull in the directions the energy most wanted to flow, along the continent's fault lines. But he would control it. He had to.

The rumbling in his ears increased to noiseless, infinite silence. He could no longer feel his body, but he kept a grasp on his staff, the only means he had of saving the world.

Take it away. Take me away. Make this city disappear. Please. Save them. Let them live.

Something swelled from deep underneath him. Energy flew across and through him in all directions.

He fell.

Chapter Twenty

"*It was... the worst thing I have ever witnessed. We did not even know if there was a world left to land in. By some miracle... namely your father, there was.*"

Darkness. Infinite and vast, yet inescapably close. Sounds, perhaps voices, rang in some distant space and expanded to echoes, drifting into nothingness as they passed over him. Everything was still, save for a quiet, abyssal pulse below, similar to the waves that rocked Arete, but far more subdued, and boundlessly larger. It was a yawning, alarming space he felt, as if the sky had reversed and he now floated helplessly above it. The dark spread forever, slumbering, yet acutely alive.

Aidan tried to open his eyes. They were dry and heavy, with a pressure against them. His right arm was twisted above his head and his left somewhere below him, still gripping his staff. He tried to lift his left arm but his whole body was caught, rigid. He couldn't even flex his claws.

He'd been entombed.

His heart began to race. He flooded the staff instinctively with energy and the mass around him began to dissolve away. The infinite darkness relinquished him as he dropped from his encasement, and the fathomless, langouring rhythm that had been connected to him faded, now separate and distinct.

His first gasp of air was a long, rasping one. Flecks of grit spat from him. As his legs and tail came free, he collapsed, shaking. He had never felt so weak in his life. After quelling the tremors in his paw, he rubbed sharp, dry grains from around his eyes to try and open them.

His lids flickered and spasmed. Flashes of white, visions of fire and dust burned his eyes. He squeezed them tightly shut and dug his knuckles into his temples to rid himself of them, but every time he opened his eyes they pummelled his senses. He groaned and rolled onto his side, shaking, curling into a ball. Everything was so dark, and cold. Biting, deathly cold. Eventually he summoned the strength to keep his eyes open, and the visions faded into the darkness that shrouded him.

The first thing he saw was his paws.

His fur was coated with tiny crystals shards that sprouted from between his follicles. He shakily brushed at them and they flaked away with a light electric crackle. He was lying on a smooth, uneven platform of rock, coloured with the blue crystal dust that saturated his fur. He rolled onto a sitting position and hugged his arms around him, trying to resist the piercing chill. More noises, the remote echoes of conversation, or perhaps screams, danced around the room. In the otherwise silence they were deafening, and danced about him like ghosts.

His shivers turned to full-body shuddering. His teeth chattered and his heavy body stiffened further as his muscles, aching and burning, tensed in the freezing air. With the tip of his staff he scraped some crystal dust into a pile by his knees. He let out a withering breath through his gritted teeth and focused everything he had on controlling his body to give the output he needed.

A tiny light blossomed from under his paw and spiralled down the crystal veins, jumping to the pile of dust. The shards coalesced into an uneven orb with a soft glow, and a radiating warmth. Aidan took hold of it and brought it to his chest. Even for being so small, barely visible through his clasped palms, it was enough to loosen his chest. He curled around it, and waited for his energy to return.

He gasped awake. He had no idea how long he'd been asleep. There was still nothing to indicate where he was, nor any light but the timid iridescence of the crystal floor.

He took in a breath to call out, but the first word he tried to speak sent him into a fit of hacks and coughs. Tiny blue specks flew into the darkness and faded against the ground. He wiped his mouth, eyeing them suspiciously, and sat back on his haunches, keeping the warm orb against his chest.

He sat for a while, meditating on where his energy should be, how to escape, or even get his bearings in the first place. After some time, and feeling his innards settle somewhat, he took the staff into his paws again.

With a gentle touch the ends illuminated, and he almost cried in relief. He stretched out his arm to cast the light on his surroundings.

He was in a tall cave; the smooth, undulating walls were black and grey, with a quality similar to melted wax. When he looked at the floor again, he saw it was crystal, but tarnished with soot. He wiped his paw across and it smeared away.

The cave stretched above him, but he couldn't see how far. With a few deep breaths to prepare himself, he rocked to a stand and gently, carefully, touched his staff to the floor. The ground creaked, jerked, and beneath him a platform began a slow ascent. He kept his staff lit, to be wary of the ceiling as it approached.

It took a long time.

Eventually he reached not rock, but something protruding from above. The metal had been melted, twisted almost unrecognisable, but rubbing his paw on the cold, burnt molten shape he knew it to be the remains of the Dhrakan generators he'd stood amongst to contain the resonance chamber. He must be underneath it.

He pushed the platform higher, so that the top end of his staff met with the fused metal above. With a gentle burst of energy the metal spiralled away, revealing a narrow opening with a ceiling of blue crystals; the small antechamber where the drill had breached the resonance chamber. He clambered up and across, having to widen the space around him as it had been compressed to barely wider than his head, but eventually he crawled back through the drill's rift, to a cavern illuminated by soft blue chroma.

The resonance chamber.

Immediately around the edge of the opening, a jagged bowl of crystal stretched across the floor and up the walls. The dome had squashed considerably, to about half its height. The crystal growths spiking from every surface made it almost impossible to tell where the walls now lay. The original staircase no longer existed, partly absorbed, partly demolished by the crystals.

The fox looked around, trying not to impale himself, and saw the tunnel he'd ejected Raikali through was still there. It was mostly blocked, but he could probably still navigate it. He stumbled forwards, flattening the crystal to a pathway wherever he could, but feeling increasingly drained and unsteady. His heavy, shaky movements were the only noise he could detect. Everything else was locked in macabre stillness and unearthly cold.

He shuffled along the cave wall he'd left only a short time ago to reverse Raikali's death ray, stopping every few steps to rest his shoulder against the smooth, cold earth. If this was the resonance chamber, what state was the city in?

The opening ahead was dark, forebodingly so. He stopped now and then to catch his breath and stop his legs from shaking. Shooting pains fired through his head, forcing his eyes shut. Every needle-like shard he passed had an inaudible sing to it, a tone that he couldn't hear, but felt immeasurably. In his exhaustion it felt like they were trying to talk to him, but he refused to listen. He needed to see, and every sound was as icy as the air around him, almost melancholic. He could not stop shaking as his mind and body flooded with worry at what he would find on the surface. Gradually, painfully, he edged closer, till he could see the tunnel's mouth.

Nazreal's buildings had fissured and tumbled to leave only a dark and broken cityscape. Those that still stood were listing husks, nothing but shells with gaping black holes at their windows like the eyes of a corpse. A thick patina of sparkling dust and choking soot covered every visible surface. The paving undulated in frozen ripples on the misshapen ground, and the calm blue glow that used to light the streets had vanished. In its place was a sharp luminescence from clusters of crystal that grew from the stone at haphazard intervals. Some were small, the size of flowers, and others towered almost as high as the buildings themselves. Aidan carefully craned his head back to look at the Tor as he stepped out. Its spires were still intact, but the beacon was dormant, and looked like it had been for a long time. Above that was pure darkness. He strained his eyes to see if it was a clouded night, or if something else was obscuring the sky. The pit in his stomach sank even further, the singing in his head reaching a frantic cacophony of sadness and terror. Chills cycled from his ears to his tail and tore at his chest, gripped his throat. He wanted to throw up, but his weak, hollow body had no energy. Nazreal's harrowing, silent emptiness pressed into him like a monstrous fog, a hunter that was ready to take its final blow and consume him. He began walking but the fear breaking down his head pushed him into a lumbering, breathless sprint to the gates. Breath tore from him in whimpers and he looked all about him as he lolloped across the stones, trying to find any sign of life, even a concrete death, anything that would give him a sign of his world.

So fervid was his panic that he didn't judge his path, and he slammed into a stone wall. He rolled back, cradling his head, feeling a damp trickle seep down his eyebrow. He raised a shaky paw to it, and saw blood and blue spreading over his fur. After shifting to his knees, he looked at what he'd hit.

The city had ended. A sheer, uneven rock face loomed over him. Following it up, he could see remnants of the paved walkways spread across it, stretching all the way over the centre of the city. Sections of building protruded at odd angles, inexorably fused with the rock. Nazreal was encased within its walls, like he'd intended. His fear deepened as the dark wall hung, silently, oppressively, as a monster's shadow.

Barely able to breathe for the constriction of horror in his chest, he pushed against the wall with his staff and forced it to arch open before him.

He pressed forwards, legs burning with the exertion of walking against both exhaustion and fear. The rock was metres thick, and the further he went, the darker his path became.

Suddenly, a sliver of light splintered the gloom.

He slammed the staff home with a desperate push, and the corridor flooded with white. He raised his arm to shield his eyes, and stumbled back as a harsh wind braced against him.

Slowly, the world came into view.

"Oh no. Oh *no*."

Desert sands stretched to the horizon, far below him.

Nazreal sat inside the peak of a vast, rocky pillar, surrounded by nothing but impervious gold dunes, and a merciless roaring wind. He spun on his hind paw and sprinted back inside the city.

"Osiris! Elysser!" he yelled.

He clambered over stones, yelling the names of his friends to every gap and crevice. No bones, no graves, no sign of anyone.

Nothing but dust. No reply but his own terrified echo among the shadows of fire and decay. Terrors filled his mind of the destruction he had wrought, the complete annihilation of the world and those inside it. His parents, the Coriolis, Arete…

At the foot of the Tor he fell to his knees and a piteous cry cracked from his throat.

"It's… it's gone. It's all gone," he breathed. He cradled his head in his paws, claws digging into his forehead, rocking back and forth on his haunches. He let his breaths out in long, slow whistles.

"No, no no no, maybe it's… maybe it just moved. Desert… there's a lot of desert on Vu-ori," he stammered, barely a murmur, as he rose to his hind paws and traipsed back to the opening in the mesa wall. The dust burnt his pads, the soot marred his clothes, which already felt like a ghost wrapped around him.

His walk had turned into a hunched limp, more laboured with each step he took towards the edge. He stood back from it and stared out at the whistling, indifferent sand.

"Long way to go," he croaked. He tried to place his staff at the precipice to create a pathway to the ground, but in his exhaustion the blade skipped off the rock and he tumbled forwards. He threw out his arms to steady himself, losing a grip on his staff, which clattered away.

He lunged for it, just as it swivelled at the brink and dropped. He scrambled after it, catching it just by the bladed head. He felt the edge slice into his digits, but refused to let go. If he was to survive at all, he needed this. He tried to curl it up towards him but his arm screamed with pain and fatigue. It began to shake. The blood dripping over the blade's smooth, flat surface forced his grip tighter, yet made it even harder to control. He could feel it sliding unstoppably to the ground below.

"Come on… *please*!"

He gripped as tightly as he could and made one last effort to haul it to safety, but the blade sliced away. He watched it fall in a dizzying spiral, his final hope, the last of him, until it was no longer visible in the fatal drop below.

He stared at the distal desert at the base of the mesa, and his body surrendered. He closed his eyes for what he knew would be the final time.

Chapter Twenty-One

"*Nazreal's desert is torturous, I'm amazed he survived."
"We are all a sum of our miracles and disasters. Your father most especially so. However... some miracles are closer tied to our past than we anticipate."*

Aidan awoke with a start, and a deep, panicked gasp. He thrashed around, trying to find his staff. It took him a moment to realise he was no longer on the cliffside, and what swirled around him were bedsheets, not air or sand. The sound of claws skittering on stone pricked his ears – he glanced to see its source, and a squirrel tail vanished through a doorway. The room was comfortably warm, lit with candles in glass bowls mounted to the walls. He could hear the faint noise of a city, or a village perhaps, but thick curtains were a barrier against the window. He tried to move and was struck with immediate dizziness. He froze in place to quell the tight, bulbous feeling at the back of his head. He thought about lying back down, but the more he glanced about the room, the more alien his surroundings appeared to be. The room was made of sandstone, the floor polished to a shine, with a thick woven rug to one side of the bed. The walls were decorated, but not ostentatiously, with torches, and carved wooden reliefs of depictions he didn't recognise. Was this Kitaia? Or Skyria?

As the swirling subsided, he shifted stiffly, aching, to the edge of the bed. Just as he tipped his legs over the side, a figure swept into the room: a female fox with large ears and resonant blue eyes, wearing a long robe of dark green adorned in gold, blue, and white patterning. On her head sat a chain headband with a drop pendant, mounted into which was a blue crystal.

Aidan gripped the bed tightly.

"How do you feel?" the fox asked, with marked rigidity. Aidan, wary, didn't move.

"I… have been better," he said carefully, watching her. Even though she bore the markings of a red fox, her fur was more golden than burnt orange. Her fennec-like ears were sharp, honed with discernment and acute awareness. "But I'm alive, which I otherwise didn't expect."

She remained stoic. "That will happen if you climb mountains like that. What were you doing up there?"

"I didn't know it was a mountain until I got out of it," he replied.

Suspicion instantly flicked across her face; her whiskers tensed. "What do you mean?"

Aidan's claws dug further into the bed; his right leg began to jitter. "I, er… I'm trying to find my friends. I need to know if they survived."

"Who are your friends? Are they in the mountain too?"

He rubbed his face firmly, massaging his forehead while his breathing became faster, deeper.

"No, nobody was. Is… I don't… I don't know where I am," he said quickly, quietly. He shook his head, trying to get rid of the sudden ringing. "I need my staff."

She shook her head. "I can't give you that until I know exactly what you were doing there. I've never seen a weapon like that before, and nobody traverses a desert so wide without supplies."

He shot her a glare. "It's not a weapon. It's a tool."

"For what?" she pressed, eyes flaring.

"Everything."

"Whose blood was on it?"

"Mine."

"Did you steal it?"

"No, it's mine. I made it."

"Where did you come from?"

"Inside the mountain," he growled.

"Nobody comes from that mountain," she barked back. "It's a desolate, dangerous place containing deadly secrets. Nobody has lived there for thousands of years yet you tell me you came from inside it? What reason do you have to go poking around in world-destroying technology?"

She stopped as she saw his face turn ashen.

"What… what did you say?" he croaked. "Thousands of years?"

He looked about. She said something, but he didn't hear it. Suddenly he threw the sheets from him and strode to the window. She moved to stop him but wasn't fast enough. He pulled open the curtains. Below him was a bustling city of sandstone in a low, forested valley. A river ran through the landscape and under the city walls. The sun shone brightly, and a gentle breeze caressed the leafy canopy beyond the wall.

He stumbled back onto the bed. "Where... where am I?"

She stood next to the window. "You're in Xayall, my city."

"I don't understand," he said, his voice cracking. "I don't know this place. This was never here when I... when Nazreal was..."

He clasped his head in his paws.

She took a breath as if to say something, but held it for a second with her paws to her chest in a motion that looked almost like an apology, then she sighed. Her expression softened somewhat, but her eyes still gleamed with scrutiny.

"I am Kaya Phiraco. I believe we have a lot to talk about."

He nodded faintly. His voice came out as barely a whisper. "So... it would seem." He swallowed hard and looked down at his paws. "How long has it been?"

"You've been asleep for several days, but... I don't believe that's what you mean. Who are you?"

He was silent for a while, feeling like his body would collapse all over again at any moment. Electric pains kept buzzing through his head, a constant throbbing that sent a deafening whine through his ears with each charge. Flashes of memories, or perhaps hallucinations, of a devastating cataclysm, and screaming creatures, crossed his eyes each time. The tension of just... *disappearing* hung in his legs like a sharp emptiness, a readiness to find a deep, infinite place to cast himself into. He forced it back down and shakily steadied his breathing.

"My name is Aidan," he said quietly. "Aidan Arc'hantael."

She paused. He saw her claws ball tightly, but the rest of her demeanour remained otherwise cool.

"What do you know of Nazreal?" she asked.

He let out a slight, tired laugh. "Everything. I built it."

She froze. "That's…" she shook her head, giving a tiny laugh. "Not possible. Nazreal has existed in that mountain for over two thousand years."

"Maybe to you," he croaked, with a deepening stare. "To me, it hasn't been even a day since…" his voice cracked, "all those people… my family…"

He hunched forwards further, claws over his eyes, shaking. His body rocked and shook as he tried to stem the cries that belted his stomach.

She released her paws, wringing her digits as she watched him uneasily.

"If… if you are who you say, much has changed," she said quietly. "However, you will be kept here until we can prove so."

He took deep, shaky breaths, then raised his head. His cheeks were stained with the blue-green shadow of resonance-saturated tears. "Was it chance you happened across the desert after I collapsed?" he asked weakly.

"I…" she began, then hesitated, as if deducing the security of her next statement. "Had a sense that something was coming, an upheaval or impending arrival, so had been observing the mesa to ensure all was stable. We had spent almost a week camping at the base of the city when you appeared."

There was a movement in the corner of the room. Aidan became suddenly aware of a black panther, clad in armour of dark grey and blue, adjusting his stance. Slung across his back, was Aidan's staff.

She gestured to the panther. "We discovered your tool at the bottom of the mesa. Commander Enyart was the one who spotted you."

"How fortunate," Aidan said bitterly. He glanced at her, and in the sun's light caught sight of the crystal on her forehead. On the backs of her paws were delicate chains with crystals mounted in rings on each finger.

"You're a resonator…" he whispered.

She nodded. "My family has protected Nazreal since it was discovered. One of my ancestors lived in the city for a time, so anything you—"

He whirled round to face her. "Elysser? Are they your ancestor?"

Kaya's eyes widened. "Y-yes. So you…" She paused, then took in a sharp breath. "Well, I can… understand your distress, Mister Arc'hantael."

He pulled his ears stiffly back as he sank into a hunch on the edge of the bed and gave a tremulous sigh.

She took a small step forwards. "Are you… all right?"

"What kind of question is that?" he bit.

She cast a tempestuous glance out of the window. "Forgive my poor bedside manner. Comes with being an Empress. Or just me." She shifted her weight. "I invite you to stay, however. There's a lot you need to know, and only one way I think you'll process it. If you could bear to wait a few days, at least."

He shrugged, giving himself a piteous laugh. "I have

nowhere to go."

She bowed respectfully to him, and turned to leave. "As a precaution, I'm leaving Enyart as your guard. You will not be allowed to leave unattended, and resonance… will be forbidden. Should you need anything, he'll summon an attendant."

She left, and Aidan remained in awkward silence, with the stern, unwelcoming Commander Enyart. His yellow eyes held a prominent disregard for Aidan's presence, and he probably remembered every movement Aidan had ever made and planned a countermove for all of them.

"Sorry to have disturbed you," Aidan muttered.

The panther folded his arms. "It's not my disturbance you should have issue with, but hers. You'll have to earn her trust before mine is granted."

Aidan lay back on the bed. "Perfect. This will be fun, then."

Chapter Twenty-Two

"*I can't imagine what that must have felt like.*"

"*We all suffer great pains that may never be adequately quantified. The best we can do is offer comfort where we can. For all of his own sorrow, your father helped me with mine.*"

For the next few days, Aidan remained virtually silent. He spent most of the time in bed, not only from exhaustion but a complete, catatonic dejection. As suspicious as Enyart appeared to be, he at least had a perfunctory concern for Aidan's safety, recommending bars be installed on his window. Aidan watched as they were hammered into place, bitterly wondering if it was out of genuine concern or simply a need to protect the questions Kaya had yet to ask. Enyart was a taciturn being with a particular dislike for Aidan that he could not surpass. His eyes were just as critical at the fourth day as they were on the first, and his demeanour just as prickly. Aidan made no effort to communicate, but the times he needed escorting to a bathroom or reluctantly poured himself a drink, the panther's piercing gaze mirrored the disdain he had for himself. Even facing the wall, Aidan felt the panther's gaze pressing into him like a heat on his shoulder. His sleep was terrible enough anyway, but now it was rendered almost non-existent.

When the seventh day after his awakening in Xayall arrived, he had orchestrated a conversation to break down the barrier between them, but in the time he took building confidence to ask the first question, Kaya returned, bearing a new set of robes for him to wear.

She held them out to him: a fine jade cloth with a stiff weave and heavy drape. It reminded him of Elysser's clothing. He stared at them for a while.

"I understand if this feels like undue charity," Kaya said. "Should you wish to have something that doesn't smell like resonance char, these are yours whenever you like."

Aidan glanced briefly at Enyart, who he guessed would find a criticism for either his denial or his acceptance. He found something comforting about the cold, prickly dust that clung to his old clothes. It was all he had left of his old world. To step into something new felt like he would walk out of his own skin, and he wasn't ready for that yet. He took them with a grateful bow and laid them on the bed.

"Thank you for the offer. I… will change eventually. I don't wish to carry the smell of apocalypse through your halls for too long."

She bowed respectfully. "In your own time. For now, though… would you wish to see the city?"

Aidan froze, taking a cautious glance out of the window. "Maybe… maybe just this building for now."

"Very well." She gave a commanding nod to Enyart,

who stepped to behind Aidan's shoulder, and the three of them entered the corridor.

The building, although adorned in obscure, new fixtures, had a familiar layout. Much like Nazreal's Tor.

"How old is Xayall?" he asked, his voice grainy through lack of use.

"Almost as old as the disaster. Elysser drew out the plans for it as a place to recover and regroup. So you may recognise its architecture somewhat."

He ran his paw over the brickwork, letting his pads feel the lines, the corners, and smooth stone edges. For having been around so long, the walls were still strong, and thick. It was, just as much as Elysser's other work that he got to experience, immaculate. "They were… always very good."

Kaya stopped at a window and gestured outside. "Xayall had some natural features that Nazreal didn't, like the river, so use was made of that too. The Tor was the first building to act as a beacon for survivors to find. The further out the city spreads, the newer it is, so it may become less familiar as you go."

He nodded. "Well, two thousand years is a long time," he said, with a hint of resentment. "I can hardly expect things to stay static. But… how has Nazreal stayed secret for so long?"

She hesitated, folding her paws together. She looked to Enyart, who gave her a quiet, subtle nod. "The desert keeps many from being able to trespass. Part of my duty as Xayall's governing family is to ensure we have resources to protect it, and uncover secrets that may threaten it. It's clear that Elysser, and the other survivors, held you in high regard for what you managed to save. But they were wary of making a legend of you or the city, as that would lead to it being found again, and many in the outlying lands didn't yet know of it, or those that did were killed in the cataclysm."

Aidan fell quiet for a long time. Kaya would demonstrate things of note, but he took little interest in them.

A sprightly opossum approached and presented her with a scroll.

"For you, Your Imperial Majesty," he said cheerily, then gave them all an enormous bow and skittered down the hallway. She flicked it open with a claw, read it briefly, then handed it to Enyart without another word. He tucked it into a small knapsack, and gave Aidan a warning glare as the fox followed its path with his eyes.

"So how big is the empire of Xayall, Your Imperial Majesty?" he asked pointedly, lingering a little too long on the last syllable of her title. "Elysser didn't strike me as the type to conquer."

Kaya's ears flicked at his tone. "Just this city."

"A grand title for someone who's essentially a mayor by inheritance," he sniffed.

She shot him an explosive stare. "Don't get pithy with me, nor Elysser. I'm sorry I'm not my great beloved ancestor, but a lot has changed in two and a half millennia. That isn't our fault. We and Skyria set up outposts to help the world recover. We gave them aid, shelter, helped them with governance. When they were able to sustain themselves, we granted them full independence and autonomy. 'Empress' was a term gifted to my family for the work that we did to secure order after the great schism." Her stare hardened. "And all this while resonators were demonised as the destroyers of the world, so they had to ever hide their abilities from those they had a duty to help. It was not frivolous, but punishing. Be grateful there are still denizens here to speak the words you scorn."

Aidan's jaw tightened and he once again stalked into silence. The city outside wasn't his. None of this was. He never even saw the world he wanted for himself, or the family he longed for.

"It's… a hard adjustment," he laboured through gritted teeth. "I had intended to be around to see these kinds of structures form."

"I'm not expecting you to be pleased," she responded, regarding him with stern reproach. "But you will have to accept the way things are. The world could have been nothing but dust. Isn't this better?"

He kept his eyes away from her. She wasn't wrong. He knew that, but it was too much to admit. *His* world had ended. Everything that he'd been proud of, all his struggles, the people he'd touched and tried to help… nothing was left. It had moved on from him, and he would need to find a place all over again, if there was even somewhere he could fit. A world that hid resonance out of shame or fear was a universe far removed from his ambitions where they could be guardians and champions of a brighter future.

She looked out of the next window they passed. It was a slight movement, but he noticed her digging her claws into her palm again. "This is owed to you, you know. One way or another, this world would be infinitely worse without you. Even if it will never know, you should. For the stories my family passed down, to hear what you did… I'm grateful. It was inspiring and horrifying in ways I couldn't have imagined. I'm sorry you didn't get to fulfil your ambitions. But please, don't diminish what they struggled to build without you."

He finally looked up and saw her features had softened. They still held a wary, almost disappointed expression, but he believed her. "Thank you," he whispered.

She raised an arm to indicate the doorway beside them, screened off by heavy green curtains. "But… perhaps I'm the wrong person to tell you that. Please, meet my advisor."

Aidan tilted his head as she strode to the curtain and lifted it, gesturing for him to step inside. He paused for a moment, trying to rid himself of a chill that crept over his arms and down his spine, then ducked under the curtain.

The sun was framed almost completely by the enormous window; he squinted to see through the light. Within seconds, a huge shape loomed into view and obscured it; giant golden wings cast Aidan into shadow. Crimson armour shone in the sun's rays, and two rapiers hung at the belt of the towering, bulky figure.

Aidan stumbled back, eyes wide in a wash of fear and disbelief.

"You… is it… *Osiris?*"

A huge claw grabbed his shoulder and pulled him forwards. The gryphon stared deeply into his eyes. He was so much older, his glorious white feathers painted with grey, the gold sheen fading from the end of his wings. His eyes, unmistakable, were still as fierce a red as they ever were, and brimmed with relief the likes of which Aidan had never seen.

Osiris shook his head "I never believed it would happen. I swore if we ever found you that you'd be nothing but bones." He clasped his claws on Aidan's shoulders again, still shaking his head, looking him up and down. "How, Aidan?" he effused. "How are you here? What trick did you pull to bring yourself back after all this time?"

Aidan could not hold back his emotions. He threw himself onto Osiris and flung his arms around him, fists clasped and shaking. "I don't know…" he cracked. "I just woke up under the resonance chamber. I broke my promise, Osiris. I couldn't protect anyone. I wasn't there. I killed them all, I lost everything. I failed you. I failed everyone."

Osiris gently laid a claw on Aidan's tremoring back. "This was not your doing. You ensured us a chance at rebuilding. And we are here. The world lived."

Aidan pulled back, hearing Kaya enter the room. She kept a respectful distance, taking a seat at the table opposite them. Aidan kept standing, breaths heaving from him as he tried to keep his body stable, feeling like it threatened to explode and collapse at the same time.

"How… how bad was it?"

Osiris pointed to a seat, in front of which was a thick, ancient journal. He recognised it instantly.

Elysser's.

Aidan refused it with an anxious shake of his head, instead gripping his claws into the wooden backboard while trying to wash away the cold waves of apprehension that flowed down his back like ice water.

"None of us had ever seen anything so cataclysmic," Osiris recounted, gravely. "Even in the clouds, the shockwave almost brought the Coriolis down. We had to climb higher, and we lost sight of Nazreal completely. The sky below turned to a storm of dust and thunder. It took days to find clear waters to land on, and even longer to traverse back to solid ground. When we did... the land as we knew it was torn apart. You created an ocean where there had been nothing but desert." He looked to the wall. "Have you seen the maps?"

Aidan swallowed hard, trying to quell his stomach contents. "What do you mean?"

Kaya watched the two carefully, twisting the crystal pendant on her forehead between her fingers.

Osiris walked to a chart on the wall. Slowly, he laid a claw on its centre, a large expanse of ocean known as 'The Great Rift', flanked by two continents, one a crescent and the other a piece that may at one point have nestled into it, but both were worn, jagged and uneven.

"Do you see it?" Osiris asked softly.

Aidan stepped towards the frame.

"I don't understand," he croaked, his paws trembling.

Osiris shifted his claw to Xayall's location, on the lower section of the crescent continent to the left. "We are here. This continent is called Cadon." He traced his claw along the eastern coastline to a bay about midway up the continent. "That's where Nazreal *used* to be."

"Andarn..." Aidan said quietly. "But that's not where I was found."

"No. Nazreal," he dragged his claw back down to a section east of Xayall, "is now here. It moved, and split Vuori in two."

Kaya stood up and moved to Aidan's side. "The energy you released was astronomical. Uncontrolled resonance energy is always unpredictable, but looking at the formation of the mountains in the new continents, it seems as though the initial explosion sent shockwaves under the ground and reformed the tectonic plates, splitting the continent and pushing them apart. There's an enormous trench in the ocean on the other side of the world where they're moving under one another. Had it gone the other way, you would have created a third continent."

Aidan swayed a little, his eyes glazed, distant. Pains shot through his head again. He tried to shake them away, but each new city he saw on the map drew up visions of carnage and ruin. "Could… did anyone on the ground survive that?"

"Some did. Mountain tribes, those in the open plains in the centre of each continental quadrant, or on stronger plates to the north-east. Skyria's resonance chamber and other earthquake preparation mitigated a lot of their damage, but not all. They were instrumental in ensuring the world didn't die immediately afterwards. It was cold and dark for a long time."

Aidan's paw crept to his chest. "And Arete?"

Osiris paused. "They… did not survive," he said quietly.

Aidan shakily turned the chair round and sat on it, hunching over.

"The resonance chamber was not strong enough for Arete's proximity to the blast," Osiris continued. "I promise it was not for your modifications." He traced a finger from Andarn in a line that roughly followed the coastline out and down. "The path the city travelled made the intensity that much greater for Arete. Between the oceans' swell and the land, there was nothing left of it. Our towers disappeared under the continent's movement."

Aidan raked his claws over his ears. "I'm sorry…" he cracked. "I'm sorry…"

Osiris let out a long sigh. "I have long since said my farewell to it, and to all who are gone."

Aidan hung his head over the table. "So Dhalen, Teratai, Elysser…"

Osiris was solemn. "The only one who could have withstood such longevity other than myself was Teratai, and she… passed soon after. After we rebuilt what we could from Skyria, Dhalen and the Kitaia moved back to the remnants of their homelands, now on Ohé, and Elysser, well…" He gestured to Kaya, who was holding her ancestor's journal. "They took it upon themself to continue your work in your stead. They saved countless numbers of us."

Kaya softly drummed her claws on the hardened leather cover of Elysser's journal. "Osiris stayed with our family to make sure we could always guard Nazreal, and that we knew the history behind it. This journal, and yours, were passed down for each of us to read, to understand our powers, what the world gained, and lost."

Aidan looked sadly to his old friend. "You've been awake this whole time?"

Osiris shook his head. "I stay for a few years, then sleep for longer. I was always available if needed, but my body is no longer what it used to be. At the beginning I was always there, until…" he trailed off.

Aidan already knew what changed. "Until they died," he said quietly.

"After that, I awoke every few years to oversee new constructions and search the world for Nazreal's artefacts, safeguard the journals and carry them between here and Skyria, where they normally stay in their resonance chamber.

Teratai dedicated her research of bionics and augmentations to them also, and they have used it to heal wounded across the world for as long as they have had the capacity."

"What artefacts do you mean?" Aidan asked, not really aware of his own question, eyes glazed.

"Nazreal broke apart along its path, and created large amounts of crystal residue as it travelled. Most of that is now in the ocean, and inaccessible. In addition, some of Nazreal's research left with their owners before the cataclysm, and we had no way of knowing what these were, or how dangerous they could be. Whatever we found, crystals or otherwise, we either stockpiled or buried, where appropriate. I keep a mark on these so I can refuel the Coriolis when needed."

Aidan gave a small laugh. "I'm glad the ship's still working. Those two… really made things to last, didn't they? Unlike me."

Osiris frowned. "Do not berate yourself, Aidan. This was unprecedented. You were the most powerful resonator in the world. We stand now because of your sacrifices."

"In spite of them, maybe," he spat. He caught Osiris' vehement look and shook his head. "I'm sorry, I'm still… getting through this." He sighed and cleared his throat. "With the world as it is… should we destroy Nazreal completely?"

Osiris and Kaya looked to each other. "That has never been decided. In deliberation with Skyria we opted to keep introducing new developments as the world grew mature enough to accept them. But for all our work, we did unfortunately little that could be gifted to the world on an equal scale. Nazreal was unto itself in advancement and application."

Aidan looked to Kaya. "And what of us, the resonators?"

Her eyes flicked with suspicion. "What do you mean?"

"I'm starting to feel they're right about us being abhorrent."

Kaya stiffened. "We are born as we are. If you're going to condemn someone for having a gift that is no fault of their own, you will find reason to condemn anyone in the world."

He dug his claws into the table. "That's not the same. We're different, and dangerous."

She glared at him. "Do you find me dangerous?"

He paused, locking her stare in his. For a second Elysser flashed before him, creating a countenance that he longed to see again, and never would. Anger welled in his chest. "I don't know what you can do."

"You don't know what *anyone* can do, resonator or no."

"I know what *I* can do. That's enough."

She strode towards him, and thrust Elysser's journal into his chest, pressing it harder with every sentence. "What *you* do means nothing when you scrutinise others. What you *did* means nothing to those who have never met you. How dare you presume us all to be criminals through your own savage guilt. You spent your days collecting and training resonators to help save the world. You were so beloved, and mourned, and here you sit in mourning for yourself." She pointed at his staff, still in Enyart's possession. "The danger in us comes from the world we are subjected to. Can you blame us for hiding away or lashing out when we have always been believed to be full of nothing but vengeful demons?"

She pushed him and the book away; he cradled it in grim silence. "You have never ruled a sovereign like I have. You have never hidden a secret many would kill you to use while the whole world watches. You may have incredible power, and experienced nightmares beyond anyone's imagination, but you are here, in a new world, that has never known you. You have lived. So did Elysser. That has to be worth something, if you were worth anything at all. They seemed to think so, and perhaps you would deign to discover their feelings on it if you were not so wrapped up in your own."

She gave a polite nod to Osiris, who nodded in return, and she strode from the room. At the curtain, she turned. "They said you were a saviour. I do not wish to believe otherwise, but I have yet to see it."

Aidan glared at the doorway for a time, then collapsed into his chair.

Chapter Twenty-Three

"We... we take familiarity far too much for granted."

"It is easy to become complacent. That is something I ever tried to instil in your father, but my view is jaded by too much cynicism. There is a balance to be struck, but I am too far past to discover it."

Aidan sat in silence for a time, breathing heavily, while Osiris stood before him in equal silence, albeit one Aidan could feel pressing into him more every second.

"Power and strength really are different, aren't they?" he said eventually, quietly, not taking his eyes from the battered tome of leather and parchment in his clutches.

Osiris bobbed his head in thought. "You trained, and left a world of comfort for one unknown, and again you ride into a world that lived long after you disappeared. It is a different means of survival than being born into a hierarchy you did not ask for."

Aidan looked back at the doorway. "Resonators are kept

hidden now, she said."

The gryphon folded his arms, his sigh swirling the dust particles that caught the sunbeams. "Overall, yes. There are far fewer in the world now than there used to be, primarily because the crystals are underwater, or buried far from most settlements. For one to be discovered in a position of power as Kaya's could start a dangerous rift in the Senate."

Aidan's fur bristled. "Senate?"

Osiris blinked. "I forget how much you do not know. Yes, there is a structure to Cadon's government now. Kaya is not only Empress of her lands, but also a Representative of them within the Senate."

Aidan rubbed his eyes. "So, these countries—"

"Sovereigns," Osiris muttered.

Aidan's paw dropped to his thigh, and he looked through his eyebrows at his friend. "You… you actually call them that now?"

Osiris rolled his shoulders and gave a brisk, sharp sniff. "It's accurate."

Aidan threw up his arms. "Honestly Osiris, I leave for twenty-five hundred years and you screw everything up, I don't even know you any more." He leant back in his seat and there was a tense moment of silence, before Osiris broke into an unintentional smile.

"Your charm has not suffered in the years, I see," he chuckled.

Aidan was relieved to see his friend granted some levity, and he laughed back in return, a welcome, tired, break in his torpor.

"I should apologise to Kaya," he said quietly. He gripped the journal tightly. "And read this."

"That you should," Osiris replied.

"The Empress will be busy for some time," came Enyart's deep and dismissive voice from the corner behind them. He stepped forwards, pulling Aidan's staff from the leather sheath he'd kept intense guard over. He gave a perfunctory bow to them both and presented it to Osiris, who took it gratefully. "I am sure she will be grateful for your company later, Tallon."

The panther then swirled out of the room and disappeared in an instant.

Aidan sucked the air through his teeth. "I mean, he could have handed it to me."

Osiris shrugged. "Commander Enyart is remarkably protective of Kaya. He takes a long time to warm to strangers, if at all. But consider this: he at least confirms your identity and right to hold your own possession, even if he may see it as a threat to her position."

"That's… remotely comforting, I guess."

Aidan left the journal on the table, then walked to Osiris and stroked his pawpads over the stave's crystalline veins. He wondered how it, or he, could have remained in one piece following such a surge. A coldness rushed over him as he remembered the darkness he awoke in, the light that had swallowed him, the two surrounding and enveloping him all at once, and existing inside him. Osiris put out his claw to steady the fox. Aidan snapped back to the room, his eyes foggy.

"S-sorry, I, er… I'm still tired, I think," he said, a shake in his voice. He reached for the tankard of water at the centre of the table and poured it into a silver goblet, before raising it, trembling, to his lips and drinking deeply. Osiris watched him with concern.

"You have indeed been on an adventure," he remarked. "Very few creatures are made for living such a long time. I barely am, in all truth, and most has been spent in deepest sleep." He ran his claws over the pommel of his rapier, looking distrait, towards the floor. "It… is good to see you again, my friend. We were devastated to have lost you."

Aidan smiled sadly, standing stiffly. "I'm sorry to have left you for so long. It feels like no time for me. But…" he closed his eyes and shivered. "Waking up in Nazreal, black and ashen…" He shrank a little. "It was covered in death. I felt it inside me. The devastation it wrought, the hurt. When I stepped outside and saw the desert, it overwhelmed me. It's a living death, that place. And I…" He clasped his fist tightly. "As I lay there… part of me wanted to disappear. At that moment, I felt I deserved nothing more than to vanish in the sand along with the world I thought I'd destroyed."

Osiris slowly tugged the feathers at his throat, his face a sympathetic shadow of grim sadness. "We all have moments of absolute darkness. Mine… have been plenty. Sometimes we are not so lucky as to save ourselves, but be saved by those around us. What we do with the time that follows is our means of repaying it." He laid his claw on Aidan's shoulder. "Such as we all thought when you saved us. Had you not been there to channel the energy, the world would be dead for certain. You controlled it enough to save the distal nations, and quelled the explosion enough for us to escape. Remember that, always. The crystals may have infinite power, but *you* directed it."

Aidan nodded as tears broke from his eyes and rolled down his muzzle. He hugged Osiris again, a little harder than he intended, clashing his head against the breastplate with a loud 'thunk'. There was an awkward pause.

"I felt that from in here," Osiris said quietly.

"Love hurts sometimes," Aidan muttered, rubbing his forehead. "Thank you, Osiris. Thank you for still being here, through… through things I could never have imagined."

"I will tell you about them, in time," Osiris said softly. He put his arm around Aidan's shoulder "For now, there are some things I wish to show you."

Osiris toured him around Xayall, its walls bright in the sun, and pointed out the innovations Elysser and Teratai had brought to the new world. It sounded like an incredible feat to Aidan to lay down the foundations for a whole new beginning. Even though Osiris had spoken of the necessity of his apparent sacrifice, Aidan could not escape the guilt of his absence when he saw the illustriousness of their achievements.

There was something comforting in the city, however. Despite how much had been done without him, Aidan couldn't help but warm to the peaceful bustle of Xayall's atmosphere. It was how he'd wanted Nazreal to be. The sheer normality of it was something of a novelty when all of the places he'd lived before, between Arete, Mahrae, and Nazreal, were either fantastical in scope or had resonance abilities in their very foundations. Xayall had no resonance chamber – Osiris had mentioned there had been neither need or resources for one – and maybe the quiet absence of such was what made it feel so different. It was a sad realisation that perhaps the world was better off without the powers that had brought him so much enjoyment and purpose. He grew quieter as they travelled, but responded kindly to Osiris' fond demonstrations of the world and the city.

They circled back to the Tor when the evening drew in, and at the base of the grand, wide staircase were Kaya and Enyart. Neither looked especially happy to see them, so Aidan's approach was as humble as he could make it. Osiris gave them both a neat, polite bow, which they returned, while Aidan's bow was longer and more penitent. As he raised himself, he looked to the Empress.

"Kaya, or, Your Imperial Majesty, I mean," he said quickly, glancing at Enyart, who seemed appeased. "I'm sorry for speaking out of turn. I know… well, you know more about this world than I ever have. If you'll have me, I'll read over everything that happened in my absence, and stay as an advisor to Nazreal, and, well…" he gave a tired laugh and shrug. "I have nothing else to offer. But I can promise it comes with respect for you and your family. I'll do my best to adjust." He looked up at the Tor and sighed. "I've done it before, so I can do it again."

She looked briefly to Enyart, who seemed tacitly dismissive, but he gave a small nod of his head all the same.

"Aidan, I owe you an apology too. I have not been sympathetic. There are… very few we can share our powers with, so my defences are always high. But for one to know not only of the power but also the secret history on which the world is built, I should not have been so curt. Thank you for understanding. It will be an honour to have you stay, and maybe we can advise each other where our knowledge fails."

Aidan smiled, and gave her another bow. "I'll be glad to

oblige and assist in any way I can to keep the world peaceful and steady."

"In which case, if you feel ready," she said cautiously, "tomorrow we're leaving for the Senate. Would you attend with us?"

Enyart looked alarmed; his eyes widened and his whiskers tensed, but he kept anything he was due to say to himself.

"I'll leave that to your judgement, Your Imperial Majesty," Aidan said, very formally, with another bow. "I've no pretentions about my position; I'm a transient at best, and very much a novice in everything here. I don't want to risk your position with my naïveté."

She shook her head. "Not at all. I believe it the best place to start, and in fact, this may be a matter very suited to your experience." She gave Osiris a stern look, then turned on the stair and began ascending them, her robe billowing behind her. "I suggest wearing those robes I gave you."

Chapter Twenty-Four

"Ugh, I need to prepare for my first Senate meeting, too. I'm not enthusiastic."

"I would worry if you were. But I will not permit you to travel until we are sure it is secure."

"I appreciate that. I doubt I may ever be free of danger, though. If I have to rise to meet it... I know I'm already in good hands."

The next day, Aidan, Kaya, and Enyart were packed into a carriage that rocked its way down a small road which traced the river to the east. Osiris was due to meet them at their destination: the Coriolis. The ship was too big to fly into the city grounds, and too prominent to stay secret. While many illustrious galleons had been made and sailed around with great pride, the Coriolis was still so advanced that it would bring immediate suspicion onto the city if it were seen close by. As such, Aidan sat with his staff in a tight leather bundle, clutching it to his lap, while Enyart sat opposite him, keeping watch outside the window. Kaya kept glancing at

Aidan, and he back, but his mind was in too many places to make small talk.

"You should consider making something more subtle," she said eventually. He looked down at the staff and rubbed the soft leather against the handle.

"I… could. This is just something I'm very proud of."

"Oh, I understand. I don't mean to scrap it, just something to wear instead and leave that in a secure place." She held up her hands. "Jewellery rarely catches an eye for security, but your staff definitely will. Weapons are barred from the Senate, and you may not be able to excuse it as a walking aid with such prominent blades."

He frowned. "Well… I could try reshaping it into a pole at both ends so it *does* look like a walking stick, but honestly I'm afraid to exert it too much in case the structure was weakened in the cataclysm."

"I think until we have a really deep look at it, we won't know for sure," she said softly. "As we don't know how you were kept in such a state for such a long time, whether it was down to the staff, you, or the crystal around you, it's best not to risk any of those things unnecessarily. Enyart will keep it safe."

Aidan nodded appreciatively to the panther, whose stoicism was beginning to grate a little. In a novelty of expression, the Commander nodded back, but swiftly turned his attention to the rickety world outside.

Some time later, the carriage ground to a stop. Enyart opened the door and leapt out in one fluid motion, like a liquid shadow, and appeared moments later at the opposite door to open it for Kaya.

They had stopped before the end of the trail, which

narrowed to little more than a footpath and curled around the water's edge to the left, where it widened considerably to a long bay.

Aidan helped himself out, pulling at the robes to make sure they didn't catch anywhere. He had never worn anything so formal before, being used to the comfortable clothes from his desert village and the loose-fitting robes better suited to the often-humid air of Nazreal. The high collar, stiff, tapered waist and tight sleeves were alien and brushed his fur in the wrong direction with every movement. He did his best to hide his physical discomfort, accustomed to it as he was with the sensations caused by resonance use. One thing it helped a little was his stability, although somewhat at the cost of his breath. He had felt unable to fully breathe since waking in Nazreal, and the board-like front of his robe was putting an even shallower limit on his capacity. Cold rushes descended through his legs, which felt empty at the top, with his hind paws incredibly heavy. He managed to stay stable thanks to the restriction around his core, but had to walk at a slower pace than he was used to. Every so often the pain in his head would rise, as if threatening to strike with an electric charge again, but he managed to quell it with focus.

Kaya dismissed the carriage driver, and they walked the trail beside the water. Enyart was the one who looked back when Aidan began to falter.

"Are you all right?" he called, stopping for him to catch up.

"I think I'm still exhausted from being inside the mesa," Aidan breathed, giving him a thankful smile.

Enyart nodded. Aidan could just catch sight of a scar on

his neck under his fur. His dark grey armour was the right shade to make it innocuous in shadow, more so than black. The dark blue highlights along the armour's edges gave sharpness to his silhouette in the sun, but had an almost illusory effect in shadow of blurring his movement. Aidan couldn't tell if it was his fatigued eyes or something in the paint itself. The two walked side by side for a while, as Kaya stayed steadfast ahead.

"I hope I won't burden you," Aidan said quietly.

Enyart stiffened. "The secrets that the Empress' family protects are vast and grave. I haven't known anyone else with access to them as you have, and I've done my fair share of covering them up myself. Whatever your origin, it is another element that may twist at her safety, and I must be diligent." He shot Aidan a warning glance. "I assure you, any threat to her will be addressed without hesitation. You are here by her grace alone."

A chill ran down Aidan's spine. He nodded, and they continued in silence until they rounded another bend, and Aidan saw in the river a shallow yet wide vessel of aged wood, splintering at the seams, draped in tattered sails. The shape was instantly distinguishable.

"What... what happened to the Coriolis?"

Kaya didn't even glance back. As they approached further, Aidan began to understand the nature of the bizarre coating. Camouflage. The wood was lashed to the sides, encasing the hull as a custom second shell.

Standing on the bank, at the base of a gangway that looked about half as sturdy and twice as dusty as a stick of chalk, was Osiris. His arms were folded, and despite his stern stature it was somewhat of a comfort to Aidan to see his friend retain the same impassive, protective nature he'd grown to know.

Kaya and Enyart boarded the gangway immediately, while Aidan paused at its base and regarded the ship for a few moments, with the wood's aged creases and protruding knots creaking in protest with every slight jostling of the water. He glanced up at Osiris, and noticed the gryphon looking back.

Osiris growled, "Not how I anticipated you seeing it."

The fox peered around the gangway at the boards. Much of it looked like driftwood.

"How is it attached?"

A breeze swept by, ruffling the gryphon's wings; Aidan couldn't tell if he was more irritated by that or his question, but even Osiris' mild frustration was a significant degree more terrifying than the usual sentiment.

"Lashed around the hull with cables."

Osiris must have seen Aidan's eyes widen because he immediately looked away in exasperation at the fox's response.

"Cables? How do you fly?"

Osiris threw out a rumbling sigh. "This is why I could have done with more than a few days' notice to prepare for your arrival."

Aidan laughed, shrugging incredulously. "I mean, I only saw it yesterday, as far as I'm concerned. It still works, right?"

Osiris shook his head with closed eyes. "It does not fly in its current outfit. But overall it even has some improvements, in fact. The maiden voyage was a much more intense and dangerous effort than we thought it would be."

An awkward silence descended between them, which Aidan aborted with a click of his tongue. "Do you at least have an emergency release system?"

Osiris' sigh was enough to signal the negative.

"All right. I'll design one for you." He turned to the gangway, then spun immediately back round, pointing a claw at his old friend. "And I promise it won't affect the aesthetics or aerodynamics, all right? It'll be secure and fast."

Osiris shook his head and dismissed him with a wave. "Fine, whatever you want. But we shall discuss it at sea, or else be late."

Aidan mounted the gangway, trying to keep his eye on the path ahead and not let his mind linger on the platform's unsteadiness. He felt Osiris' heavy footfalls behind him and increased pace, darting onto the deck in seconds. Osiris hauled the plank up and cast it alongside the railing, then marched to the sterncastle. Aidan almost had to run to match his speed, and the interior blurred past as they mounted the stairs to the navigation room. Even at speed he could see some of the additions but had no time to study them. It was more detailed, stronger, weathered. The urge to stop and run his claws over it was immense, but the pursuit of his friend was stronger.

They finally entered the flight deck, and for the first time Aidan saw the splendour of the ship from where Osiris conducted his journeys. The captain swivelled a golden horn to face him and bellowed into it.

"All of you, prepare to sail."

From below came sudden movement, and crew members emerged from their stations to operate the sails. The ship rocked as the anchor rumbled into its socket, and in a few short moments the ship began to drift to its course. Aidan watched in heightening wonder the landscape shift around them, and felt the inertia impress on his body.

"This is exhilarating!"

A modest laugh swelled in Osiris' chest. "You say this after I personally flew you to Arete?"

Aidan flustered. "Well, I mean, I just, the ship is so big!"

"You built it."

"Barely," he scoffed. "Teratai and Elysser did most of it. *And* it wasn't moving then," he exclaimed, pressing his paws to the window. "It felt like a building. Now it's something new."

Osiris smirked, a wistful spark in his eye. "You should have felt it fly. We would have needed to peel you from the ceiling."

They broke free of the river mouth and began a wide, slow arc to the left. The compass on Osiris' control deck twitched and swung accordingly. Once Osiris was confident in their heading, he barked into the horn once more.

"Lerris, to the helm."

A sleek fossa bounded up the stairway and saluted the captain, then took hold of the wheel.

Osiris tapped the compass. "Keep to this bearing for twenty leagues, then bear twenty degrees north-west."

"Aye, sir."

Osiris flicked his head towards the lower levels, and Aidan followed. Now walking at a steadier pace, he could see the relief on the wall. They seemed to tell a story of sorts, in abstract design with many geometric lines and shapes. He could see figures, landscapes, and further along, the broken plates covering something cataclysmic.

"A history," Osiris murmured, "in case there was nobody left to recant it but us."

Pain bled through Aidan's skull; he closed an eye and held his paw to it to try and quell it, but seeing Kaya and Enyart on the deck ahead, he withdrew, opting instead to bear it in the hope it subsided of its own accord.

The Coriolis' first level below deck was now furnished with rows of golden cannons, their barrels stowed behind locked hatches. Lining the walls above them were great metal rods angled towards a massive scaffold-like rail set at the very bow, and either side of this he saw dormant engines attached to the same ball lightning generators he'd demonstrated to Elysser just before the Leviathan arrived.

"It's a warship."

"Once, as we needed," Osiris rumbled. "Now it is merely cloaked, and has not seen combat in many decades."

Aidan let out a bitter laugh. "Well, that's some comfort, I suppose…"

Aidan's paws slipped around each other, a heaviness again seeping into his chest. He'd hoped to be part of all of these journeys and discoveries, and in what felt like a day it had all vanished. This routine must be so heavily ingrained in Osiris, his presence was probably inconsequential now.

"I really missed a lot."

There was silence for a time, broken only by the slow tilting of the boat, the rising of the water against it, and the wooden shell creaking and clunking in reciprocity.

"I cannot deny that," Osiris said sombrely. "But you will have to accept what cannot be undone. Even though the world is new, and growing, we have been chasing the shadows of the old one for many years."

Aidan glanced round. "How so?"

"This Senate hearing is important for many reasons. Your timing, in fact… is somewhat of an omen."

Aidan glanced to Kaya, who gave Osiris a grim look.

The gryphon's voice lowered. "We were not the only survivors."

Aidan had never seen a city as busy as Sinédrion. Even when Nazreal was at its most populous, it never had as many conjoining cultures as this sprawling cityscape did, with such foundations that history seeped through its every stone. A state of constant run and bustle, an eminence and purpose coursed through its streets and the walls of its buildings. *This* was what he'd anticipated Nazreal becoming, but to see it now was exhausting.

They had left the Coriolis at the closest inlet, which was still a considerable distance away, and had travelled inland via carriage again, drawn by the lithe reptilian Theriasaurs. He would have taken all of the city's rich visuals and intricacies more to heart if he wasn't so preoccupied. Something burned at his chest, and felt it would twist from under his skin at any moment. Pulling up alongside the Senate building, with its incredible dome and entrances flanked by companies of guards, did nothing to set him at ease. Even Enyart seemed alerted to his energy and regarded him a little more warmly.

The attendants smartly pulled open the door, giving each of them a bow as they disembarked. The sweeping, sloped ceiling loomed over them like the lid of a hungry box trap and channelled the wind away, leaving an eerie stillness just before the door. With his tight robes feeling even tighter on his neck, chest, and ribs, Aidan was sure the aerodynamics helped Representatives stay presentable in their entrances, but it reminded him too much of the empty, infinite quiet of Nazreal's tomb. For the third time in what to him was as many years, he entered the already fast-flowing current of a deep and unknown world, in anticipation of a great crisis about to unfold. He steadied his breaths, and kept pace just behind Kaya's left shoulder.

Dignitaries swept by in opposite directions, some talking, others stoic, all marching along the padded carpets as if they were the only ones who existed. Aidan spied an approaching possum with a necklace of bright crystals in a fan pattern around her neck and leant in close to Kaya.

"Does she know, is she-?"

"No, and say nothing."

"Isn't that irresponsible?"

"Better to have them treated as a treasure, guarded and seldom revealed, than set a scare that brings further power dynamics into the equation. We have more to worry about than a firecracker in someone's earrings."

They reached a set of eminent doors, already open, behind which lay a slowly-filling auditorium. Enyart gave them a bow at the door and hung behind.

"Personal guards are not permitted to enter," he said ruefully, in response to Aidan's quizzical look.

"Ah. I'm sorry."

"This is not a plea for sympathy. I'll be here when you return."

Aidan nodded, respectfully, despite feeling Enyart

would sooner prefer to have his tail plucked off than give Aidan space in coveted authority and proximity to Kaya. Politeness was to be his shield and best attempt at peace, however.

The amphitheatre had been built from sparkling, pristine stone that glinted in the light from the domed window above, while wooden benches gleamed with thick coats of varnish. Embossed leather covers lined the seats and ornate, glass-housed torches hung from wooden posts above them.

The auditorium was about half-full when they entered and made their way to their section of the bench, on one of the upper levels to the left. Armrests at intervals indicated the allocations for each sovereign, some bigger than others. Xayall was among several small sets of seats, while the levels below held wider benches. Instinctively Aidan kept thinking he'd see Dhalen, and could do nothing to kill the expectation that each new entrant to the room would be a face he recognised from Nazreal. Osiris refused to attend, affirming that Arete was dead, and his presence would only antagonise and detract from the matters at hand.

"I have no land to represent. My place is no longer of talking but of doing, and that in itself being far beyond the sight of others," was his edict. And, from what Osiris had told them on the voyage over, it was even more imperative he kept hidden.

The delegates milled briefly around their seats to a murmur of activity, until a coarse-furred badger with strict eyes entered the podium below, flanked by two deer, a cheetah, and a stoat. The congregation quickly sorted itself to sit, and the badger rapped a gavel on the table before him.

"Representatives of the Senate," Tyrone began, "please

rise and state your attendance for record of this session."

In turn, each sovereign and member stood and declared their name and for whom they were attending. There were more attendees than provinces, but still more nations than Aidan had anticipated. Once the last had given their address and they had been recorded by the stoat, who had to push his glasses back up his nose every time he sniffed (and apparently had some kind of cold, making this a common action), the badger gave a crescendoing cough and rolled open the large scroll in front of him.

"Members of the Senate, the first order of this session is a request for membership. As per our rules, the prospective member sovereign is not granted access into these halls in an official capacity until the current Senate has agreed to their presence and admission. However, The Senate is permitted to interview an elected delegate in order to ascertain their capacity to adhere to the governance and contribute effectively to our confederacy. If you have prepared your questions, we shall begin."

Aidan dug his claws into his robes, staring at the doorway to the far left, where two attendants gripped the handles in preparation.

"Enter," Tyrone boomed.

The doors swung open, and a set of hushed whispers bristled around the room. Aidan's stomach lurched.

Striding into the room, wings part shredded, dressed in charcoal armour that seemed to both reflect and absorb the light around it, came the dark red creature. Yellow eyes scanned the room, and a long tail flicked sharply behind him.

The dragon straightened to his full height, head high,

and rested his claws in his belt. His scales had greyed around the edges, he was covered in small scrapes and nicks, and at least for now his movement seemed slowed by his sheer increased muscle mass, but it was unmistakably him.

Kaya gave Aidan a sideways glance. "Was Osiris right?"

He nodded. "That's him."

Tyrone glanced about, trying to pinpoint the sources of the whispers, which seemed to die out wherever he cast his stern gaze.

"You come before us to seek membership in our chambers," Tyrone barked, reviewing Fulkore with the same dismissive scrutiny he did the rest of the room. "State your name and sovereign."

"Fulkore Crawn, of the nation of Dhraka."

"What do you seek to gain as a member of the Senate?"

"Knowledge, and fair treatment for my people."

"What will you contribute to us?"

Fulkore's eyes flicked to the badger. "We are a nation with a long history. We have resources available for trade and a passage around our coastline that we are willing to open up."

Aidan leant forwards, cupping his muzzle in his paws as a burning cold rushed through him. More questions were presented to Fulkore in turn, which he answered with perfunctory, sometimes vague, responses.

"It's too easy," he hissed. "They don't know anything."

Kaya's back was against the chair. "If they're inducted to the Senate they will be held to its standards, and have sanctions imposed. It should be easier to observe them."

"Or easier for him to take advantage of the system."

Kaya watched Aidan sink further into his paws, closer to

the wooden railing separating him from the edge of the balcony.

The chamber reached a lull as questions subsided.

"Is that all?" Fulkore asked, a shadow of a grin appearing at the corner of his scaly mouth.

"What is your military capability?" came a booming voice. Aidan was on his feet, fists clenched.

Fulkore's eyes narrowed. He paused, eyeing Aidan with intense scrutiny.

"Minimal," he replied.

"So your armour's ceremonial, is it?"

Fulkore's head lowered slightly as his impassive demeanour stiffened and a glower appeared in his eyes. "In part. It has been in my family for generations."

"What kept you from the Senate previously?" Aidan continued, his face barely restrained from a snarl.

Fulkore raised his head. His vertebrae cracked audibly. "We… underwent a great sickness that kept us underground for many years. Now we have seen the world anew, we wish to gain accord with those around us."

"What motivated this change?"

Fulkore's eyes flared. "Change?" he hummed, with a blossoming grin. "What do you mean?"

Aidan froze.

Fulkore spread his arms wide, gesturing to the auditorium. "There has been no change. We have *always* been interested in the greater good of a world we could be part of. We were simply…" he licked his lips, fixing Aidan in a knowing, piercing glare. "…prevented."

The dragon extended a hand to Aidan. "If you will, introduce yourself. I didn't catch your sovereign."

Aidan stammered. "I…"

Tyrone bashed his gavel several times on the desk. "This is not in accordance," he barked. "This time will be for questions given in their proper format or not at all, and it is certainly not an opportunity to broadcast personal grievances."

Fulkore bowed his head. "Of course, Your Honour." He shot Aidan a final glance before turning back to the door. "If the questioning is done, I believe I must exit. Is that correct protocol?"

"It is," Tyrone muttered, scribbling on the parchment.

The dragon marched out, wings swelling and teeth bared in a rancorous smile.

"It is now time for Representatives to deliberate, and then the vote shall be conducted."

Aidan sat heavily down in the chair, pulling at his collar.

"Sit back," Kaya implored, pulling him against the chair to straighten him. He closed his eyes.

"It'll happen again," he whispered darkly. "It's just as before."

"You can't predict that. I will not let my sovereign, or anyone's, fall to ruin." She stood and began an address with someone across the balcony.

Around him the room faded to muffled noise. In a sort of stupor he relived the timeline that brought him here, all of the moments he could have chosen a different path to make something better. Beside him, Kaya felt somewhat like Elysser, albeit colder, making her an even more arrant reminder of what he failed to protect.

"Against," she asserted.

His attention snapped back to the room. The vote.

Tyrone took down the last few tallies, and cleared his throat.

"Decisions like this do not need to be unanimous, but discrepancies should be taken into account. However, as it stands, the current vote is twenty-six in favour, three abstentions, and two against. If there are no changes to be made, they shall be confirmed and recorded, and Dhraka shall be inaugurated at the next session."

Aidan dragged his clawtips down his face, letting out a low, anguished growl.

They exited the Senate chamber as quickly as they could, curtailed by the meandering impediment of the other Representatives walking at an interminably slow pace, and with such obstruction as to make the aisles impassable.

"If I had my staff, I could just," he made a gesture to demonstrate the ground opening up under the two pine martens in front of them.

"I feel you," she sighed, "but let's get out of here without causing a diplomatic incident."

"*You're* a diplomatic incident," he muttered.

"Don't tempt me."

Enyart met them swiftly, with a look that set Aidan on edge.

"To the carriage, immediately," the panther warned. As soon as they broke into the corridor that encircled the chamber's lower level, they heard a rising commotion behind them. With a quick glance Aidan saw Fulkore marching through the crowd, directly to them, with opposing pedestrians no obstacle to him as they bounced off his armour or brushed under his wings. His eyes were hungry, focused. They quickened their pace, rounding the corridor far enough to get out of his sight.

Aidan grabbed Kaya's paw and held it tightly, then pulled both her and Enyart against the building's outer wall. Enyart drew back to punch him for a moment, but Aidan's determined, glowing eyes forced him to stay the action.

In seconds, the wall folded in front of them, and they were outside.

"What are you doing?" Kaya hissed.

Aidan released her paw. The crystals in Kaya's bracelet shimmered into dormancy, and he let out a deep, shaky sigh.

"We need to hurry."

"Practicing resonance in the middle of the Senate could start a *war*!"

He shot her a steely glare. "There will be worse if we let him anywhere near us, or Nazreal. Go!"

At heightened pace, they returned to the carriage and set it in motion immediately. Enyart kept watch, paw on his sword, as they rattled along the roads, and did not relent until they arrived at the Coriolis.

Once their voyage was set, Osiris followed his companions below, where Aidan perched on the edge of a low bunk, with Enyart and Kaya standing in front of him. His eyes met Osiris' as soon as he stepped into the room.

"Dhraka made it to the Senate."

Osiris nodded gravely. "As I suspected they might. I am sorry that we did not do enough."

"He hadn't changed," Aidan shuddered. "If anything… he was worse than before. I think he recognised me. He didn't get close, but he tried." He ran his hands over his muzzle and groaned. "How did he survive? Wasn't he in the

Leviathan?"

With a shake of his head, Osiris gave a grim recount of his story. "He was with his own machines inside the Dhrakan highlands; the Colossus and Gargantua, likely in preparation to advance on Arete. They were mostly buried in the initial burst, and together we thought we destroyed and sealed them away for good. When Kaya's grandmother warned me of the dragons' resurfacing, he had not been present. When I heard of the meeting today, I had hoped it would be someone new."

"What do we do? Be grateful it isn't Sarr?" Aidan scoffed.

Osiris folded his arms. "Do you see my rapiers?" He nodded towards a rack on the wall of his cabin. Six thin-bladed swords, in vastly different styles but all with shining silver blades, golden findings, black inlay, and red gemstones, hung on its rails. "Each of those has a different mechanism designed to inflict the most harm on a Dhrakan assailant. Designed by Elysser and Teratai, after our... incursions following Nazreal's destruction."

"When you said Dhraka survived, I... hoped they'd be different. A whole race can't possibly be so indoctrinated for hate."

"We have all waged crimes against them," Osiris said spiritlessly. "I tried to lock them within their own volcanoes. For a long time it worked, but they found their perseverance much like myself, and you. The damage may now be irreparable, and our lives once again inescapably entwined."

Aidan rocked to his feet.

"Take me back to Nazreal. Right now."

Chapter Twenty-Five

"*I only saw Fulkore for a short while, on the Gargantua and again in Nazreal. He seemed vicious.*"

"*That, he was.*"

"*And you fought further with him, after Nazreal's fall?*"

"*That... is a story for another time.*"

The desert sand once again blew around Aidan's hind paws. The sky roared with the strength of the winds, a ceaseless, harrowing cry that seemed to scorn the ground it battered. The fox looked up at the mesa with its edges rough and haggard, and felt he was looking into a mirror. Far above them was the hole he'd emerged from. It reached to him even from here, as if it had impaled a cold anchor into the small of his back.

"Take me up."

From behind, Osiris crossed his arms in front of Aidan's chest and flew him up to the mesa's gaping mouth. Upon landing, Aidan stood uneasily for a while, staring into the tunnel that vanished into the inky depths beyond. He could see it even from here, every rock and crystal outcrop, as if it was part of his own body. Osiris departed to bring Kaya and Enyart, and for a second Aidan was alone again just as when Osiris had left before, facing the city. His city, but no longer full of what had made it his in the first place. His hopes, his friends, his world. What it contained of him now was pain and fear, synchronised in his grief over all he had lost, and could yet lose.

Wingbeats and footfalls behind him brought him away from his recession to the darkness. Kaya was next to him.

"This is the closest I've ever been," she whispered.

"I'm surprised, for how much you studied it."

"Your journal was very explicit in its construction… and Elysser's in its danger. My mother saw it, only once. She said it was like the enormous grave of something that refused to die."

Aidan stared into the cave. "She was right. I want to seal it away, close off my exit."

She looked to him, then to the darkness ahead, and stepped forwards. "I'm here for too short a time to be held back by fear." She turned back to him. "Show me the world you created, Aidan. Even just once, before it disappears forever."

He froze for a second, caught by the ardour of her eyes. Reminiscent of Elysser, but completely new, independent, and powerful in their own right. For the first time he saw Kaya as something more than an unfamiliar copy of something dear, and as someone new. Together they broached the archway of shadows.

Nazreal was in a strange, unsettling flux, the product of

an interrupted termination, both dead and alive. Twisted into something that barely resembled what it began as, yet filled with a terrifying, dormant energy that slept just below every surface. It was an undercurrent that would sweep you to oblivion's depths, a pile of embers with a heart that would burst into a roiling flame given the slightest provocation.

Aidan and Kaya trod pathways coated in the soft blue dust that prickled and fizzed as they stepped over it, in harmony with their resonance abilities. Their eyes glowed softly in the ambience. Further behind echoed the steps of Osiris and Enyart navigating the warped stones.

Kaya's gaze moved from far to near, studying all she could. She ran her claws over the stonework, brushing sputtering clouds of dust from reliefs and carvings. She twirled rivulets of crystal between her fingers, which shone as they crumbled and plumed glowing blue smoke that disappeared into the silent air.

"There's something… very beautiful about it."

Aidan looked bitterly aside. "All I see is a failure, a monument to overambition and blind ignorance. It took so little greed to end the lives of so many." He picked up a stone, a splinter from a wall next to them that had turned to rubble. It glistened, sparkled, even under the crust of fine soot.

"It has to stop. While Dhraka is still here, Nazreal is a liability and we all remain in danger."

"It didn't seem he knew where we were from. We have time."

He gave a deprecating frown. "Only till the next Senate meeting, when you'll have to introduce yourself. He'll be here within minutes."

"If they've taken this long to move, why do you believe they'll act so quickly?"

A scornful laugh hissed from his mouth. "He wouldn't reappear without a motive. He needs something, either an opportunity or a resource, and it will ultimately come at great cost." He sighed. "I gave him, and Raikali, so many allowances. Fulkore even seemed vaguely placatable at first, but they were too driven, kept sabotaging everyone and themselves for the slightest advancement in their self-perception. I tried to see their best, and was met with their worst. And I don't believe in inherent evil." He dropped the stone and kicked it into a crevice, where it rattled to places unknown. "I feel for those left under Fulkore's rule. I had wondered if this place could again be shared, until I saw him on the Senate floor. That cannot happen."

She slid her digits under her bracelets, rubbing them gently as if nursing a burn or an itch.

"You feel it too?" he asked quietly.

She nodded. "Such a strange energy. It's–"

"Volatile."

She pierced him with a look for interrupting. "Interesting, how raw it is."

"This is what the Zenith used to feel like, before Nazreal took its place. Before…" he trailed off, "…everything."

She tilted her head towards him, the gem on her forehead radiating faintly. "Do you want to stay, honestly?"

"I'm sorry?"

"I cannot hold you to a place that causes you such pain, but… your help in monitoring and maintaining Nazreal, and our efforts to keep it secret, would be immeasurably appreciated. You know more about this than anyone ever will. You could change everything for us."

He began to nod, but violently clutched his head again. She started towards him, but he dismissed her with the paw holding his stave.

"Do you hear that?" he groaned through heavy breaths.

Her ears twitched, she looked about for a sign. "I don't."

"Just as well," he grimaced. He flicked his head, as if trying to shake something from his ear.

"It… Nazreal remembers. It could hear the world, the people, screaming, trying to flee…" His paws began to shake; he clenched his eyes shut. "I didn't see any of it, but it lives in me somehow. There's a break in the world, a scar that won't heal, and it's in me." He looked to her, as a glowing tear rolled from his right eye. "I feel it… in everyone."

He took in a sharp breath and forced a smile. "I'm sorry. We came to seal this place off, I shouldn't be…" he paused, as a slew of words he wanted to say swirled before him. '*Here*' was what kept edging closer to his tongue, but he could not take that step.

"Speak, Aidan," she stressed. "It will wear you out and break you if you let it take root."

"You make it sound so easy," he scorned. "Within me… in this place, is the deep, infinite memory of destruction, death. I felt the fear of the planet crawling through my bones, wrapping around my mind. Do you know how big the world is? Have you ever seen inside it, the roaring, raging nothingness at its heart? I see it… when I sleep, when I wake, hear it in the wind through the trees.

You haven't seen what we lost, the life that should have been. It kills me again every single day. And… I…" he tilted his muzzle back to look at the black cave above them. "It stares back into me. I wanted… I want, sometimes… to join it. Because I can't escape how much of this was my fault. But I… I know they wouldn't want me to give up." He balled his fist. "This pain is mine. My penance and my duty. I will not inflict this burden on anyone else. It is… too great."

"Do not disrespect me by believing I am not strong enough to hear your feelings, Aidan," Kaya replied, quietly, but with bitter consternation. "I am an Empress, not a child. I may never know the scope of your pain, but for your sake and mine, and the greater world's, let me help you. Do not crusade to your own destruction out of scorn for a world that has long since survived thanks to the kindness and determination of those within it. I will never stop trying to save Eeres in any way I can, even if you believe diplomacy is worthless. You know how to do it in ways I can never accomplish. The secrets within you are dark, vast, and sinister, but if you die protecting them, the world will be destroyed again. You, the one person who holds the key to protecting it…" She took his paw. "Don't turn your back on it."

Aidan flinched slightly at her touch, then relaxed into her grip. He collapsed against her, holding her tightly.

"Thank you, Kaya."

They stood together in the cold, sparkling city, and for a time, Aidan felt a small sense of peace. He knew the darkness existed around them, and within him still, but he could see the smallest sliver of himself existing beside it.

From the shadows emerged Osiris and Enyart. Aidan withdrew from Kaya, a little sheepishly, wiping his eyes. When he stepped back he saw a small fleck of blue under her eye too, but she wiped it away within moments.

"I think we have what we need," she breathed. "Are you ready?"

Aidan nodded.

Together they walked back to the hewn archway. At its edge, Aidan swept the blade of his stave across the ground. The wall below them rose up and around, creating an alcove that hid the opening from view. Then, striding back into the cave itself, Aidan placed the staff against Nazreal's broken, cobbled path. From the floor grew a staunch doorway that pushed the tunnel's ceiling higher. Crystal tendrils snaked jerkily up and across the stone, embedding itself in its surface. Aidan lifted the stave, still glowing, and pressed it into the door. It sunk inwards, making a perfect impression into the centre. The crystal shone brightly, then light careened along the veins and vanished beyond. Aidan's eyes were shut tight, his legs shuddering. He pushed himself hard against the door for a few more seconds. The light ebbed to a soft glow, then to nothing, leaving them in the dim alcove. He stumbled round and fell back against the door, pulling at his collar.

"It's done," he rasped, barely keeping hold of his stave. "If anyone tries to enter without this, the walls will disintegrate. Despite my reappearance, it should be to the world as if Nazreal remains a whisper of legend, and nothing more."

Osiris came to his friend's side and supported him, walking him to the cave's outer level. Aidan gave a weak laugh. "That's how the Coriolis will be secured, by the way."

The gryphon tensed. "A self-destruct mechanism?"

"No!" Aidan cried. "No, no no. It'll blast the wood off with pressurised air."

"All right, good. Because if that happened, even as its captain, I would not be the one going down with the ship."

"Noted."

Chapter Twenty-Six

"That was why Raikali needed to channel me to open the city. With her powers warped, she couldn't use the crystals without breaking them apart, which would have destroyed Nazreal."

"I am sorry you ever had to deal with any of this, Faria. It was our war to finish."

"It's fine. Like I said when we first met, I won't stand by while a war is fought in my name. If others can take on these struggles… it's only fitting that I do to."

It took Aidan some time to recover. He drifted in and out of sleep, while Enyart, Kaya and Osiris took turns monitoring him. He awoke to a different face each time, which made things confusing when he fell asleep mid-conversation and awoke with a start to try and continue it to someone with no memory of the first part. Several times he woke in the dead of night in a cold sweat, shivering, his breath hacking from him. Over time he subsided to a regular rest schedule, which for him was relatively little, as the resonance energies kept him awake in the early morning hours, much like Kaya, whom he met several times wandering the halls of the Tor. While they were tentative about conversing at first, unsure of each other, they cooperated well, and under Osiris' guidance, Xayall expanded further, generating prosperous farmland and fisheries. Talk between the foxes often turned to shared experiences with the crystals, and inevitably, how to deal with the shadow of the Dhrakan presence.

Aidan excused himself from being present in the Senate chamber but still attended with Kaya, listening covertly through the wall when waiting outside. True to his irregularities in Nazreal, Fulkore did not always attend himself, usually sending a second in his place. They seemed to be asking for access to libraries and arable land. Even though Dhraka had rich grassland from near the volcanoes, it had very little wood, and their supplies of fuel were close to exhausted. Lands like Andarn, and a large swathe to the South of it, were abundant with forests and trees, and Kyrryk had a copious supply of renewable plant life that was of excellent use in weapon staves and small-scale construction. Dhraka seemed to take particular interest in them, despite being on the other side of the continent. It was difficult to question their motives from the outset, and with Senate meetings only every few months, with targeted correspondence between sovereigns in the interim, it made monitoring them without direct communication, and hence arousing suspicion, difficult.

Aside from learning the structure of the world as best he could, over the months, Aidan found some solace in the gardens of the Tor, where he built a small memorial to his friends and family. The modest-sized stone stood in a sandy base atop a set of stairs, similar to the obelisk at which Dhalen had mourned Oakhe. Directly in front of it was a smooth stone bowl for placing flowers or burning tributes, and the entire structure was surrounded by a low wooden fence with hooks for lamps, and a trellis for flowers to grow over the top of it. Aidan had to be careful constructing it all, pretending to use traditional tools, so next to him was a leather bundle of stonemason equipment. Nestled in one of its pockets was a small silver rod, about a foot long, with a shard of crystal at the end. He held it as if it were a chisel, and slowly ran it across the stone. Letters morphed into the obelisk's front, and the area on which they were carved shifted out slightly to create a fake plaque. With another pass of the crystal wand, the stone shimmered; both the letters and the frame were now polished and in a different hue to the surrounding stone, such that the letters shouldn't be obscured by weathering or debris.

He stood back, holding the rod at his hip. A soft wind rustled the trees around him, and although he knew the flurry was coincidental, he still hoped it was a sign of contentment from those he missed as he read the inscription.

To those we lost. May our memories keep their love present and eternal.

He gave the stone a deep, long bow, tucked the crystal rod surreptitiously into the leather bundle, and descended to the stone pathway that led around the gardens.

As he traversed the path, he saw Kaya and Enyart approaching. He gave them both a polite nod, not wishing to impose if they weren't seeking him directly. Enyart looked content to continue, but Kaya wavered, and met him with a gentle smile.

"Is it done?" she queried, leaning ever so slightly to peer over his shoulder in case it was within sight.

"It is," he said, with a reserved, tired smile. "It's not the tribute I could have given but... for now, it's something."

"You could have put it closer to the mausoleum," she suggested. "I'm sure we could find a way of moving it."

He shook his head. "No, I'm... I've had my share of tombs for now. I'd rather remember them in a place of life than death."

She nodded, and hesitated, a breath caught in her chest. Just as Aidan went to ask her if she was all right, she turned to her bodyguard.

"Mai, I'm sorry to ask this; could you prepare the council chamber for us, and make sure Osiris is there too? I want to make sure we're up to date with developments regarding Kyrryk."

With reticence, Enyart brought his fist to his chestplate and bowed, a stiff and punctuated moment which he finished with a disapproving eye directed at Aidan, then fleeted away through the gardens. She gestured to the path back from where Aidan had come, and they began a slow walk together.

"While I don't wish to presume, what plans have you now the memorial is complete?"

He rubbed his neck idly. "Well, I may work on some small carving projects, or plants... did you have anything in mind?"

She laboured on the answer for a time, her whiskers twitching as thoughts parsed in her. "I had meant... in the long-term. I know Xayall has meaning to you given the need for Nazreal's protection, but I don't want you to feel held hostage by habit or…" She laced her digits together and twisted them against each other, looking distracted. "…or otherwise."

An anxious swell rose in Aidan's stomach. The paw rubbing his neck moved to his shoulder, which he began squeezing subconsciously.

"Even for not having seen the world yet I'm certain this is the best place to stay, so I didn't have plans to leave. I may join Osiris on a venture or two, maybe finally see Skyria, but…"

She took in a sharp, impatient breath. "I just know this isn't your world. I would rather you be here to make of it what you want, and not out of some self-imposition." She directed him a sharp look. "Because I know that habit well. I'm sure it resides in you as much as it does in me."

Aidan looked down, somewhat caught out. "Well, I can only choose my duty based on what I know, but I appreciate your consideration. This isn't where I'd intended to be, but… it's an easy trap to love retrospectively, isn't it? To think the world was so much better and larger back then than it is now. I can't deny my purpose feels… well, I'm not even sure of my purpose except as custodian of forbidden information. Maybe you should keep me in the library," he said with a laugh.

Her stony face sent him back to looking at his paws, now turning the leather bundle over between them.

"I knew so much more back then, but I was still naive. The world was a canvas to cast a future onto however I wanted. I met people who could do the same. Now they're gone, and I'm…"

She glanced expectantly to him, her tail curling round her ankles.

"I'm sorry," he flustered. "I shouldn't... be saying this. It's inappropriate, and I would insult you."

Her laugh rang in the wind. "I don't doubt it," she clipped. "But, I had hoped we passed the barriers of candour some time ago." They stopped as they reached the memorial. She wrung her paws again for a moment while gazing at the stone, and the trellis that covered it. "If I might ask," she said quietly, "had you given thought to your name, as you're here? Were you intending to keep it, or...?"

Aidan shrugged. "Well... aside from my body, it's all I have left."

She gave him an admonishing look, and pointed at the memorial. "You have your memories, knowledge, your quest which you just described to me. These are more than trivial. For all it brought, you're still the architect of Nazreal."

"That isn't a proud legacy," he exhaled.

"You can't escape it, as much as you may want to. Despite how it fell, you constructed it with noble cause and great skill. What caused its entombment should never be forgotten, but it's up to you to decide whether your name carries too much of a risk for you in this time."

He thought for a long time, listening to the wind in the trees, staring between the bundle in his paws, in which he could see the glint of the crystal rod's silver handle, and the memorial, in which he could feel the shadow of his old world.

"I don't know."

She shifted nervously. Her tail stiffened as she took in a deep breath. "Because... if for no other reason than as an alias… I would offer you my name."

"Aidan Phiraco. I…" he swayed a little and his cheeks felt hot. He pulled at his sleeves. "Are… you're not proposing, are you?"

She paced slightly, moving from hind paw to hind paw, her tail flicking in abashment, the first time Aidan had seen her not completely at ease with her focus. "No, I mean… I have to consider that resonators are rare to come by and there's an expectation of me as Empress and Nazreal's guardian. I… I wanted to know if you had aspirations to start a family, if you even wanted to be part of this world to begin with…" she rubbed her fists, looking flustered. "…this was not how I intended this proposition to go."

Aidan held up his paws, pads outwards. "It's alright. I had expected that I would, eventually, I just… didn't know when. Being inside an exploding city tends to destroy your focus a bit."

She rubbed her forehead. "I've no doubt. With everything you've been through… can you still have children?"

He froze again, feeling his heart pounding in his head. "Er… I haven't… I don't know."

They stood at the memorial for a time, neither one looking each other, until she turned to him and their eyes met again.

"Are you busy tonight?" she rushed.

Aidan tensed. "Isn't this immensely against tradition? You're an Empress, and I'm, I'm just, Enyart would eviscerate me in seconds."

She swallowed, and looked down to the floor, speaking quickly. "I have many duties; some of them will extend past tradition if it means a better future. Enyart's right to be protective, but sometimes his focus is a little... limited. I have to consider things far beyond that, and take opportunities as they arrive." she sighed, looking up to the clouds breezing across the pale blue sky. "Please trust me when I say I've considered this, that I'm not so lonely in my station that I'd advance anyone who came close to me with a minimum of compatibility. And as suitors go, you would... you would fulfil that duty."

Aidan chewed his next sentence for a few seconds, then mumbled it aside. "I mean... I hope I'll be more than a duty."

She stepped past him, and said surreptitiously, "If you do well enough, a duty can be a pleasure."

She stepped quickly away, leaving Aidan blinking in shock.

Chapter Twenty-Seven

"I didn't... is that really how I was seen, as a duty?"

"Do not sell yourself short. Children often are conceived or discussed as such, and grow to be infinitely more. I am sure Kaya would have been ecstatic to see what you have achieved."

"I wish I could have spent more time with her. I don't remember how she died. I remember being carried in by the nurse, and seeing her in the dark, and holding her, but... I didn't understand then. Can... can you tell me that?"

"I will. I think it is your father's last secret, and perhaps his hardest to bear."

Pattering pawsteps echoed in the Tor, accompanied by light, animated giggles and squeals as the three-year-old Faria ran circles around her father and spun behind the flowing curtains of their enormous bedroom, while her mother signed documents at the doorway. Radiant evening sunlight poured through the wide, arched balcony entrance, and particles of dust floated through the rays like miniature stars, swirled into cascading disarray by Faria's energetic game. Leaning against the wall, in the reddening shadows, was Mai. The panther's expression had softened with the presence of Faria, but he still held a stern discountenance, emphasising his protective duties as an absolute priority. He and Aidan were at least on speaking terms now, given their joint fondness for Kaya, and now Faria as well.

It had been the first day Aidan had felt this energetic in a while. He had been kept to a bed or chair almost constantly in recent months, as he grew tired and wan. He put it down to exhaustion over looking after Faria all day while Kaya was at Senate meetings and covering Representative duties, but his ability to stay upright was slowly decreasing. He pushed through it for the sight of his daughter, and to counteract the exhaustion that Kaya felt herself in conducting her duties at all hours of the day. The compromise had been that she worked in their bedroom some of the week, so that they could all be together. Today had been all but perfect so far.

"Daddy," the young Princess chimed, "do I have your eyes, or Mummy's eyes?"

Aidan smiled, following her trail around the room. "You have your own eyes. A gift from us both."

She giggled and thrust herself back into the chase.

Kaya gave a thankful nod to the messenger, who saluted and bounded away. She watched Aidan swipe playfully at Faria as she danced and bounded around him, trying to break his pursuit by hiding behind furniture, or throwing pillows at him. He saw her and smiled, and as she smiled back, a pillow hit him in the back of the head.

"Got you!" Faria preened, giggling. Aidan picked up the

feather-filled missile and raised it above his head, taking aim. She squealed and ran to Enyart, grabbing his leg.

"Help meee!" the kit squeaked. Enyart raised an eyebrow in warning to Aidan.

"You better be a good shot, because I'll hit back a lot harder than she does."

Aidan grinned. "You always say that, I've yet to…"

The smile faded from his face. Sound disappeared from the room. The ground seemed to pitch and list in circles. He saw Enyart suddenly reaching towards him, and as he tried to cry out, everything went black.

When he awoke, it was night. He was on his bed, with Kaya sitting next to him. He gently raised his paw and touched her side; she darted round.

"Thank goodness," she sighed. "You were barely breathing."

He swallowed. His throat felt dry and raw. "Ah. Well… can't say I feel great. What… what happened?"

"I was hoping you might tell me," she fretted. "This… is similar to how I lost my parents."

He closed his eyes. "How so?"

"You… understand very few active resonators have survived into their thirties?"

"Gygel did tell me that," he croaked. "I had… hoped to ignore it." He leant up, looking over at where their daughter was sleeping in her bed across the room, separated by a fine gauze partition. "For a while longer, at least."

Kaya's face was severe, and dark as the shadows in the corners of the room. "Do you know why it happens?"

Aidan shook his head.

"It's called crystalline ossification. Essentially, your body is hardening, turning into crystals as a result of continued exposure to its radiation. You saw it in a small part when we were inside Nazreal, the glow in our tears."

Aidan winced. "So... I'll be a crystal statue?" He burst into a coughing fit, and blue flecks once again landed on his paw, this time accompanied with small drops of blood. Faria stirred.

Kaya grimaced dolefully, handing him a towel from their bedside to wipe his paw. "You won't get that far. Your organs will fail and the rest of you will decompose before that happens. It's a reaction to your body's energy, so when there's no energy left to feed on, the process stops."

He pulled himself to a sitting position, rubbing his ribcage. "So... shouldn't I have died in Nazreal?" he rattled. "I felt... the energy there was immeasurable."

She shook her head. "I can't tell you. Sometimes channelling the energy is less damaging than absorbing it, and you may have been surrounded by enough of it that it dissipated along paths of low resistance instead of lingering within you. But..." she took his paw. "...it seems like it caught up with you, and much sooner than most. Under normal circumstances you should be able to live another ten or twenty years."

She pulled a pendant from around her neck; a small prismatic crystal with a spiral cage of silver and gold encircling it, and a small metal orb at the top. She unbuckled the clasp, and held it in her palm. He gently pushed it over with his claw.

"What's this?"

"It's a reservoir, essentially. When you began having your headaches, I was... I began working on a means of trying to collect extra resonance energies that were floating around your body. But over time you seemed to weather them less, and I just… I assumed a little too much about your health, and between Faria and the Senate, I had thought our tiredness was shared. I'm remiss not to have noticed, not to have felt a single worsening change or deepening of your condition. But I had been prepared for this ever since I saw you first recoil in pain."

He stroked the back of her paw. "We adjust to pain when it's constant, and often the change comes so incrementally that we aren't overtly affected until it's too late. Which… I hope this isn't…"

Carefully, she cradled the prism in her paw and touched it to his chest. It glowed softly through the gaps in her fingers.

Her eyes widened, and watered.

"Oh… Aidan, you… This… may be it."

His breathing quickened, but was shallow. "How much can be channelled away?" he rasped.

She shook her head. "This orb is tiny. Even if I were to draw out as much as I could, it would have nowhere else to go, no container. It would have to pass into something bigger, and transfuse you with body and blood that had been overtaken."

They looked to each other desperately.

"Don't," he whispered.

She said nothing, looking at the prism ebbing in her paw.

"Kaya, don't," he repeated, more urgently. "I'm not worth your loss."

"One of us will be gone either way," she wavered, paws

tremoring. "You… you know more of Nazreal's secrets than I can ever hold, can do far more with your resonance than I can dream."

He shook his head as she spoke. "You know what this world needs, how it works; this is where Faria lives. I had my world, and left it. I'll always be a visitor here."

Her eyes were fierce, with a burning, passionate sadness. "You… you will never see your value, will you? You walk into a room with an apology at your lips and your tail between your legs when you have as much right to be here as any of us. We are all here *because* of what you managed. Do you…" she stopped to let a few unsteady breaths escape her. "Do you know when Osiris first told me your story in my childhood, I thought you were one of the strongest creatures that could ever have existed. I read your journal, and Elysser's, over and over again, imagining the world you could have created together. I read their sadness at your loss. I felt it in every page. They spent their life trying to create a world that you may, somehow, see again."

"And now you're here, and… this is it. I'm the one you found. I'm part of their legacy, their tribute to you." She wiped a tear from her muzzle. "They loved you. As I have been lucky to."

She stood up and paced distraitly. "I hoped, if I were ever in that situation, I could make my life worth as much as either of yours, and give even one person a future for the better. I have been privileged. I've had no need for resonance battles or forging entire cities by hand, but that's why I embraced my duty as an Empress, to bring some measure of peace and justice to those under my sovereign, and further afield if I could. When you appeared, after centuries burnt into the stone… I could scarce believe it. The more I saw you escape this past, the more I come to love what they saw in you, what you at one point even saw in yourself."

She sat back down, facing him. "I don't care what you think this world needs. Politics and academia are nothing in the face of true kindness, honesty, and bravery."

Aidan's voice was barely audible as he spoke against his choking cries. "I haven't deserved so many to give so much to me. Can we get to Skyria, can they do anything-?"

She closed her hand over his. "Osiris is already on his way there, and by any normal ship you would die long before we arrive."

She held him tightly as tears rolled down his cheeks.

"If one of us has to stay, I choose you," she said, resolute.

"I don't."

"You never would." Her voice was a quiet mix of admonishment and determination. "Please, don't disrespect me with pity. I am not a child or virgin sacrifice. You know what it is like to lose your world. Faria will see both of us die, sooner rather than later. I'm not the comfort and stability she'll need to get through that and go on to see this is a place worth saving for love, and not just duty."

Aidan rubbed her paws in his, breath rasping.

"What do I need to do?"

She held the crystal tightly. "Just lie back."

He closed his eyes and did so. He felt her press the crystal to his sternum. A second later, he flashed his eyes open and clasped her paw.

"Wait!"

She paused. He could feel her claws shaking, ever so slightly.

"Don't... don't take everything. Don't leave just yet."

She smiled. "I know what I'm doing."

He felt a glow blooming in his chest, then passed out.

He awoke with a start, air rushing into his lungs with a cold freshness he had not experienced in years. He was dizzy, and his limbs still stiff, but his whole body felt lighter and his head clearer. He glanced around through the dimness. The pre-dawn sky lay hidden behind ashen-grey clouds. Next to him sat Kaya on the edge of the bed, squeezing her paws. He shifted next to her, and she gave him a tired, wan smile.

"It... worked?" he said quietly.

She leant into him. "It did. I feel terrible," she said groggily. She pushed herself off from him and cleared her throat, a rattle in her breathing, then walked to Faria and gave her a soft kiss between her ears.

"Come on, Aidan. We've... got a lot to cover."

Aidan shadowed Kaya for the next few weeks, attending every meeting, every study and engagement. She insisted in taking the lead even if she was too tired to speak, but even with her fortitude and the constant use of the crystal pendant, the creeping sickness began to overwhelm her, and before too long she was unable to rise from her bed.

She had just sent an envoy away. Thick curtains were

drawn tightly to mask off headache-inducing light from the afternoon's brightness. Aidan left the candlelit desk, having just sealed several scrolls for dispatch to the Senate, and knelt by Kaya's bedside. Behind him, near the window, Faria slept in her bed. He rested his head on Kaya's lap, stroking her paw in his.

"I'm sorry."

She shook her head. "I told you not to pity me. I anticipated I'd be less tolerant to resonance than you. It's… unfortunate, but this is my choice."

He looked back to the desk for a second, to see if he'd left anything unfinished, then back to her. "Well, I can get–"

Next to him Kaya lay with her eyes closed. Her shallow breathing made her chest rise and fall in short, sharp motions. She clutched at her chest with a trembling paw.

Aidan sprang to his feet and sprinted outside. At the next door along, he skidded to a halt and slammed his paws against it repeatedly.

"Mai!" he yelled "Mai, quickly!"

The door burst open, Enyart's sword was drawn. His face fell when he saw Aidan's desolate expression.

"Get help."

He wasted no time, vanishing down the corridor.

Aidan returned to their bedroom, where he saw Faria had woken and climbed out of her bed to sit next to her mother. She kept trying to rouse her, shaking her shoulders; all Kaya could do in response was wince. Aidan ran quickly to his daughter and scooped her into his arms. "She's sick, love. Just… someone's coming, okay?"

Faria made a distressed whimper, and tried to reach for her mother again. Behind them, a slew of physicians and nurses ran in, led by Enyart. Aidan took Faria and shrank to the back of the room, collapsing into a chair, holding his daughter tightly, as Kaya disappeared behind the frantic mutters of the team.

Enyart came to face him. He stood for some time, looking not at Aidan but somewhere through or beyond him.

"When she told me what she did... I wanted to slaughter you for it," he said eventually. "But knowing this was her will, to protect the world she had made with you, and for young Faria... I have no right to object."

Aidan held Faria tightly. "You have every right to object to an unfair world, Mai. You have every right to yell and scream at every hurt handed to you, or others, and want for better. What we haven't yet been able to change, we should keep trying."

They stayed there for a few hours while the physicians worked to stabilise Kaya. One of the nurses took Faria away to care for her and help take her away from the stress of the room. After even longer, almost into the evening, they managed to get Kaya sitting upright and breathing moderately steadily, at which point they began to depart one by one.

Aidan knew what it meant. They had done all they could.

The nurse carrying Faria returned and handed her to him, then left with a solemn bow. Aidan bounced his daughter a little on the short, but infinite walk to Kaya, as Mai accompanied them.

The Empress opened her eyes and gave a weary smile to them all.

She looked to Mai as Aidan took her paw, and Faria crawled gently beside her. "Thank you… for being here… For all that you've done, Mai."

He bowed his head. "I am the richer for serving you," he said solemnly. "It has been my highest honour to see you grow, flourish, and conduct yourself with the greatest charity I have ever known." He took her other paw and held it to his forehead, descending to his knee. A second later, he stood again. "If you would excuse me, I must prepare."

She nodded. "Thank you, Mai."

He left, and the three foxes sat together on her bed.

Kaya looked to Aidan. Despite her tiredness, the pallor of her fur and now pale lustre in her eyes, she was still as resolute as he had ever seen.

"Don't pity my choice," she said quietly. "I lived in service of my sovereign, and now my family. You can't tell me… you weren't ready for the same… back in Nazrcal."

Aidan swallowed down the lump in his throat. "I don't think I was brave enough to even think I'd die. Let alone… take on the pain of another like this." He gritted his teeth. "I pity the world that wakes without you."

"Such as it did for you. Yet you were strong and kind enough to return."

Her eyes flickered closed. She pulled Faria close to her one last time. "Thank you… I love you both…"

Aidan watched her paws gently fall, and pulled both Kaya and Faria to him tightly, in the hope Faria may not yet have noticed her mother was gone. They sat there together for some time, as he held back his cries, until the physicians returned to prepare her for rest.

Chapter Twenty-Eight

"*She was... incredible.*"

"*Her strength is the foundation on which we stand. For every moment she breathed, she gave hope and protection to all she could. Though you may not have known her for long, by knowing the good in yourself you meet her, every day.*"

Osiris returned two days later. Aidan waited at the canal for his arrival, and gave him the news immediately. Kaya was lying in state. Together they visited her tomb to pay tribute. It was a muted day; the whole city had been quieted by the news. Citizens moved solemnly from one task to another, as funerary processions began to form and ceremonies planned. Aidan took himself from the mausoleum, unable to face the throes of people coming to mourn or give regards.

He and Osiris stood together on the Tor's highest balcony, leaning on the railings in the red twilight sun. The wind was gentle, yet cold. Like the passage of time, Aidan thought bitterly.

He let out a long, whistling sigh. "I'm tired, Osiris… I hadn't realised how much I relied on her for guidance."

The gryphon breathed deeply. "I have wandered the sea for centuries, and spent even longer in slumber. Neither of these have done as much good as you, or her. I think there is greater satisfaction to be found in building a world and learning from others, rather than running from either. I very much admire you for that."

Aidan smiled. "Thank you. I'm glad to still have you here. And Faria, she… she is my foundation right now, keeping me grounded, giving me a purpose."

Osiris stood next to him, arms folded as the wind rustled his feathers. "How are you going to teach her about Nazreal?"

Aidan gave a pathetic shrug, staring out over the twilight city. "Slowly. Or eventually. I need her to be a good person before she knows about the power it holds. For now, she needs love and to live in the present."

The gryphon folded his arms. "Will you have time for that?"

Aidan stroked a claw over the stone railing. "I don't know. But I can't rush her. She has to live in hope, always, never in fear. Even if things get bad, she needs to know there's good in the world. If she thinks I'll die at any second, if she's anything like me, it will consume her. Those who spend their whole lives in fear rarely act in compassion. You see it in those who are greedy; Raikali especially. She was terrified of losing power, both her resonance and influence. She died cocooning herself in fear, and unleashing it on the world. Faria deserves to be taught love and hope like it's all she knows. That's what Kaya wanted for her, and I think for me as well."

Osiris clicked his beak in thought.

"I'm not naïve anymore," Aidan continued, half-looking across his shoulder at the avian, whose wings bristled in the breeze. "I'm not going to pretend the world isn't dangerous. Kyrryk's been at war for years. We may forever become hunted if word gets out about us, or Nazreal, which we may yet have to destroy. But among the dangers are millions of peaceful lives. Faria has the power to protect them, any and all. I want her to know, as she experiences the world, that it's worth protecting, instead of giving in to the dark that makes us want to throw it away." He paused, clutching the railings tightly. Around his neck lay Kaya's pendant, glowing softly against his fur. If he held it, he could feel her warmth and spirit. "Could you keep our journals in Skyria? Just… so I know they're safe if anything happens to me?"

The gryphon nodded. "Teratai's will be glad for the reunion, I'm sure." He glanced to the room behind them. "Are you in need of a new bodyguard, by the way?"

The fox arched his eyebrows. "Surprisingly, not yet. Enyart agreed to stay to train his two protégés – you know Kier and Bayer, the fox resonator and the ocelot from Kyrryk?"

Osiris's derisive snort brought a smile to Aidan's face. "Those two sound like an adventure in themselves."

The fox shook his head, with a quiet laugh. "They are, apparently, but he's surprisingly patient with them, more so after Kaya. But I have my own quest to begin shortly, as the new Emperor and Representative. And sole father." He leant back and looked up at the reddening evening sky, and the vermillion clouds that swept close overhead.

"I have to do this. I need to make it worth every second of time Kaya sacrificed. So…" Aidan continued, watching the gryphon grasp the railing in his golden-scaled claws, weathered with scratches and scars. "Will it be another twenty-year sleep for you?"

Osiris snorted. "It will not."

He pushed himself from the balcony to stand straight. "I am not hibernating any more. This is where I intend to stay. As long as you are alive then there is a battle worth fighting. But if you feel I may raise too many questions for Faria, or from the city, there are things I can do to keep the Dhraka from your doors, and protect the interests of both you and Skyria in the shadows."

Aidan smiled, a little sadly. "I'll need all the help I can to keep the world peaceful. But stop in whenever you can, please."

"Always, Aidan."

Epilogue

Osiris let out a long sigh. "That is all I know."

"'*All* you know'," Faria scoffed. "Like it was trivial."

"I do not like to embellish," he replied, with a hint of smugness. "My memory is generally accurate despite my age. I daresay there were details I missed, though."

Faria nodded, tracing a claw over the surface of her table, watching the fading candlelight play shadows over the shiny veneer. "Well… it's enough for now. Thank you. It gives me something to think on while I prepare to address the Senate. I would hate to stand there in ignorance of the truth. I just…" she sighed, tracing a claw over the grain of the wooden table by her arm. "I wish he could have found a time to tell me."

Osiris leant back in his seat. "I believe he meant to, had we all reached Skyria as intended. That's where the Nazreal libraries are kept now. For Aidan, happiness was always a cherished thing, especially so after he came back. Nothing stabilised him as you did. For what he, and we all, went through, I could not blame him if the horrors were too much to pass on, if every time he saw your face was to feel truly at peace. We both became too guarded; for his part he put compassion ahead of all else, in the hope history would take a new path. Isolation was my vice."

She nodded sadly, flicking her claws nervously. "Do you think they'll believe me?"

Osiris sat upright and rustled his wings. "To an extent their belief is irrelevant. You will present yourself with more truth behind you than they could hope to see in their entire lives. They may choose to become your allies, but you alone have the key that will lock us together. Are you ready for this?"

She wrung her paws briefly, then took a deep breath. "If being ready was a choice, I would say no. As it isn't… then I am."

He smiled, and looked to the staff on the table, resting in its two halves, with assorted crystal fragments around it from places it had been fractured by Raikali. "Will you fix it?"

She gently picked up both halves and gripped them. A light glow pulsed erratically through each end.

"No. It… it doesn't feel the same anymore."

He tilted his head. A shadow of sadness crept over his face, but it dissipated in a second. "Did she change it?"

She shrugged. "I don't know. I'm still so burnt out, it could just be my oversensitivity. But either way, this was his, and…" Her fingers tightened on the staff. She brought it closer to her for a second, as if there were some lingering thought, or feeling, or perhaps a whisper of his voice coming from the staff's breath-like glow, then laid it on the table. "...he deserves to rest. What I need is something new, for this world."

Osiris stood to leave, and as he passed her, laid a claw softly on her shoulder.

"Sleep well, Faria. I will see you tomorrow."

She watched him depart. Once his wingtip had slid through the curtain and she heard the door's soft closing, she shifted in her seat and dragged the small chest out from under the table. It rattled softly as she lifted it, unsteadily, to the tabletop.

Carefully opening the lid, she was met with a familiar blue glow. Dozens of resonance crystals sat before her in a nest of golden fabric. Gently, she picked up the biggest one.

She closed her eyes, and the crystal began to shine.

Dear Reader

Thank you for reading *Ruin's Dawn*. If you enjoyed this book (or even if you didn't) please visit the site where you purchased it and write a brief review. Your feedback is important to both me and my publisher, and it will help other readers decide whether to read the book, too.

Acknowledgements

I honestly hadn't intended these books to release every four years, but it's interesting to see at how I've changed over each. I feel no less idealistic – if anything now I'm even more so, just with a hefty dose of radicalisation.

Ruin's Dawn has been in my mind ever since *Legacy*. That has its bonuses, and its detriments: while it's had the most time to evolve into a stronger tale, it's also stayed beholden to some less-than-progressive tropes. Had I known then what I know now, there would be a lot of differences in the world and its characters. I still love them completely, but from here I aim to create a deeper authenticity that retains what they meant to me when they came to life so many years ago.

I have so much to be grateful for. My amazing family in Mum Coral and Dad Rob, my older sister Dulcie, her husband Matthew, and their clutch of lovely creatures, Toby, Alex, and Sienna; my younger sister Venetia and husband Simon, my uncles Roger and Bruce, Christine, and of course my wife Madison, whose faith in me I always hope to live up to, and our dog Tohru, who never ceases to make me swell with love with even the tiniest gesture.

On themes of inherited duty, I always think of my grandfather Hugh Jackson, who braved artillery fire in Italy to save eighteen soldiers, then developed safety measures to prevent accidents to untold numbers of children. I hope to carry that same passion for making the world better, with my own voice and in my own way.

I'm immensely thankful for friends who've shown me their bravery and helped me find mine. People like Aaron, whose generosity is a gift to this world; Chris Bleil, whose constant enthusiasm is unparalleled; Daniel, who gave me so much of myself; Jeremy and Su-Yang, who despite my awful ability to stay in contact haven't lost faith in me; Jenny and Chris, who show immense kindness over and over again; Roger and Amanda, whose passion for being themselves is a beautiful thing, and who're patient enough to let me DM for them, Nate, Seth and Shara; Paul, who still inspires me with humility, truth, and kindness every single day. And David, who, between him and his progeny George, James, and Lucy gave me one of the most treasured stories I will ever hear, and will keep with me forever.

I want to give a specific shout-out to fellow Inspired Quill author Craig Hallam, who showed exceptional bravery and vulnerability in his autobiographical book *Down Days* about battling anxiety and depression.

I've been lucky to find so many wonderful people over social media, who've talked, listened, shared incredible artwork, and made me pay attention to a world I could easily hide from. Those who helped me find my best forms of self-expression and identity, and given me incredible purpose in my trans-nonbinary self. CarcinLoring, Sisk, True_N8ure, Carcass_HH, Hanji_Shaddon, AnonSergal, BroccoliFox, VexWerewolf, Tonya Song, Azure_Husky, Kaithral, Eric_Fullswipe, Jordan, usagisenshii and Bukkaroo; all of you have shown me what it means to survive and persevere. You are nothing short of inspirational and I hope every day to live by doing you justice.

I could very easily copy and paste a list of my Twitter follows, but there are people I specifically want to mention, whether for art or personality, generosity, or overall badassedness: GlazedScales, Necrotext, Serpentsaurus, StixilFox, DutchieGoNyah, Nuregator, injytech, Ivic_Wulfe, Mervyn Fox, WiredInZero, HoppNate, Ashes and Jenny, Chaosqueen97, Smatterbrain, AK_illustrate, kaijukisses, ChocolateQuill, Paradox, ottdoqbuns, wottermelon, Peppermint_Punk, Zalno, Mike Hamilton, Sorren, AngosturaCat, foundbysara, losthiskeysman, RussellTehFox, Splash, Gills, OC_Pawprints, Sprocket, Oasus, Lauren Rivers, Mikey, Sentvri, itsyaboiphoenix, i80and, conreeaght, Rybark, Eevachu, JackalopeWren, Mizuno_Aoi, PunkYeenLilith, remygryph, DonryuArt, RamuneTigress, lykanprince, Viddy, kofukitty, XydexxUnicorn, floofytailed, rd_doodles, WordsBySC, WolfMamaCorner, CayennePupper, kayfey, RiotTheRenegade, leporibae, Rhaenspots, Comburos, TheHGSantori, KnoProblem, Wolfofthenyght, and a huge plethora of others ;w;

Once again I'm indebted to the incredible work of Katie Hofgard, whose cover art I cannot praise enough, and whose integrity, strength, and creativity is constantly inspiring. Thank you for creating a window into so many heartfelt, beautiful worlds, and for being an extraordinary presence in our own. If you love her art, please support her Patreon (patreon.com/Eskiworks)

None of this would have been possible, and may not have even continued past *Legacy*, if it weren't for the behemoth energies and enthusiasm of Sara-Jayne Slack and Laura Cayuela. You are both amazing, fantastic, and I owe you several more books' worth of thanks to effectively impart what this has meant to me, and for your faith in my journeys both literary and personal.

Thank you everyone who has picked up a book, shared a post, sent me kind messages, put up with my political ramblings and fursuit nonsense, and given kindness to those around you. You make this world worth living in.

I'll see you in the next book.

P.S. Trans rights

About the Author

Hugo is a British-born author living in North Carolina. They began life as a starry-eyed creature with a fascination for fantastical adventures, heroes, and animals, and invested as much time in their own imagination as they did on animations, video games, and music.

In 2012 Hugo moved to the United States to live with their wife Madison, who is a native to North Carolina, where they both enjoy as much barbecue and biscuits as health will reasonably allow, and together dote over a lovely corgi-cross named Tohru.

In their spare time, Hugo is heavily involved with the furry fandom, standing as an advocate for LGBT+ rights, mental health awareness, inclusion, and artist/author visibility and fair treatment. They talk about many of these things on their intermittently-updated blog, Writesaber, and occasionally produces their own videos. Hugo makes all of the costumes that they wear (or scrounges materials from charity shops), and attends whichever conventions they can.

Find the author via their website:
hugorjackson.com
Or tweet at them: @phoenixtheblade

More From This Author

The Resonance Tetralogy

Book 1: Legacy
Her power is unmeasured. Her abilities untested. Her destiny inescapable.

Faria Phiraco is a resonator, a manipulator of the elements via rare crystals. It is an extraordinary and secret power which she and her father, the Emperor of Xayall, guard with their lives. The Dhraka, malicious red-scaled dragons, have discovered an ancient artefact; a mysterious relic from the mythical, aeons-lost city of Nazreal.

When her father goes missing, Faria has to rely on her own strength to brave the world that attacks her at every turn. Friends and guardians rally by her to help save her father and reveal the mysteries of the ruined city. She soon realises that this is not the beginning, nor anywhere near the end. A titanic war spanning thousands of years unfolds around her, one that could yet cost the lives of everyone on Eeres.

Book 2: Fracture
The shadows are coming…

Months after the tremors that shook the world, repercussions of battle still lie in Xayall's broken streets. Among the debris stands Bayer, former bodyguard to Faria, Empress of the city state. His position redundant, and his injuries still healing, he struggles to find new purpose.

Unrest between nations is already stirring. A Councillor from Andarn has been murdered, and only a handful realise that sinister machinations are blackening the root of the whole continent. Questioning his duties, Bayer finds himself escorting Captain Alaris on a mission from which neither may return, although their failure may spark a brutal and catastrophic war.

As blades rise, threats both new and old emerge from the darkness and bare their teeth at the world.

Available from all major online and offline outlets.

www.ingramcontent.com/pod-product-compliance
Ingram Content Group UK Ltd.
Pitfield, Milton Keynes, MK11 3LW, UK
UKHW041409180426
11947UKWH00007B/28